"Sweetheart..."

Her lips brushed his, a soft sweep of flesh on flesh, her tongue flicking out for a tiny taste. And hell if she didn't taste as sweet as she smelled.

"I'm *not* your sweetheart," she said, a slight tremble in her voice.

And no. Despite how she tasted and smelled, there was nothing sweet about this girl, especially now. And because he didn't think—couldn't right now even if he tried—he tangled his fingers in her soft hair and pulled her to him.

She hummed a soft moan when he palmed her breast. And when he pinched her hardened peak, she gasped—and then sprang up like he'd set her on fire.

Her hand flew over her mouth, and she shook her head. "I can't. *We* can't."

She spun and, without another word, bolted toward the front door.

"Shit." He tried to get up but knew she was too fast for him unless he risked making his situation even worse. "Lily!" he called after her. "You don't have to"—he heard the door slam—"go."

But she did have to leave. Because now that she wasn't pissing him off or kissing him, he had a second to do that thing he tried to avoid—think.

No matter what had gone wrong in their marriage, he couldn't do this to his best friend. Lily Green was and always would be off-limits.

PRAISE FOR *SECOND CHANCE COWBOY*

"A fabulous storyteller who will keep you turning pages and wishing for just one more chapter at the end."
—Carolyn Brown, *New York Times* bestselling author

"Cross my heart, this sexy, sweet romance gives a cowboy-at-heart lawyer a second chance at first love and readers a fantastic ride."
—Jennifer Ryan, *New York Times* bestselling author

"Ms. Pine's character development, strong family building, and interesting secondary characters add layers to the story that jacked up my enjoyment of *Second Chance Cowboy* to maximum levels." —*USA Today* "Happy Ever After"

"5 Stars! Top Pick! The author and her characters twist and turn their way right into your heart."
—NightOwlReviews.com

"This is a strong read with a heartwarming message and inspiring characters." —*RT Book Reviews*

Also by A.J. Pine

Second Chance Cowboy

Saved by the Cowboy (novella)

TOUGH LUCK COWBOY

PAPL
DISCARDED

A Crossroads Ranch Novel

A.J. PINE

FOREVER
New York

This book is a work of fiction. Names, characters, places, and incidents are the product of the author's imagination or are used fictitiously. Any resemblance to actual events, locales, or persons, living or dead, is coincidental.

Copyright © 2018 by A.J. Pine
Excerpt from *Hard Loving Cowboy* copyright © 2018 by A.J. Pine

Cover design by Elizabeth Stokes
Cover copyright © 2018 by Hachette Book Group, Inc.

Hachette Book Group supports the right to free expression and the value of copyright. The purpose of copyright is to encourage writers and artists to produce the creative works that enrich our culture.

The scanning, uploading, and distribution of this book without permission is a theft of the author's intellectual property. If you would like permission to use material from the book (other than for review purposes), please contact permissions@hbgusa.com. Thank you for your support of the author's rights.

Forever
Hachette Book Group
1290 Avenue of the Americas, New York, NY 10104
forever-romance.com
twitter.com/foreverromance

First edition: August 2018

Forever is an imprint of Grand Central Publishing. The Forever name and logo are trademarks of Hachette Book Group, Inc.

The publisher is not responsible for websites (or their content) that are not owned by the publisher.

The Hachette Speakers Bureau provides a wide range of authors for speaking events. To find out more, go to www.hachettespeakersbureau.com or call (866) 376-6591.

ISBNs: 978-1-5387-2710-2 (mass market), 978-1-5387-2709-6 (ebook)

Printed in the United States of America

OPM

10 9 8 7 6 5 4 3 2 1

ATTENTION CORPORATIONS AND ORGANIZATIONS:
Most Hachette Book Group books are available at quantity discounts with bulk purchase for educational, business, or sales promotional use. For information, please call or write:

Special Markets Department, Hachette Book Group
1290 Avenue of the Americas, New York, NY 10104
Telephone: 1-800-222-6747 Fax: 1-800-477-5925

ACKNOWLEDGMENTS

Thank you to the amazing team of people who let me keep making words into sentences and sentences into books—that have lots of kissing and stuff. Agent-extraordinaire Emily, Word-beautification specialist Madeleine, and sanity-protecting partners-in-crime Lia, Jen, Chanel, Natalie, and Megan. If my cowboys rode flying horses, you'd all be the wind beneath my Pegasus wings.

Thank you, readers, for coming back for another happily ever after—and for reading the acknowledgments! That's dedication, and I'm forever grateful for it.

And always, thank you, S and C, my two most favorite people in the world. I love you infinity times infinity. Plus infinity.

TOUGH LUCK COWBOY

PROLOGUE

Three years ago...

Despite the setting sun and the fact he'd been working since the damn thing rose that morning, Luke Everett wasn't about to call it a day. He had Cleo saddled up and ready to ride—and only a week left before his first rodeo. His trick riding was good. Real good. He wouldn't settle for anything less than top-notch. When you excelled at one thing and one thing only, nothing but the best would do.

He was on Cleo and had barely made it into the arena when the black Audi RS 3 rolled up next to the stable.

Luke pushed the brim of his hat up, wiping the sweat off his forehead and squinting at the emerging driver.

"You do like to make an entrance, don't you?" Luke called over the arena fence. "Still enjoying your graduation bribe, I see."

Tucker Green hopped out of the driver's-side door, and Luke couldn't help laughing. There was his buddy, dark hair cropped close and neat, a collared shirt and clean dark jeans, and a car that cost three times as much as his truck. Luke glanced down at his faded, dirty jeans and scuffed boots. He gripped Cleo's reins with rough, calloused hands that boasted fingernails in need of a good scrubbing...or seven.

"It's not a bribe if I actually want to stay in Oak Bluff," Tucker said. "As long as my father thinks he got his way, I'll take the car and seed money to start my own business. By the way, got any business ideas?"

Luke shook his head and laughed. He didn't begrudge Tucker the perks the guy grew up with. They were just so—different—the two of them. Yet his friend had had his back for too many years to count. And Luke would always have his.

"What are you doing here, Green?" Luke asked. "I got shit to do."

"Jessie ended things, and in case you can't tell, I'm a mess. I could have married her, you know. If she didn't move back to Ohio after grad school."

Luke shook his head. "Why didn't you chase her?"

Tucker held out his arms. "And leave all this? You know as well as I do that people like you and me always come back to Oak Bluff. It's in our blood."

Luke couldn't argue with that. There was something about this place that called you back. Sometimes it was easier to simply not leave.

"You think every woman is the one that's going to get you to settle down. But they never are."

Tucker laughed. "And you don't think any woman will get you to settle down."

Luke raised a brow. "And do you ever see me crying about a broken heart?" He knew better than that. After seeing what love did to his father and how it almost ruined his brother Jack, too, he wasn't about to walk down that path.

"Look, man," Tucker said, smile fading. "This one stings, okay? I might have even loved her. I can't sit home with Charles and Judith tonight. I need to blow off some steam, and from the looks of it, so the hell do you."

Luke shrugged. "This *is* how I blow off steam. It's also how I make sure I'm not gonna get myself killed when I compete for the first time. I'd say that's a win-win situation."

Tucker strode toward the fence, stopping only when he couldn't go any farther, then crossed his arms.

"Okay, then. I need a wingman. You can, at the very least, be that."

Luke pulled his riding gloves out of his back pocket and slid them on.

"No can do, my friend. I already have a date with this pretty lady tonight." He patted Cleo on the neck. "What kind of man would I be if I bailed on her now?"

Tucker raised a brow. "Drinks are on me."

Luke hopped off the horse. "Gimme ten minutes to take a quick shower."

"A line dancing bar?" Luke asked when they pulled up in front of the Lucky Star Saloon.

Tucker put the car in park and pulled the keys from the ignition. "You know who likes to go line dancing, my friend?" He didn't wait for Luke to answer. "Women like to go line dancing. And you know my favorite way to blow off steam..."

Yeah. Luke knew. It was one of his favorite ways to blow off steam, too. But there hadn't been time for that the past few weeks—not with running the ranch, training for the rodeo, keeping his unpredictable younger brother Walker in line, and making sure his ailing father, Jack Senior, ate enough each day to soak up the booze.

No, Luke Everett hadn't had the privileged upbringing his friend had. At least, not after his mother died and his father had taken to drinking and raising his hand to Jack Junior. The worst was behind them, but life still had a way of piling up every now and then.

"You were right," Luke said as the two men headed toward the swinging doors of the Lucky Star Saloon. "I needed a night off."

Tucker clapped him on the shoulder and grinned. "I know, Everett. I'm always right. Now get in there and be the life of the party I know you are."

In a matter of minutes Luke had a beer in hand and a barstool view of the dance floor where the line dancing was in full swing. It didn't take him long to spot her—the pixie-cut blonde in the short denim skirt and green tank top. But it was her smile that nearly knocked him off his stool.

"I'll be right back," he said to Tucker.

"Are you shittin' me? You don't actually know how to line dance, do you? Or have you been holding out on me?"

"Never done it in my life," Luke said. But he'd do just about anything right now to see that girl's smile up close.

He ran a hand through his blond waves and took a swig of his beer as he made his way onto the floor.

She was right there in the front line, so he burrowed between her and the woman to her right, a tall brunette with a severe ponytail who crashed right into him as she stepped left.

Luke expected chastisement from Ponytail. Instead he was greeted with a flirty "I'm sorry" as the woman blushed and smiled.

He offered her a friendly grin as he cross-stepped to the side, trying to keep in time with the line, not that he had any clue what the hell he was doing. "Not necessary. It was my fault."

Luke turned his attention to the woman on the other side

of him, the one still dancing without so much as a missed step even as she gave him the side-eye.

"You look lost," she said, and they were suddenly moving three steps forward.

"I beg to differ," Luke replied. "I'm exactly where I want to be."

She pointed at his beer, and they were now taking three steps back.

"Makes it hard to do all the moves with that. Just an FYI. Though I'm guessing you don't know any of them."

He flashed her a smile. "Oh I know moves, sweetheart." And because his timing was perfect, that was exactly when he stepped right just as everyone else was stepping left.

She burst out laughing as he crashed into Ponytail Girl again, causing him to stumble forward and—thankfully—out of the line. Somehow he managed to save his beer.

His chest tightened at the sound of her laughter, not from embarrassment but from the sheer joy radiating from her, and he was sure the only cure for whatever her happiness was doing to him was to hear it again.

"You might have *some* moves," she said. "But they're not out here." She grabbed him by the wrist and pulled him off the dance floor, and he followed more than willingly.

"You got a name?" Luke asked.

"Lemme have some of that and I'll tell you."

He handed his still-cold bottle to her, and she drew a long, slow sip.

She licked her lips and offered the bottle back to him. "I'm Lily."

"I'm Luke. Buy you a fresh one of your own?" he asked, taking his beer back.

She reached a hand toward his face, pressing her fingers

to the back of his neck and brushing her thumb along his jaw.

His pulse went into overdrive.

"You got a little smudge of something..."

He laughed. Sometimes it didn't matter how many times he showered after a long day's work. A little piece of the ranch always seemed to stick with him.

Her thumb slowed as she felt the scar beneath his stubble.

"First time getting thrown from a horse," he said, answering her unasked question.

"First time?"

"Sure," he said. "This one was an accident. The other times I was asking for it." The corner of his mouth quirked up.

Lily cleared her throat. "There," she said, dropping her hand. "All better."

Luke raised a brow. "You sure you weren't just looking for an excuse to get your hands on me?" Her cheeks went crimson, but she held his playful gaze. So he leaned in close and spoke softly into her ear, "I'm gonna tell you a little secret, sweetheart. You never need to make excuses with me."

He straightened just in time to spot the ponytailed line dancer he'd almost knocked over twice bounding toward the two of them.

"Hey, you guys! I was wondering where you went!" She bumped her hip against Lily's, then hooked her arm through Luke's. "I think Mr. Sexy here needs some dance lessons. Don't you agree?"

Mr. Sexy?

Lily shook her head and laughed. "Dina, this is Luke. Luke, this is my friend Dina—line dancer extraordinaire."

Luke cleared his throat. "I'd shake your hand but—you're sorta holding it."

She'd slid her hand from his elbow to his palm and

was now gripping it firmly. She was pretty and sure as hell not shy. But there had been some sort of connection when Lily's skin met his. And hell if he wasn't going to see where that led.

"Is this guy bothering you, ladies? He's been known to leave a trail of broken hearts wherever he goes, and I'd hate to see that happen to either of you. Just say the word and I can take care of him for you."

Luke turned to see Tucker eyeing the three of them with a look on his face like he was ready to kick someone's ass. And it was pretty damn convincing. Only Luke knew that Tucker Green would never chance messing up that pretty face of his.

"No!" Lily said. "He was just—wait—trail of broken hearts?"

Tucker tilted his head back and laughed, and Lily's lips pursed into a pout.

"Lily, Dina…meet Tucker." Luke freed his hand from Dina's. "Tucker, stop being an asshole."

"Fine," Tucker said, crossing his arms. "Drinks are on me. Anything to keep your sorry ass off the dance floor, Everett. That was painful to watch." He turned to Lily and Dina. "Shall we, ladies?"

The four of them headed back to Luke and Tucker's table, and soon there were beers in everyone's hands.

"You both from around here?" Luke asked Lily and Dina.

"Born and raised," Dina said. "I'm getting certified to teach yoga at a local studio. My instructor says I'm the bendiest person in my class."

Lily coughed as she sipped her beer.

Luke patted her on the back. "You okay there, sweetheart?"

She coughed again, then cleared her throat. "I'm great. Just wasn't aware of Dina's bendiness." She pressed her lips into a grin.

Luke's hand slid down to rest on the back of Lily's stool. She was safe from choking on her drink, but he wanted to stay close by—just in case. That was a logical enough excuse without admitting to himself it could be anything more, especially when he didn't exactly do more.

"You ladies don't discuss degrees of flexibility?" Tucker asked. "Because that's pretty much all Everett and I talk about."

Lily lowered her chin and laughed, but there was a nervousness to it. She straightened and smiled coyly as she chewed her bottom lip. Well shit. It wasn't nerves. She was flirting.

With him or Tucker? The joke had clearly been about both men, but Tucker was the one who said it. And dammit, when was the last time he'd silently dissected a woman's behavior to determine whether or not she liked him?

The answer was never. They'd *always* liked him. Not being able to read this woman was maddening.

"We just met a couple weeks ago—me and Dina. She needed a roommate, and I'd just moved here from Phoenix and needed a place to stay, so here we are."

"Why'd you leave Phoenix?" Luke asked. He wanted to know, sure. He also wanted to keep her attention, to find any excuse to stare at her emerald-green eyes. Tucker might have been right with his *trail of broken hearts* joke. But it wasn't like Luke set out to love 'em and leave 'em. He just never saw the point in long-term. His brother Jack fell in love in high school and got his heart crushed. Their father had loved their mother something fierce, and look what that did to him. She died, and he all but joined her, letting the bottom of a whiskey bottle kill the man who'd raised them and turn him into a violent stranger. So no, love wasn't something Luke Everett sought. Yet this girl he'd known for the better part of an hour had him thinking *What if?*

Luke shifted slightly on his stool, leaning his elbow on the high-top table and angling more toward Lily. He wasn't openly ignoring Dina and certainly didn't want to be a dick. He did, however, want to make his interest clear. In the past he'd found his leaning usually said more than enough.

Lily smiled at him and then shrugged. "I finished culinary school and needed a change of scenery. And now I need a job." She laughed. "Sometimes it's good to wipe the slate clean and start fresh. Leave the past behind and all that. You know?"

She was playing at nonchalance, the sparkle dimming in her eyes a dead giveaway.

Hell yeah he knew. He'd had that fresh start back in high school when he and his brothers were removed from their father's custody after the man almost killed Jack by pushing him down a flight of stairs. But Crossroads Ranch was the family business. He understood why Jack left, but ranching was in Luke's blood. He could never truly leave his past behind.

"I get it," Luke said. His hand shifted, his fingertips accidentally brushing her shoulder. She shivered. "How are you liking—"

"Wait," Tucker interrupted. "Wait, wait, *wait*. Did you just say *culinary school*?" He slapped a palm down on the table. "I just had a damned epiphany!"

Luke straightened and instinctively pulled his arm away. The shift in the air was immediate yet noticeable only to him. Whatever Tucker was about to say was going to change everything. It was Tucker's way—a big personality with even bigger ideas that drew everyone into his orbit whether they wanted to be or not.

"I just finished business school," Tucker continued. "And I have this start-up fund that's sitting in the bank waiting for me to figure out what the hell to start up. You're a chef looking for a job. It's all so damned perfect. How do you feel about barbecue? I always thought Oak Bluff could use some good barbecue. Also doesn't hurt that it's my father's favorite. I do like to please my investors." He raised a brow. "Plus, I know this great ranch nearby, so all recipes would come from locally sourced beef." He gave Luke a conspiratorial grin.

Lily's brows drew together. "So, I've actually never cooked barbecue before. My influence is more, um, eclectic? You know, farm to table, the menu always changing…"

Tucker nodded. "Sure, yeah. I hear what you're saying. I'm just sort of spitballing ideas here. What if we talk about this more in the light of day? I'll give you the grand tour of Oak Bluff, show you why it needs barbecue, and let you put together some menu ideas. Tomorrow morning sound good?"

Lily's hesitant smile bloomed into something radiant, her green eyes sparking back to life. Luke realized the foolishness of his *What if?* Tucker could literally give her the world, and he couldn't compete with that.

"I went to Berkeley!" Dina called out as if they were playing some game and she was claiming her turn. "What about you, Luke? Where'd you graduate from?"

His smile fell for a second. Then he painted it back on. "Los Olivos High School," he said matter-of-factly. "Hey, man. If y'all are staying for a while, maybe I'll call an Uber or something. Got an early morning."

Tucker clapped a hand onto Luke's shoulder. "My man

Luke here isn't telling the whole story. Did you ladies know he's competing in his first rodeo next week?"

Luke shook his head. "They don't want to hear about bareback or bronc riding."

"I do," Dina said. "I could drive you home, and you could tell me all about it."

Lily said nothing, which only sealed the deal. Tucker might be a little self-absorbed sometimes, but he was a good guy. The better guy in many respects. When they were in their early teens, he was there for Luke during some of the hardest years of his life. No matter what sort of spark he felt with Lily when they met, she deserved someone more like Tucker, and Tucker deserved a win. He wouldn't stand in the way of either of them getting what they wanted.

"I think I'll take that ride, Dina," Luke said.

"You sure?" Tucker asked, and Luke nodded. "I'm happy to take you home, Lily. We can talk more about Oak Bluff's culinary future. I mean, no pressure or anything, but if you're really looking for a job as a chef…"

Lily hesitated for a second, mouth hanging open. "Sure…I mean, this is what everyone wants, right?"

Luke shrugged and slid off his stool, taking a step back from the girl who, for a brief second or two, made him think he was ready for something more. "I can't offer a girl a restaurant. Just stories about cows and horses." He took himself out of the running, though he guessed Tucker never really knew he'd been in it.

"What a coincidence!" Dina said. "I adore cows and horses." She linked her arm through Luke's and pulled him close. "You're good with getting a ride from Tucker, right Lil?"

"I'm good," Lily said.

Tucker hopped off his stool. "Then I guess we're all heading out."

The bar filled with the opening of Billy Ray Cyrus's "Achy Breaky Heart," and Dina squealed, "Classic! Oh, we have to stay for this one. Please?"

She batted her eyes at Luke, and he blew out a breath. "I guess we're going to be a few minutes behind you," he said to Tucker and Lily.

"I guess this is good night, then," Lily said.

"I'll catch you tomorrow, Everett. *Later* tomorrow. Nice to meet you, Dina."

Luke said nothing as he watched Tucker slide his fingers through Lily's. Then the two of them turned toward the swinging saloon doors.

Maybe this place was a poor replica of the Old West, but he'd swear he just dodged a bullet, one that was aimed straight for his heart.

"So," Dina said. "Wanna go dance and then blow off some steam?"

Luke chuckled at her choice of words. He was good at blowing off steam. It was stupid for him to think he'd be good at anything more.

"Yeah," he said. "I think I do."

CHAPTER ONE

Lily Green stood outside the entrance of the Crossroads Vineyard tasting room. The place was still under construction and not yet open, but Jack Everett was expecting her. She glanced back at the Audi RS 3, the car that had impressed her the night she met Tucker Green. Now it was listed in the sheaf of papers under her arm as one of many assets turned over to her in the divorce agreement. She'd signed and initialed each and every page in the stack, read them through again, and then once more before leaving her house this morning.

"Well," she said aloud to no one in particular. "There you have it."

Lily Green knew what it was like to be left. At the ripe old age of twelve, her own father decided that both marriage *and* parenting weren't his chosen path in life. And after cleaning out the joint savings account he shared with Lily's mother, he disappeared from both their lives. His not loving her mother anymore would have been enough. But what about his daughter? He hadn't loved Lily enough to stay in touch, let alone in town. That had been fifteen years ago, and she and her mom were still rebuilding the foundation he tore down with that one little decision.

"That's why I did everything by the book," she said, answering her inner monologue. Good grades, scholarships to offset loans, marrying the guy who promised stability and a future for both of them. *Her* life path consisted of planned-out decisions that were supposed to be foolproof. Instead she'd fooled herself into thinking history wouldn't repeat itself. She just hadn't expected *she'd* be the one to leave.

Lily Green, the girl voted most likely to teach life who was boss—because yes, that's exactly what her senior superlative had said—was twenty-six and had been thoroughly schooled by life instead.

Scratch that. Twenty-seven. Because of course she was finalizing the details of her divorce on her birthday.

"Guess there's nothing left to do but make this official, right?"

But no one answered. She was still talking to herself. Prolonging the inevitable.

A shiver ran through her, and Lily wondered if it was the crisp October afternoon or the realization that a carefully cultivated plan could still run off the track. She squinted into the sun, which shone bright over the burgeoning California vineyard. The Everett brothers were sure as hell showing life who was boss, and despite the weight on her chest, that thought elicited a smile.

She fingered the silver wishbone pendant that hung at her neck, the only gift her mom could afford when she'd graduated culinary school.

"I always knew you'd do better than I did at figuring life out," she'd said. "Look at you—on your way to doing such great things. I'll never stop being proud of you."

Great things, huh? She was jobless, almost divorced, and completely and totally lost. How could she tell her mom that?

She couldn't. Not yet. She'd call home eventually. When she could think of the right words. When she would be ready to hear the disappointment in her mother's voice.

Right now she squared her shoulders and pushed through the tall wooden door, ready to get down to business, and stopped short at the scene before her.

At a workbench stood the owners of the Crossroads Ranch and soon-to-be Vineyard—three tall, strapping men all in well-worn jeans and well-fitting T-shirts that were sprinkled with sawdust or dirt. This was all juxtaposed with their raised hands, each awkwardly gripping the stem of a wineglass.

"You need to swirl it first, like this, letting it breathe."

Across from the rugged blond Everett brothers stood a beautiful redhead. Ava Ellis, Jack's fiancée and resident wine expert.

"Why the hell do crushed, fermented grapes need to *breathe*?" the youngest of the three men—Walker—asked.

Ava let out a sigh and narrowed her eyes at her *almost* brother-in-law.

"It's oxygenating, opening up. This softens the taste, lets you truly get a sense of the aroma so you can learn to identify the ingredients."

Walker turned to his brothers. "Aroma?" He grunted. "Tell me she's not going to make us sniff the damn grapes."

Lily stifled a laugh. They still hadn't noticed her enter, and she did not want this performance to end on her account.

"Pay attention, asshole," Luke said. He was grinning.

"If Ava wants you to sniff the damn grapes, you're gonna sniff the damn grapes," Jack added.

Walker set his glass on the workbench in front of him and crossed his arms. "You fuckers can sniff. I'm waiting until it's time to drink."

Ava just shook her head and laughed, dipping her nose toward the rim of the glass. She breathed in, eyes closed, and sighed with a smile.

"Earthy, with a hint of black cherry," she said, then opened her eyes. "What do you think?" she asked Luke and Jack.

The two men swirled the wine in their glasses, both sloshing it over the rim.

Ava giggled. Walker shook his head.

"I just smell—wine," Luke admitted.

Jack looked at his fiancée and cleared his throat. "Totally earthy," he echoed. "And black cherry—ish."

She crossed her arms. "You just smell wine. Don't you?"

He winced and then nodded. "Just wine. Sorry, Red. But you're sexy as hell trying to teach our sorry asses how to do this." He set his glass down and leaned across the workbench to kiss her, and Lily's heart squeezed tight in her chest.

She faked a cough, silently berating herself for interrupting the moment, but she could no longer stomach being the outsider looking in. She just wanted to do what needed to be done and get out.

Everyone's heads shot up and toward the door.

"Nail gun," Walker said, breaking the silence. "I need to, uh, do some manual labor involving a nail gun. That's why I'm here." He strode off to a far corner of the space where there was another workbench piled with tools.

Lily couldn't help laughing. Then Luke's eyes found hers, and she felt suddenly exposed. Luke was Tucker's best friend, the only person who knew her ex-husband better than she did. Yet the way he looked at her—jaw clenched and eyes narrowed—showed exactly where his sympathy lay. Not that she was surprised. Luke Everett had never really been her biggest fan.

"Lily," he said with a curt nod as he ran a hand through his cropped blond hair. And then he strode right past her and out the door.

Her mouth hung open.

The two of them were far from best friends, but she'd never known him to be openly cruel. Luke Everett *knew* what today was, on both accounts. And he had the audacity to just saunter on by like it was any other day that ended in *y*.

"What was that?" Ava asked.

Lily shook her head. "Nothing." Her brow furrowed. "He thinks I was a controlling shrew with Tucker, and I thought a married man should come home before dawn when he was out boozing it up with his buddies."

Ava knew about Tucker's late nights out with the boys as well as his showing up at the Everett ranch at 2:00 a.m. the night Lily had walked out and crashed on Jack and Ava's couch. He'd begged her to come home.

Lily hadn't told anyone about the infidelity, though. It had stung too much at the time it happened. Plus, it wasn't anyone else's business. Lily didn't place all the blame for their divorce on Tucker's actions. It took two to make a marriage work, and she owned her part in all of this.

Ava gasped. "He called you a controlling shrew?"

Lily huffed out a breath. "Well, not exactly in those words. But he has told me to lighten up or relax on *several* occasions, and I know all together those boil down to controlling shrew."

"Ugh," Ava said. "I hate those words. Jack, if you ever told me to relax—"

"He wouldn't," Lily said, coming to Jack's defense.

Ava smiled wistfully at her fiancé. "No, he wouldn't."

Jack and Luke may have been brothers, but their personalities were miles apart. So Luke Everett found her uptight and felt the liberty to say so on more than one occasion. Why should she care? Did wanting to be organized or have some semblance of a plan make a person controlling? What was wrong with knowing what came next?

Lily sighed.

Ava pursed her lips. "Aw, honey. I'm sure Luke never meant to be an ass. I love him like a brother, but he's just a big kid, you know? If it's not a party, he wants no part in it."

"Yeah," Jack added. "Other than ranching—and I will admit he does a damn good job around here—he's sort of shit with the grown-up stuff. He'd rather be riding a horse or a bull than have to truly interact with the rest of the human race."

"I'll let you two get down to business," Ava said, giving Jack a kiss. "And I'll leave the wine," she added, her eyes now on Lily's. "Just in case."

Lily forced a smile. "Thanks. I actually could use a glass. Or three."

Ava hugged her. The two had gotten to be close since Jack, Ava, and their ten-year-old son Owen had become frequent diners at BBQ on the Bluff—the main asset Tucker was retaining.

"Come over for dinner after. If you're up for it," Ava said. "Everyone's going to watch Luke at the rodeo. I could hang back and work on my paper for my art history class. I wouldn't mind a small distraction."

Lily shook her head. "I'm gonna be terrible company tonight. Trust me. Thank you for offering, though. Plus Jack might bill me extra hours if I cost you valuable work time."

Jack winked. "I hadn't thought of that, but now that you mention it..."

Ava poked him square in his broad chest. "You behave,

Jack Everett. Lily's practically family, so I trust you're giving her a family discount."

He just shook his head and laughed, his eyes lingering as he watched his fiancée stride out the door. Then he nodded toward a different door, a small one in the back of the space. "Shall we head to my office?" he asked.

"No time like the present!" Her words were forcefully more enthusiastic than she'd intended, but whatever. She followed Jack to what might someday be an office but what certainly was *not* one today.

He motioned for her to sit on one of the few pieces of furniture in the room, a futon that was at present in couch position. Other than that, a coffee table, and a small desk and chair, the room was empty. They were surrounded by unfinished drywall, but the air had that new house smell. She liked it. It was the smell of new beginnings.

"Sorry," he said. "We can head back to the ranch and go to my real office if you want."

"No, no." She plopped down on the futon, and a cloud of dust rose to greet her. She coughed. "I wanted to see how the place was coming along. We can do this, and then you can give me the tour."

Jack dropped down next to her, and she narrowed her eyes.

"What?" he asked, leaning back, an easy grin taking over his chiseled face.

She let out a nervous laugh. "In faded jeans and a dirty tee, you just don't look like a"—she switched to a whisper—"divorce lawyer."

Jack chuckled. "That's because I'm a contract lawyer. You can still bail if you want the real deal."

She shook her head. She wasn't one to bite the hand that fed her pro bono work. "It's pretty cut-and-dry. The settlement, I mean. Tucker and I talked it all through. Plus, I did spend two full weekends at the library reading up on divorce law in whatever books and databases I could find."

Jack raised a brow. "That's pretty thorough. You sure you need me at all?"

She forced a smile. "Of course I do, but I like to make sure all the *i*'s are dotted and *t*'s crossed. Then you can double-check before I double-check again." She took a breath. "I'm keeping the house and car. He's buying me out of BBQ on the Bluff, which will give me the funds to start something just for me. I guess there wasn't too much history to divide up."

"Something just for you?" he asked.

She chewed on her bottom lip. "Always wanted my own restaurant." Jack opened his mouth to say something, but she answered his question before he could ask it. "I know I already had that with Tucker. But it wasn't really mine. I brought his ideas to fruition, but I wasn't exactly passionate about barbecue."

Jack frowned. "But you were so damned good at it."

This made her laugh. "And someday I'll be good at bringing my own ideas to reality. Until then I figure I could do some catering. You know? I get to cook without the overhead of running a whole restaurant until I make enough to open my own place."

"Will you still make your corn bread? For Owen, of course. He loves it."

She nodded. "Anything for that sweet little boy of yours. I may even let him share it with you."

Jack pulled out a pen from where it was hidden behind his ear and then held out his hand.

"You gonna give me that envelope or keep hugging it?"

She dipped her head toward her chest where she was, in

fact, clutching said envelope to her torso like it was a life vest and she was floating in the middle of the Pacific.

She hugged it a little tighter, like she was saying goodbye to an old friend. "I know this is all just a formality, but it's formalities that make things real. You know? Tucker and I split six months ago, and despite everything that happened between us, I know it was the right decision for us. But after today I'm gonna be divorced, and I never planned on being divorced."

Jack wrapped his strong hand over the top of the envelope, and she finally relinquished it.

"You always live according to a plan?"

She scoffed and reached into her oversize purse, pulling out her giant planner. She opened it, leafing through the pages of color-coded lists, highlighted dates, and—the part she was most proud of—zero mistakes needing to be crossed out. *Unless* she went back to her planner from three years ago and crossed out the weekend when she and Tucker eloped. Because yes, she still had it.

"Whoa," Jack said, whistling softly. "That's a little intense."

"It's my life," she said, her finger landing on today's date, where nothing per se was written. There was just a drawing of a black arrow in the shape of a U.

"A U-turn," Jack said, stating the obvious.

She nodded, sitting up straight. "Today is the day I turn it all around. I messed up. Married the wrong guy. Put my dream on hold for his. I detoured. Today I get back on track."

Jack leaned forward and pulled the papers from the envelope, leafing through them as he spoke.

"You know," he said, "there's no shame in detouring."

She was afraid of this. The pep talk. But pep talks were

meant for people who needed to be pepped. Buoyed. Propped up. But she'd managed on her own for six months already. Now wasn't the time to start leaning. It was time to get back on track.

U-turn.

She stood quickly, straightening out nonexistent wrinkles in her skirt before grabbing her bag and dropping the planner back inside. "If nothing looks out of place on first glance, I think we can do that tour now. You'll let me know if I missed anything, right? Or if Tucker snuck something past my own contract scrutiny." She let out a soft laugh. Nothing got past her scrutiny. Well, other than her ex-husband's infidelity.

"I've said it before and I'll say it again—you're going easy on him. You could have asked for a lot more in the settlement and gotten it easily."

Lily shook her head. "It's more complicated than that. He did a bad thing, but he's not a bad person. I don't want to punish him with years of alimony or whatever. I want a clean break." She brushed the dust off the back of her skirt. "I'm just going to wash my hands," she said, turning toward the small bathroom.

Jack pressed his lips into a smile. "Just don't close the door all the way. The doorknob on the inside is a little temperamental." He laughed. "Walker got stuck in there for two hours a month back."

She laughed softly as she turned on the sink and left the door wide open. "You didn't know he was here?" she asked over the running water.

"No. We knew. Just thought he could use a couple hours of silent reflection."

She was still laughing when she emerged into the office space once more.

Jack rose to meet her, shaking out his right leg, the one he'd broken last spring.

"Still hurts?" she asked.

"Just a little stiff," he admitted. "Must be a storm coming in. Hell, we need rain after the summer we had." He held the door open for her. "I'll get back to you no later than tomorrow afternoon if we need to contact Tucker's attorney for any last-minute issues. But I'm thinking we're all good."

Lily almost tripped over a dusty cowboy boot as she exited the office. Luke Everett straightened and caught her elbow before she went down. Talk about mixed signals—ignoring her birthday/divorce day and then saving her from face-planting on the wood floor. Then again, he had been one big pile of mixed signals the night she first met him.

Was his grip this strong three years ago? Or his fingers this warm?

"Shit. Sorry. I was waiting for Jack."

"It's all worries," Lily said. Then she shook her head. "I mean, no good."

Luke's brows drew together, and Lily jerked her elbow free as she willed her brain to unscramble.

"What's up?" Jack asked, but he was already glancing over his brother's shoulder to the tall, slender blonde circling the perimeter of the space.

"Can I help you?" Jack called, walking toward her.

"Jack, I—" Luke stammered, but his brother ignored him in favor of the stranger, who seemed to be casing the premises.

Lily and Luke were on Jack's heels, and if she didn't know better, she would have thought Luke was racing her.

When he stepped in front of her, effectively cutting her off, she slammed into his back.

"What are you doing?" she asked, but he held up a hand, waving her off. "Hey!" she said, poking Luke in the shoulder. "What's your problem?"

He spun to face her, blue eyes full of ice and his jaw tight. "Jeez, Lily. Not *now*, okay?"

"Screw you," she whisper-shouted, but Luke had already turned back toward his brother.

She maneuvered in front of *him*, trying to keep him from whatever he wanted to say. She didn't care what it was, only that she came out victorious in this little battle of wills.

"*Jack*," Luke said again, but his brother had already caught up to the mystery woman who was several paces ahead, squatting on the floor, running her hand along the unfinished baseboard.

"Knotted pine," she said, standing. "Very rustic and ranch-like. A good fit."

"Thanks," Jack said, his brows pulling together. "We're not open till late next summer, though. Maybe even early fall. Depending on the crop, that is."

She smiled and rested a hand on her flat belly. She wore a simple blue T-shirt and dark skinny jeans that ended at a pair of ballet flats, though her legs seemed to go on for miles. Her hair was in one of those messy buns, her face seemingly free of makeup, and she was—gorgeous. Lily had this niggling feeling she'd met the woman before, but she couldn't place her.

Instinctively, she ran a hand through her still-growing-out blond pixie. She glanced down at the wedges she wore to make her five-foot-four frame seem longer. Then she silently chastised herself for the comparison.

"I know," the woman said. "But I heard about your place from my boyfriend. I mean fiancé. Wow, I'm so not used to calling him that." She was talking like she was on fast-forward. "And anyway—okay. This is gonna sound crazy, but my fiancé and I are unexpectedly expecting, and we want to get married before the baby comes. And while I can still fit in a dress. So I thought, a Thanksgiving wedding! But it's October, and everything's booked, and we're not looking to have a giant affair. Just our family and close friends, and even unfinished the winery would do. Then I'd just need music and a caterer and—"

"I'll do it!" Lily interrupted. "The food, I mean."

This was definitely not in her planner. But hell, she was making a U-turn, right? She was almost officially divorced and absolutely officially jobless. And what safer place to cater her first party than with the moral support of her friends?

"Fuck. *No*," Luke said, glaring at her as the two of them caught up to Jack and the stranger.

Okay, so Jack and his fiancée, Ava, were her friends. She could ignore the second eldest Everett—if he would just stop talking.

The other woman's eyes darted toward the younger of the two brothers.

"Luke!" she said. "I thought that was you. Wow do you two look alike." She glanced back and forth between the brothers.

He opened his mouth to say something, but Lily didn't care who the woman was or what this little reunion between her and Luke meant. She was going to seal this deal. *Now.*

"Jack," she interrupted, "the interior should be done by the beginning of next month, right? That's what Ava said. You could put the place on the map before it even opens, and I can do this, my first catering job." She turned to the other woman. "I swear I can cook. I used to run a restaurant, but I left it to open my own business.

I can even cook up some menu samples this week as a résumé of sorts."

Jack scratched the back of his neck, and the beautiful stranger beamed.

"A wedding?" he said. "That was never the plan for the winery, but it's not a half-bad idea."

Luke grabbed his brother's shoulder. "It's a *whole* bad idea. Trust me."

Jack narrowed his eyes. "I'd have to talk to the contractors first. Then I'd have to draw up some sort of contract. You really up for this, Lil?"

"Don't say I didn't warn you," Luke said under his breath.

He was the only one who seemed put off by the situation, which made zero sense, but she didn't care. Not one little bit. She was making her U-turn right here and now, and hell if she was going to let Luke Everett ruin it for her.

Jack shrugged. "Why don't we all head on up to the ranch, where we can iron out the details." He held out his hand. "Jack Everett," he said.

She shook. "Sara Sugar."

Lily gasped, recognition finally setting in. She *had* seen the woman before. On television. She looked so different that she hadn't put the pieces together. But that's not how she *knew* her. "You—you have that show on the Food Network."

Sara beamed. "*Sugar and Spice.* Yeah. The baking show. I know. I look nothing like my TV self, right? I get that all the time. It's the hair and makeup, I guess."

Her heart beat like a sledgehammer against her chest. She'd finally gone and done something impulsive—put herself out there like she never had before—and look what she'd done.

She should run out the damned door and never look back. Except then she'd leave Jack in one hell of an awkward situation after he'd just done thousands of dollars of work for her for free. And the buyout she'd received from Tucker for BBQ on the Bluff? She couldn't live on it forever, especially if she was going to use it as seed money for her own business…and that whole paying-the-mortgage issue.

She needed a job. And this was so close to being the perfect one.

"Tucker Green is your fiancé," Lily finally said, trying as hard as she could to make her wince look like a smile as she shook the woman's hand.

"Aw shit," she heard Jack say under his breath, but Sara must have missed it. She just smiled and nodded.

"Yes!" she said. "How did you know?"

"I'm Lily Green." She fought to keep her voice steady. "Tucker's ex-wife."

CHAPTER TWO

Eight seconds. That was all Luke needed. Just last eight seconds with his hand in the goddamn rope, and he would qualify for the finals in Phoenix and be able to take the holidays to rest up.

"Focus, Everett," he said under his breath, the bull beneath him huffing out a breath as the two stared down the gate. He watched the timer. Three seconds till showtime, and then hang the hell on for eight.

Two.

One.

"Here we fucking go, partner."

The animal darted through the gate, and Luke's legs hugged the rough hide while his left arm flew in the air. Then in a flash of vision, he saw her, that stricken expression on her face before she hid it behind that bullshit mask of perfection. Christ, what the hell was Lily Green doing in his thoughts? She had no place there. No right to distract him *now*.

And that's when it happened. He hadn't seen or felt the glove slide off his wrist. Hell, had he forgotten to tighten the strap? The split-second thought didn't matter. Glove or not, he'd lost his concentration just as the bull kicked its hind legs into the air, bucking so hard his hand slid free with a wild jerk.

He heard his shoulder pop before he was thrown, and then the air was knocked out of him when he hit the dirt. Pain seared through his right side so hard he swore one of his lungs had collapsed. The last thing he remembered was the rodeo clown running between him and the bull before he blacked out completely.

He woke in the ambulance to see his aunt Jenna staring down at him, her eyes narrowed. He took in a breath and winced.

"Well," he said, forcing a smile. "At least you're not Jack." He wasn't in the mood for a lecture about the risks he took with his physical safety.

She just shook her head, her blond ponytail swinging. He wasn't quite sure, but there might have been two of her sitting beside him.

"He sent Ava and Owen home in the Jeep. But you best be sure he's following right behind."

"And Walker?" Luke asked.

Jenna shrugged. "He took off with what looked like a bachelorette party after he saw you weren't dead."

He laughed, then hissed at the pain. "At least someone's ending the night on the right note."

"Easy now," a male voice said on his other side as Luke tried to lift his head. The EMT. "You've most likely got a concussion. Got the shoulder back in the socket while you were out, but we won't know about other injuries until we get in for X-rays."

Ah, he thought. That was the pop he felt when he was forced to let go.

"How many seconds?" he asked Jenna through gritted teeth, each breath bringing back that searing pain in his side.

Her gaze softened, and he knew. She didn't even have to say it, and he could tell from the look on her face that she didn't want to, either.

"Fuck," he growled. "How close was I?"

She chewed on her top lip and then blew out a breath. "Six point eight seconds. I'm so sorry, Luke."

"*Fuck*," he said again, his head pounding. "There's still Anaheim at the end of November. My last chance to qualify for the National Finals. I'll just—get back to training."

The EMT was checking his pulse as the ambulance came to a stop.

"Keep him in the waiting room," Luke said.

His aunt's eyes widened as she opened her mouth to protest.

"Hell, Jenna. Let them patch me up in peace before I have to listen to the top ten ways Luke Everett takes his life for granted. Better yet, I'll recite it for him when they release me. Just keep him in the goddamn waiting room."

The doors in the back of the ambulance flew open, and the two EMTs lowered the gurney. Jenna followed. And there was big brother Jack, already pacing just outside the entrance.

"Christ, he must have been driving faster than we were," one of the EMTs noted.

Luke's eyes met his brother's, and all he saw was a storm of fury. So he winked and grinned at the man who was more of a father to him than his bastard of a drunk—and dead and gone—one was.

"All in a day's work, big brother." He grinned through the pain, putting on the show that everyone expected. "See you on the other side."

Jenna pressed her hands to Jack's shoulders. She may have been eight years his senior, but his brother towered over their aunt. Still, he let her hold him back. And only when they were out of sight did Luke let his head fall back on the gurney, his teeth threatening to grind to dust as he surrendered to the pain.

Nope, he thought. *I sure as hell don't need the lecture.* But he'd get it. Hell, he'd get an earful because that was Jack. He cared too much. After taking the brunt of their father's fists and sometimes boot for five years when they were teens, he still couldn't let go. Couldn't stop trying to protect him even now that they were grown men. But Luke couldn't live the careful life he had back then.

"My terms," he mumbled as someone from patient registration started asking him questions about his name, his address, whether or not he had insurance. And when they wheeled him off again to be X-rayed, there was Jack, just outside the curtain. He hadn't listened to Jenna at all.

"I'm taking Jenna home," he said. "But I'll be here when they bring you back."

Luke nodded and closed his eyes, and his brain decided to fuck with him again. Because there was Lily Green, popping up where she didn't belong, derailing his life in 6.8 seconds.

Jack's knuckles were white as he gripped the steering wheel, his jaw tight.

"How the hell's Jenna gonna make it over for Sunday brunch tomorrow if you got her car?" Luke asked. His intent was a subject change, but all it seemed to do was make Jack clench his jaw tighter.

"We're putting brunch on hold. You need your rest. I'll worry about the car tomorrow." He shook his head. "I've kept my mouth shut about the bruises. The stitches. The other *two* concussions," his brother said, and Luke forcefully cleared his throat. "Fine. I've *mostly* kept my mouth shut. But fuck, man. A dislocated shoulder, two fractured ribs, and concussion number three? At what point does this stop becoming sport and finally turn into reckless endangerment?"

Luke bit back a laugh only because it would fucking hurt *not* to, and he wouldn't give his brother more ammunition.

"Shoulder's already back in place," he said instead.

Jack shook his head but kept his eyes on the road. "So they got you in a sling just for fun?"

Luke rolled his eyes. "To stabilize it for a week. I'm just saying it's not as bad as it looks. I'll be fine to train—"

"Four weeks," Jack said through gritted teeth. "You are out of the goddamn saddle for four weeks. Doctor's orders. And *mine*."

Luke laughed. And fuck it hurt to do it, but he couldn't be expected to sit on his ass when his last chance to qualify for the finals was at the end of those four weeks. Plus there was a ranch to run, a vineyard to bring back to life. He wasn't going to rest. Luke Everett *didn't* rest.

"There are two new calves that need tagging," he said. "And what about Gertie?"

"Walker and I got the calves," Jack countered. "And Gertie's still got at least a week or two to go before calving herself."

Luke groaned. "I just hired that new stable boy to work weekends. High school kid who lives in town. He needs training."

Jack shrugged. "Ava has a Saturday morning class, so I'm on Owen detail. Your brother will have to drink a little less on Fridays and wake a little earlier."

Luke snorted. "Have you met Walker?"

They rolled up into the driveway of Crossroads Ranch,

their childhood home, where Jack now lived with his fiancée and son.

"Someone hit *you* on the head, asshole, or did you forget I don't live here anymore?" Luke asked.

Jack climbed out of the vehicle and walked around to the passenger side, obviously anticipating the struggle it would be for Luke to open the door without the use of his right arm.

"Well, shit," Luke said under his breath.

"You're staying here," Jack said, pulling the door open. "At least for the week while you're in that damn sling. And maybe another week after that."

Luke swung his leg out and planted his boot firmly on the ground, then gripped the frame of the door as he pushed himself up to stand.

"Fuck," he said, louder this time.

"Still want to tag the calves?" Jack asked with an *I told you so* grin.

"Fuck you."

His brother raised a brow. "Consider yourself grounded for the next four weeks, cowboy."

Despite his desperation for the prescription they filled on the way home, Luke couldn't help but push back. Limits were *not* okay.

"And what the hell am I supposed to do until then? That gives me zero time to train for Anaheim. And shit, we have a business to run. *Two* now that you said yes to that damned mess of a wedding."

His brother smiled, which was not a good sign. The only things that made Jack Everett smile were Ava and their son, Owen.

"You're freaking me out, man," Luke said.

Jack nodded. "The wedding," he said. "It's perfect.

You're in charge of getting the space ready for the wedding. Tucker's your buddy. You can make sure the Callahans stay on task with finishing the interior, and you can help Lily with the food stuff. Hell if I know why she still wants to cater this thing, but I bet it'll help if she has an ally." He slammed the car door shut behind Luke. "And *she* can make sure you stay the fuck out of the stables."

Jack didn't wait for a response, just turned and headed for the front porch where despite the late hour, Owen had just thrown open the door, his chocolate Lab Scully bounding down the steps. Luke struggled to keep up the pace behind him.

"I don't need a chaperone!" he called after him. Certainly not Lily. She was the goddamn reason he was in this situation in the first place.

Jack dropped to his knees to give Scully, who was already stretched out on his back, an enthusiastic belly rub. Then he caught up to Luke. "Well, then consider yourself lucky. You've got *more* than you could possibly need." He slapped the small white bag from the pharmacy against Luke's leg. "Ava has your old room all ready for you. Take your meds and get some rest."

And since the events of the night had finally caught up with him, Luke didn't argue. He just crossed his fingers the painkillers would knock him the hell out and let him sleep in peace, with no unwelcome thoughts of a certain blond caterer invading his dreams.

CHAPTER THREE

Do I have to do this blindfolded?" Ava asked.

Just for that, Lily tightened the tie they'd stolen from Jack's side of the closet.

Ava laughed. "Guess that answers my question. Still don't see how this makes me better qualified for the job, though, if at all."

Lily sat across from her at the kitchen table. "You grew up learning how to identify the ingredients in a glass of wine just from sniffing its *bouquet*." She overemphasized that last word. "I'm gonna venture to guess that you have a very discerning palate. The blindfold is so you don't let presentation influence your vote because these are just sample cakes. What the final product will look like is still up for consideration." She bit her lip and stared at the seven Tupperware containers in front of her. "The bride is a freaking *Food Network* pastry chef. I have to make sure I'm bringing my A-game when she does the official taste test."

Ava lifted the tie and peeked out with one eye. "The bride is also marrying your ex. Are you sure *any* of this is a good idea?"

Lily lovingly slapped Ava's hand away from the blindfold.

"This is what I've always wanted to do, and if anyone can put me on the map as a go-to caterer, it's Sara Sugar."

"Tucker's fiancée."

She nodded even though Ava couldn't see her. "Tucker's fiancée."

"Who's pregnant," Ava added.

"Who is definitely pregnant. I *know,*" she said. "It's probably the worst decision ever. But something in me just sorta snapped, I think. I said yes before I knew who she was and then once I did, I couldn't figure out how to say no. Especially when she was all, *This was supposed to happen.*"

Ava snorted. "And you're sure you're over—"

Before the woman could get another word in, Lily tore open one of the containers, pinched a piece of cake between her fingers, and shoved it into Ava's open mouth.

Ava's palms splayed against the top of the wooden table, and her head fell back as she let out a groan. "Oh my God," she said.

Lily beamed and clapped her hands together. "Tell me what you taste!"

Ava's tongue swiped at a bit of frosting still on her bottom lip. "It's not buttercream. I'm sure about that." She pursed her lips. "There was fruit, too. The tiniest bit tart but mostly sweet. Raspberry, I think." She did a little happy dance in her chair, and Lily knew she'd figured it out. "Not buttercream but white *chocolate*. White chocolate raspberry. Oh, Lil. How can any of the others be better than this?"

"Looks like I'm missing the part— *Shit.* He's got me chaperoned even when I'm in the house?"

Lily's gaze darted past the kitchen—and to a half-naked Luke Everett who'd just emerged from the hallway. Her hand flew to her mouth as she gasped. "What the hell happened to you?"

Angry purple bruises mottled the right side of his torso, and his right arm hung in a sling. And she couldn't help it. Her eyes dipped to where his dark jeans hung just below his hips. She swallowed, hoping no one noticed. But then ogling kind of came with the territory when you were near any of the Everett brothers. If you were into that whole blond-hair, blue-eyed cowboy sort of thing. Which she certainly was not.

"The rodeo was not kind to our Luke last night," Ava said, pulling the tie over her head.

"Neither is all the damn commotion out here," he said, his initially playful tone growing cold. "How's an injured man supposed to sleep with all this—" He stepped closer to the table, leaning over to peer at the lined-up containers. Then he sucked in a breath through his teeth. "Well damn. Guess I'll have to add leaning to the list of things that hurt like hell."

Ava snorted. "Commotion? Poor baby. Next time we'll simmer down so you can sleep past eleven."

He didn't smile, just strode past the table and to the coffeemaker that still had a cup or two left.

"What else hurts?" Lily asked, his back to them as he awkwardly poured the coffee with what she could tell was his nondominant hand.

He moved toward the fridge, still not looking at her as he answered, "Breathing. Getting out of bed. Being woken up earlier than I'd like to be."

Ava rolled her eyes, which gave Lily permission to do the same.

The jug of milk he set on the counter was brand-new and therefore not yet open.

"You want help?" she asked. "I can open it for you."

He looked at her, then at the jug, and slid the milk back onto its shelf in the refrigerator.

"I'll drink it black," he said coolly.

I'll drink it black, she silently mimicked, only Luke turned around before she finished.

Busted. Yet his expression remained impassive.

He leaned against the counter, still shirtless. Did he know he was still shirtless? She was sure now that he wasn't a lefty, his hand not quite steady as he took his first sip.

"Where's Jack and Owen?" he asked Ava, but she'd already sneaked another taste of the white chocolate raspberry cake, and her mouth was full.

"They left for the park about fifteen minutes ago. Something about pitching practice, I think," Lily said. "They were complaining about two hours in the car this morning."

Ava nodded and groaned again. "Brought Jenna's car back. Park. Pitching. Yes." She licked frosting from her fingers. "Sorry. I'm a little preoccupied with orgasm-inducing pastry. Don't mind me."

Luke raised a brow, but absent was that ever-present grin he wore whenever she saw him with Tucker. Well, unless *she* was with them, which wasn't often. Tucker liked his boys' nights separate from date nights, and Lily liked to pretend that the boys' nights didn't exist.

"Do you—want a taste?" she asked him, holding up the almost empty container. "Before Ava leaves your brother for this last bite?"

"Oh I might," Ava said, trying to stab the last morsel with her fork, but Lily flinched just in time. She grabbed a clean fork, got up from the table, and strode right up to Luke.

She had the ridiculous urge to rub her fingers over his bruised ribs, to soothe what she assumed must be more painful than he was letting on, even if he was complaining. And the sling. What was that for? She knew injury was par for the course when it came to rodeo, but something about this time was different. She could see it in those ice-blue eyes.

She forked the last piece of the first cake and held it in front of his mouth.

"I can still feed myself," he said.

She could smell the coffee as his warm breath filled the space between them, the scent far less bitter than his tone.

She cleared her throat. "You gonna put that coffee down, then, and take the fork? I was just trying to—"

"Help," he interrupted. "Yeah. I know. Fine. I'll eat your damn cake." And he nearly snarled as his lips wrapped around the fork, wiping it clean. His eyes widened, and Lily allowed herself a smug smile. "*Shit,*" he said, and though it was not the sweetest of words itself, the way he said it made her think it was the nicest thing he'd said to her in quite some time.

"You're welcome," she said, then spun on her heel and turned back toward the table where she again sat across from Ava. "Time for blind taste test number two!"

Ava's phone buzzed with a text as soon as Lily opened container number two. Lily watched her friend smile and knew that it must be Jack. Ava had a certain smile that was just for him, and as much as she loved that she could recognize it, it also made something in Lily's gut ache.

Had she ever had a smile like that for Tucker? Or he for her? Ava and Jack's connection spanned more than a decade. She didn't know their whole story but had gleaned enough to know that even when they weren't in each other's lives, that connection hadn't faded. And now that they were together again, she felt like she was watching a snippet of a romance movie every time she saw them together.

Ava's smile turned to a wince when she looked up from her phone screen.

"You're leaving me alone with all this cake. Aren't you?" It wasn't a question. Lily knew that look.

"Well…?" Ava started. "Owen and Jack drove through town on the way to the park and saw on the signboard that Baker's Bluff had Owen's favorite grilled cheese sandwich on the menu today, and they're going to lunch and wanted to know if I could meet them. But you know what? I can totally stay. This is important, and I promised I'd help you. I'll just text him back—"

"Stop," Lily said, laying her palm on Ava's hand. "I'm not going to keep a friend from spending time with her almost-husband and child. What kind of a monster do you think I am?"

Luke snorted, and her head shot up.

"What was that for?" she asked. "Did Tucker call me a controlling monster or something?"

He shrugged, then winced. "I'm not saying he didn't…"

"Luke!" Ava said. "What's gotten into you?"

Lily waved her off. "I walked right into that one. I'm not saying your almost brother-in-law isn't an asshole for saying it, but it wasn't wholly unexpected."

"Noted," Luke said.

She felt a little triumphant that his dig at her had caused him physical pain—but also a little like an asshole herself for relishing in someone else's misfortune. The truth was, he looked terrible all banged up like that—yet downright gorgeous. How could a man put his body through the ringer like Luke did and then roll out of bed with that sexy swagger that never seemed to leave?

She sighed. It was an Everett thing. The gene pool had been kind to all three brothers—at least in the physical respect. Ava got the nice one, and Lily had been verbally sparring with Luke for the better part of three years. What happened to the charmer who made a fool of himself on the dance floor just to talk to her?

"I know you're in a lot of pain," Ava said to Luke, "but Lily didn't deserve that. You know what? You can make it up to her by helping her with the cake tasting while I meet up with Jack and Owen. And, Lily, you can make sure he ices his ribs and keeps his arm in the sling." She pointed at Luke. "No being an asshole, and *no* sneaking out to the stables."

"I don't need a damn babysitter," he mumbled into his coffee mug.

"I'll just taste my own cakes," Lily said under her breath.

Ava laughed. "I think you two can call a truce for the sake of wedding cake," she said. "Can you both promise to behave for an hour or two?"

Lily did need an outside opinion to tell her which flavors were her true A-game. Otherwise she'd just choose her own favorite, lemon curd, and call it a day.

Lily crossed her arms and sighed. "*I* can behave."

Luke narrowed his eyes and lowered his coffee mug. "I'm only doing this because that first cake was fucking good."

Ava raised a brow. "Say you'll behave."

Lily watched the muscle in his jaw pulse once before he spoke. "Fine. I'll behave."

"Good!" Ava stood and handed Jack's tie to Lily with a wink. "Time to blindfold your victim."

CHAPTER FOUR

A throat cleared in the kitchen entryway.

Lily yelped while Luke simply chewed the next bite of cake he'd been fed, pulled off his blindfold, then gave their party crashers a sly grin.

"Mornin', Sheriff. Who's your friend?" Luke raised a brow at Sheriff Cash Hawkins and his lovely brunette guest.

"Sheriff!" Lily said. "I was just—I mean, Luke was helping me pick a cake for the wedding."

Cash narrowed his eyes. "You two are getting married?"

"Hell no!" Luke said. Didn't matter how good she smelled or that she could bake the hell out of a cake. Marriage wasn't on his radar, especially with the woman indirectly responsible for his broken ribs and dislocated shoulder.

Lily gave Luke a pointed look, then laughed nervously. "*No*. Luke and I are *not* getting married. But my ex-husband is. To Sara Sugar. From that Food Network show *Sugar and Spice*? Right. You don't watch television. Anyway, Tucker's getting married, and I'm happy for him, and I'm sort of catering the wedding."

"What?" the sheriff's mysterious companion blurted. "I'm sorry. I don't know you, and that was rude of me, but—*what*? You're catering your ex-husband's wedding?"

Lily bit her lip and nodded. "I know it sounds crazy, but I need the job."

"And she agreed to it before she knew *whose* wedding it was. Not that I didn't try to stop her." Luke put his coffee mug down on the counter and swiped the fork out of Lily's hand. "If you all are going to keep on talking about Lily's excellent decision-making skills, I'm just going to take care of the cake." He dug the fork into the hunk of cake and stuffed it into his mouth.

"You're an asshole sometimes. You know that?" Cash said.

Luke just raised his fork in a gesture of cheers and kept on chewing.

"Jack in his office?" Cash asked Lily.

She shook her head. "Is he supposed to be? Ava just went to meet him and Owen for lunch."

Cash pulled his phone out of his pocket, glanced at the screen, and then cursed under his breath.

"What is it?" the other woman asked. She sounded worried.

"Nothing," he said. "Just missed a text from Jack." He went on to explain something about how Jack having lunch with Ava and Owen instead of being there to meet with the two of them wasn't a sign. Luke had no idea what the sheriff was talking about but didn't care. He welcomed the interruption. Because Lily Green feeding him cake after the night he had? It felt more dangerous than getting back on the bull.

"Heard about the rodeo last night," Cash said, turning to Luke. "Bull threw you pretty hard."

Luke's grin faded. "I got—distracted," was all he said. Yet here he was, standing inches from the woman who'd invaded his thoughts when he'd least expected it. It was the closest he'd been to her since the night they'd met, and the memory of her on that dance floor—of her hand in his—made him suddenly dizzy. Or maybe it was the pain of his injuries, though nothing seemed to hurt at the moment.

Lily invited their surprise guests to stay for cake, and Luke—unable to shake the feeling he might indeed need a chaperone if he spent any more time alone with Lily Green—half hoped the sheriff would say yes.

"We'll take a rain check," Cash said.

"I'm Olivia, by the way," the other woman said.

Luke opened his mouth to introduce himself, but Lily beat him to the punch.

"Lily," she said. "And this ray of sunshine is Luke."

"Ray of sunshine my ass," Luke mumbled as the two women continued to exchange pleasantries. But what burrowed under his skin was the thought that he *was* a goddamn ray of sunshine 99 percent of the time. He'd swear on it—even call witnesses. But that one percent of the time when he crossed paths with Lily Green? Cloud cover came real quick. Sometimes even a storm.

"Uh...Earth to Luke? Do you copy?"

"Huh?" he asked, blinking to realize he and Lily were the only ones in the kitchen again. Cash and Olivia were gone.

"I was just wondering—I mean, what if someone else walks through the front door. Are you—gonna put a shirt on?" she asked.

Luke lowered himself into a chair, looked down at his bare, bruised torso and then up at the only woman who ever seemed to have a problem with it. Sure, he could finish getting dressed, but what would be the point? It wasn't like he was leaving the house today. Plus it would hurt like hell to get up again.

"Wasn't planning on it," he said. "Most women actually prefer me this way."

Lily groaned. "Yeah, well, I'm not most women."

He raised a brow. "Then I guess you're missing out."

She narrowed her eyes, those green pools of poison threatening to obliterate him. What the hell was *her* problem? She was the one who got them into this mess—her baking multiple wedding cakes for her ex-husband and him benched and having to help her do it.

"Am I eating more cake or what?" he asked.

She sat down and stuck a fork in the opened container in front of her.

"You don't even *like* me," she said, and his brows drew together.

"Seems beside the point."

She huffed out a breath. "So you admit it. God, I knew I was right! I just never figured it would take me divorcing Tucker for you to finally own up to it."

He leaned forward, resting his good arm on the table.

"Sweetheart," he said, his voice low and cool, "you don't know a thing about me."

She matched him, lean for lean. She smelled like warm vanilla, like she'd just stepped out of a bakery. But he'd blame his mouth watering on the perfectly lined-up containers of cake long before he'd admit to her having any sort of effect on him.

"I know you think life is one big party, that you don't take anything or any*one* seriously, and that you think it's charming women prefer you naked than any other way because that's probably the only time you give them your undivided attention. It's no wonder anyone in your orbit would think *his* life didn't measure up."

His teeth ground together, and he gripped the edge of

the table like he was prepared to turn it to dust. "You didn't just blame me for your divorce, did you? Tucker was married to *you*. Not me."

And she was the one who left. Shit, he remembered the night it happened. Tucker, the guy who always had his shit together, was a goddamn mess, drunk off his ass at three in the morning. Maybe it wasn't his place to lob accusations at Lily like he was, but it also wasn't his place to be letting her feed him cake.

They were so close. He could kiss her if she was any other fucking woman in the world. If she wasn't his best friend's ex-wife. If she wasn't a whole hell of a lot of things.

"Yeah, well now he's marrying someone else, so why don't we just leave Tucker out of the equation."

He laughed. "So you can insult me and the way I live my life?"

Lily shrugged. "I just don't see what's wrong with acting like a responsible adult. With taking your life seriously. Or—or stopping for one second to think how your actions—like going to a strip club on a Tuesday—might influence others."

Christ. He remembered that night—and *Tucker's* suggestion that they leave the bar and do something a little less PG-rated. But what would it matter now to defend himself? He knew how Lily saw him—how she'd always seen him since the night they met—and that wasn't going to change.

He pushed back from the table and rose quickly, fueled by adrenaline. But that did nothing to mask the pain as he swore he felt something pop.

"Dammit!" He hissed in a sharp breath, but that put more pressure on his ribs.

Her eyes widened, and she was up in a flash. "Shoot.

Ava's gonna kill me if she comes home and finds you in worse shape than when she left. What do you need? Ice? Do you have an ice pack in the freezer?"

He braced his unencumbered hand on the counter and took in another breath, this time slow and controlled. "Yes. On the bottom shelf of the door." Great. Not only was he stuck with her for the next couple of hours, but now he had to *rely* on her help because he let her get a rise out of him.

She slammed the freezer shut and brandished the blue gel pack in her hand. "You probably need to lie down, right?"

He nodded. "Right."

She approached him hesitantly, like she was afraid of spooking a wild animal.

He groaned. "I'm not gonna fucking bite...unless that's what you want." He raised a brow, but she just rolled her eyes. Nope, he wasn't getting a rise out of *her*. This was their dance, though. He ruffled her feathers, her eyes sparked with anger, and he'd get the satisfaction of knowing—in some small way—that he'd had an effect on her. It was safe enough that he could justify it. But the only thing he saw in her eyes right now was pure, unfiltered annoyance.

"I'm just trying to figure out if I need to help you to your bed or just drop the ice pack on the counter and let you fend for yourself."

He blew out a breath. "I can't handle the stairs right now. I just need to get to the couch."

She pursed her lips. "And...?"

"And *what*?" he snapped. His body answered him with a sharp stab of pain to the ribs.

"And, 'Lily, I would be most appreciative if you'd assist me.'" She wore a self-satisfied smile. He'd have been wholly pissed off if not for one thing—that tiny spark in her green eyes.

"Nobody fucking talks like—"

"And…?" she interrupted.

His head fell back, and he closed his eyes, needing a moment to collect himself. Because he couldn't believe what he was about to say.

"Please, Lily," he ground out. "Can you help me to the couch?"

She jutted out her chin. "Why yes, Luke. I'd be happy to." Then she deflated, her brows pulling together. "How do I do that so I don't make it worse?" He opened his mouth to respond, but she cut him off. "And no sassy comment about how I've already made things worse."

He bit back a laugh, though he wasn't sure if it was because he knew it would hurt or because he didn't want her to see she had the ability to make him smile.

He put his good arm over her shoulders. "Put your right hand on my right hip. You just need to make sure I don't go down like a ton of bricks."

She did as he asked, and he bit the inside of his cheek as her breast, covered only by a thin T-shirt that read I LIKE BAKING MORE THAN I LIKE PEOPLE, pressed against his side. Her fingertips brushed the skin above his jeans as she placed her hand gingerly on his hip, and now that she couldn't see his expression, he smiled to himself as he heard her short intake of breath.

Maybe he got a rise out of Little Miss Responsible Adult after all.

Once they were moving, though, that grin was a thing of the past.

"You realize," she said, "that if you do go down like a ton of bricks, I can't do much more than break your fall."

He waited until they made it to the couch and she helped lower him to his back before he responded. "Maybe that was my grand plan, to crush you to dust so you'd stop being so irritating."

She kneeled next to him and laid the ice pack gently over his bruises, not taking the bait.

"Damn, that feels good." He practically groaned.

"Do you need medicine or something?" she asked, her hand still resting lightly on the pack.

He shook his head. "I took a painkiller early this morning. Can't have another till about two."

She stared at him, her brows furrowing as her soft blond hair fell over her eyes. How much had changed since she'd been the sexy line dancer with the pixie cut he couldn't take his eyes off of? She chewed that plump bottom lip of hers and just kept looking at him, like she was having a conversation in her head that she couldn't interrupt. And that damn hand of hers was still on him. On the ice pack on him, but close enough. It felt—messed up.

"Do you always do that?" he asked.

She blinked a few times, like she was coming out of a trance. "Do what?"

"Think so goddamn hard."

She nodded slowly. "I do."

"Doesn't it get tiring?"

Again she nodded, and her breathing was less even than it was seconds ago. "Don't you get tired of hospital visits. Or—or never waking up with the same girl twice?"

She swallowed hard after that one, and like it didn't know who he was talking to, his dick twitched in response as he thought briefly of waking up with *her*.

"No," he admitted. "I do what I want, when I want. My choice. And if and when that starts to get tiring, I'll consider another approach. Life's too fucking short to waste time on thinking."

It was part truth, part lie. Luke thought long and hard the night she went home with Tucker Green instead of with him. He realized then he wasn't the kind of guy women chose for the long term, so he took that off the table. And guess what? Life *had* been pretty damn enjoyable—until Lily Green got back in his head and he wound up in the ER busted up the worst he'd ever been.

She nodded absently, then quirked her head to the side, her brows furrowing. "Especially when I'm thinking the *wrong* thing."

She grabbed the arm of the couch and made like she was going to stand, but because Luke was against the whole thinking thing, he didn't have time to realize that what he was about to ask was also the *wrong* thing.

He grabbed her hand before she lifted it from his side. "What's the wrong thing?" he asked softly.

"Yesterday was my birthday," she said absently.

And the day the divorce was final. He knew. He fucking knew and said nothing because just being around her knocked him off-kilter.

It always had. But now that she was this close, all logic flew out the window.

"It was sort of the worst birthday, too," she continued. "No presents. So I was thinking...I mean, there's this heat, right? This angry sort of heat. And it makes me *want*..."

She shook her head even as she lowered it, and when her lips were so close to his that a mere breath could have made them touch, she whispered, "It makes me want this."

Her lips brushed his, a soft sweep of flesh on flesh, her tongue flicking out to tease him. And hell if she didn't taste as sweet as she smelled.

"Sweetheart... What the hell are we doing here?"

"I'm *not* your *sweetheart*," she said, a slight tremble in her voice.

And no. Despite how she tasted and smelled, there was nothing sweet about this girl, especially now. And because he didn't think—*couldn't* right now even if he tried—he tangled his fingers in her soft hair and pulled her to him.

This time they were two semis on a collision course with no possibility of slowing before impact. They crashed in a fiery explosion, tongues tangling, yet in the back of his mind he knew she was taking care not to fall on top of him. She was thinking. *Still* thinking, and he wanted to figure out how to make her stop.

He let go of her hair and gripped her waist, his hand traveling up her torso until his thumb brushed the side of her breast. Right now he didn't care if she *did* topple onto him. She could bust him up good if this was the reward.

She hummed a soft moan when he palmed her. His cock throbbed inside his jeans. And when he pinched her hardened peak, she gasped—and then sprang up like he'd set her on fire.

Her hand flew over her mouth, and she shook her head. "I can't. *We* can't."

She spun and, without another word, bolted toward the front door.

He didn't even get to eat any more of the cake.

"Shit." He tried to get up but knew she was too fast for him unless he risked making his situation even worse. "Lily!" he called after her. "You don't have to"—he heard the door slam—"go."

But she did have to leave. Because now that she wasn't pissing him off or kissing him, he had a second to do that thing he tried to avoid—think.

No matter what had gone wrong in their marriage, he couldn't do this to Tucker. Luke had had his shot, and he blew it. Since then, Lily Green was and always would be off-limits.

He glanced down to where he was still rock hard inside his pants. Looked like someone hadn't gotten the fucking memo.

CHAPTER FIVE

Lily breathed in the salty sea air and grinned at the list in her planner.

Food. Shopping for food at a farmers market. *This* was her happy place. She didn't have to think about anything other than the ripeness of a banana or the firmness of a tomato.

Firmness.

She'd had a week to forget about Luke Everett's firm torso—and the firm line behind the zipper of his jeans after she…

Good Lord, she couldn't even *think* the thing that she'd done let alone relive its aftermath.

"Kiss me over the garden gate?"

Lily gasped and looked up from her planner to a young man standing behind a booth. "What?" she asked.

"Kiss me over the garden gate." He gestured to a table full of small potted pink plants. "Are you looking to pink up your garden?"

She shook her head slowly, still trying to block out that word. *Kiss.* Yeah, she was failing miserably.

"I have an herb garden," she said. "It's got a monochromatic theme going on."

He ran a hand through shaggy brown hair and then crossed his arms. "Pink goes really well with green. In fact, kiss-me-over-the-garden-gate has green stalks and leaves. It'll blend right in."

She blew out a breath and stepped closer to the table. "If I buy a plant, will you stop saying *Kiss me over the garden gate*?"

He gave her a toothy grin and stepped out of the booth and behind the table.

"Promise," he said. "Here. The runt of the litter, so it hopefully won't grow too high." He handed her the pot.

"How tall does it get?" she asked, her interest in the dangling buds piqued.

"Twelve feet!" he said proudly. "Grow it along a trellis or over a gate or fence. Makes a beautiful place under which to get kissed. Hence its name."

She groaned. "You *promised*."

He laughed. "I promised not to say *Kiss me over the garden gate.* You gave no directive about the word *kiss* in general." He held out a hand. "I'm Zane."

"Lily," she said, shaking Zane's hand.

"Ahhh. The perennial Lily. Blooms brighter and stronger each season."

She let out a nervous laugh. He was funny. And cute, if you liked overgrown glossy brown waves or sun-kissed skin that told of endless days at the beach when he wasn't cultivating flirty flowers. And maybe he was actually *flirting* with her, which was great, right? She was single, free to flirt with whomever she wanted.

Almost. There was a certain moody cowboy she needed to stop thinking about. Made it harder to appreciate the attention of a good-looking stranger who could even make her name sound romantic. Luke Everett just made it sound like a burden to utter. Come to think of it, he couldn't even bring himself to do that much. Just his disdainful *sweetheart.*

Stop. Thinking. About Luke Everett, she silently chastised.

She flipped to the page in her planner that had a convenient little pocket for her cash.

"That'll be ten bucks and—" He dipped his head and looked up at her through thick lashes. "Your number?"

Her eyes widened and she threw the planner to the ground. Apparently she was out of practice with this flirting thing.

She dropped to her knees to grab it only to find the book resting against the dusty toe of a worn cowboy boot. Her head rose slowly, her eyes following the line of his faded, ripped jeans up to where they hung perfectly on equally perfect hips. A gray T-shirt hugged his torso, one she knew hid three cracked ribs. The sling was gone, and his arms were crossed as he looked down at her through mirrored aviators.

Of *course* that certain moody cowboy was here.

She sprang to her feet and shoved the planner in her bag.

"I—uh—" She handed Zane a ten-dollar bill and grabbed the plant. "Here. I mean, thanks."

Zane raised a brow, and she could feel Luke just standing there, watching the whole scene like it was a Netflix Original he couldn't pry his eyes from.

"Is that a no on the number, then?" He nodded toward Luke.

"Rain check," she said, and then—though she needed to head the other way—bolted in the direction from which she came. The one that would hopefully lead her far, far away from Luke Everett.

Except once she got a hundred feet away, practically back to the parking lot, she remembered that she really did need eggs, and she only bought them fresh. She also needed butternut squash, apple, and fresh ginger for the ravioli. Peas, carrots, potatoes for the shepherd's pie. And—well—just about everything for the menu of autumn comfort foods Tucker and Sara had requested. Maybe she hadn't yet figured out the cake, but she could at least ensure the dinner items were up to par.

So, plant in hand, she spun on her heel once again and strode back into the heart of the market. Luke wasn't there anymore, waiting by Zane's flower stand. Of course he wasn't waiting for her. God, what was wrong with her? Luke Everett seemed to exist for two reasons only—to taunt her or get irritated with her like he always did.

Eggs. I need fresh eggs. She let that thought buoy her to a stand called Farm Fresh. The sign was hand painted, a rustic red background with white lettering and a nest of white eggs next to the logo. A blond woman, hair tied back in a messy bun, was handing a carton of eighteen eggs to a satisfied-looking customer. As Lily approached, the woman turned and gave her a familiar smile just as a chicken flapped its wings and flew up from behind the stand to greet her. Lily stumbled back in surprise as the bird landed on Farm Fresh's table.

"Lucy!" the egg woman scolded as *oomph*, Lily slammed into something solid.

"You gonna let a little chicken ruffle your feathers?" a deep voice rasped in her ear.

And then everything fell into place. The Farm Fresh sign. The woman she seemed to recognize. The obvious presence of an Everett brother at this very stand. The *one* Everett brother she'd be happy to avoid until the end of time. Or maybe an asteroid could just hurtle toward Earth right now and put her out of her misery.

She quickly stepped away from the warmth of the body behind her.

"Oh shit!" she said, turning to face him, the memory of his injuries overshadowing her humiliation. "I'm sorry. Are you—? Did I—?"

Luke's left hand rested lightly on his right side, but he was grinning. His eyes were still hidden behind the glasses, though, so she couldn't be sure if it was a genuine smile or a sneer. She'd place her money on the latter, yet she couldn't look away. She couldn't stop wondering what his blue eyes were doing behind their mask or if he, too, hadn't been able to get that kiss out of his head.

Her mouth went dry, and she struggled to swallow. His lips had been both rough and soft—insistent yet yielding, as if he was willing to give as much as he took. And when his fingers had tangled in her hair…

An ache burned low in her belly.

"It's gonna take more than a little thing like you to bring me down, sweetheart."

She groaned through gritted teeth but secretly thanked him for breaking whatever trance she'd been in. "I'm *not* your sweetheart."

And without giving him a chance to respond, she turned back to the table filled with eggs and a rambunctious chicken.

"You must be Luke's aunt Jenna," she said, straightening her bag on her shoulder and shifting the plant to her left hand so the two could shake. She didn't know much about the woman who looked way too young to be the aunt of three grown men, but she knew enough from the times she'd seen her with the Everetts that they were close. Her heart squeezed at this. The only family Lily knew anymore was her mom, and she hadn't been back to Phoenix to see her since long before things went south with Tucker.

"I'm Lily," she said. "A friend of Jack and Ava's. We may have met a time or two at—"

"BBQ on the Bluff!" Jenna said. "Y'all have the best corn bread I have *ever* tasted, and believe me when I say I am a harsh judge."

The lilt of her Texas accent reminded Lily the woman wasn't a California native, and for a small moment she felt a connection to the otherwise stranger—someone else who possibly came to the California coast looking for something better.

Jenna's eyes brightened. "You run the place with your husband, right?"

Lily's cheeks burned. "Ex-husband, actually, as of a few signed documents and short court appearance." That word. *Ex*-husband. Would it ever just roll off her tongue? She shrugged and forced a laugh. "Didn't last nearly as long as the wedding, and there were a lot less gifts."

She expected Jenna to do that thing that others did when she told them she and Tucker had separated, tilting their heads to the side with that puppy-dog-eyed look of sympathy. But instead the woman clapped her hands together and grinned.

"Well look at you, darlin'! You get a fresh start. A do-over. When it comes to matters of the heart, it's never too late to get it right." She leaned in close. "I'm thirty-six, and I know my Mr. Right is still out there. He's just hiding *real* good, waiting until our time is the right time."

Lily narrowed her eyes. "I guess that's one way to look at it. I don't know if I believe in that whole Mr. Right thing, though. Maybe Mr. Rebound?"

The chicken flapped her wings again, and Jenna pulled the bird into her arms, pinning the wings to her sides. "*Lu-cy*!" she scolded once more. Then her eyes met Lily's.

"Sorry. She gets a little excited when she can sense heightened emotions."

Jenna's gaze flickered over Lily's shoulder and narrowed.

"Don't you go doubtin' the power of Miss Lucy's intuition, nephew. She only tries to fly when someone's emotions are on the rise."

Lily heard Luke chuckle behind her, and something in the sound made her giggle softly, too.

Jenna put Lucy back on the table and rested her hands on her hips.

"Y'all are mocking me now?" she said, her Texas twang even more pronounced.

Luke strode past Lily and bent over the table to kiss his aunt on the cheek.

"Of course not," he said. "You have a psychic chicken. There's nothing in that worth mocking."

Lily's hand flew over her mouth. She didn't want to insult Jenna and certainly didn't want to give Luke the satisfaction of having made her laugh, so she bit the inside of her cheek and focused on doing anything but.

Jenna swatted Luke away. "I need a break from you, you pain in the ass. Last time Jack puts me on babysitting duty." Luke's smile fell away as quickly as it had appeared, but he said nothing. "You got more shopping to do, honey?" she asked, and Lily nodded. "How about this, then? Save the eggs for last. You can leave your pretty plant here, and since y'all are friends, *please* take him with you so I can get him out of my hair for an hour or so? His brooding is driving Lucy crazy, and I swear that's the first smile he's cracked since we opened shop—even if it was at Lucy's expense."

Lily opened her mouth to protest, but Jenna was already reaching for her plant. "I'll give you two for one on the eggs. Just please give my stir-crazy nephew something to do."

"I don't *need* something to do," Luke insisted. "I'm a goddamn grown man, and you all have me under lock and key."

Jenna squinted into the sun and pursed her lips as she faced her nephew once more. "You've got the whole morning to spend under this great big blue sky with a pretty girl and no shortage of good food around every corner. Most people would jump at the chance to be *locked up* like you keep complaining you are. You could have your big brother watching your every move if you prefer."

Luke kicked the toe of his battered boot into the dirt, and for a second Lily saw what he must have been like as a child—petulant yet endearing. The thought unexpectedly warmed her.

"Only because I'm stranded here with you—"

"And because you love your aunt." Jenna raised a brow and then leaned forward, Lucy still in her arms, offering him her cheek to kiss once more.

He did, and then he kissed Lucy, too.

"That's just to show I love her even though she's the worst psychic on the planet," he said.

Jenna laughed and swatted him away, but Lily knew this was the Luke everyone knew and loved, the one she saw that first night when she'd met him and Tucker, and the one who—for some reason—felt nothing but disdain for her.

And there it was. Thanks to a not-so-psychic chicken, she was spending her morning with the one man she swore she'd stop thinking about—whose kiss she swore she'd stop replaying in her head.

Yeah, she thought to herself. *Good luck with that.*

"I can't believe you just haggled over squash," Luke said before pulling an apple from Lily's tote bag and sinking his teeth into it.

"Hey!" She backhanded him on the shoulder. "That's for my ravioli! Or maybe they'd prefer soup." She shook her head. "Whatever. It doesn't matter. The point is, it's *mine*."

He grinned, a hunk of apple between his front teeth. "Take it back," he said around the fruit, and she just rolled her eyes and kept walking.

"I still overpaid for the squash," she said. "But he was the only guy who had butternut, so I guess the law of supply and demand wins."

He bit off another piece of the Red Delicious, wiping the dribble of sweet juice from the corner of his mouth with his bare forearm.

"You're barbaric," she said, and he barked out a laugh.

"Sorry. I forgot my pocket hanky," he said, still chewing. "Does being so high-strung keep you from making a mess when *you* eat?"

She stopped short, her tote of apples, squash, and God knew what else she carried slipping off her shoulder. She huffed out a breath, readjusted the bag, and crossed her arms, leveling him with her glare.

"I am *not* high-strung," she insisted.

He winked. "That's exactly what a high-strung person would say."

She groaned. "I'm organized. I'm efficient. I'm—well thought out."

He snorted, and she fisted her hands at her sides.

"What? You're saying I'd be better off if I didn't give a shit what was happening one day to the next? If I used my sleeve as a napkin? My body as a plaything?"

He raised a brow.

"I didn't mean like *that*," she insisted. "You want to know the difference between you and me?"

"I lie awake at night thinking about it," he teased. "So, yes. Please. Do enlighten me with your wisdom, sweetheart."

She breathed in deep through her nose, let it out, and a certain calm fell over her. "It's really quite simple," she said. "I care."

"About what?" he asked.

"*Everything*."

She stalked off toward the next designated booth where she'd probably haggle over a goddamn potato.

"I care about shit," he mumbled. But then he found himself making a mental list.

His brothers and aunt.

Tucker.

The ranch... and soon-to-be vineyard.

Getting his eight seconds and qualifying for the finals.

Wasn't that enough? He kept what was important close and didn't give a shit about the rest. The less that mattered, the less a guy could lose.

Damn her for making him doubt himself. She cared too much. That's what it was.

He tore off the last chunk of apple and tossed the core in the trash. *One* thing was certain. He sure as shit didn't care what Lily thought of him. He'd made himself believe that a long, long time ago.

He found her haggling for potatoes this time, russet, baby reds, and Yukon gold—because apparently there weren't just *potatoes*.

"I'm going to lose a third of my product after I cut out all those eyes," she said emphatically, blowing her long, blond bangs out of her eyes. "The only way I'm giving you that price is if you throw in those three gorgeous sweet potatoes for nothing." She picked one up and smelled it, eyes closing as a rapturous smile spread across her face.

He swallowed, throat suddenly dry. *Christ.* How did she make a root vegetable look sexy? He shook his head, realizing it wasn't the vegetable at all that was stirring shit up below the belt.

"You all set there, sweetheart?" he asked as she filled a second tote—another extra thrown in by the vendor—with her potato haul. "Because that apple ain't holding me over. So if you're still chaperoning—making sure I don't take off on a bull or something—I'm going to hit the corn dog stand."

Her brows drew together, and she wrinkled her nose.

"What *now*?" he asked.

"Why is there a corn dog stand at a farmers market?"

He waggled his brows. "Because they're the best damned corn dogs in the state. Possibly the country. No. The *world.*"

She scoffed.

"You got a problem with corn dogs?" he asked.

She shook her head. "Of course not. We served them at the restaurant. I mean, I'm sure Tucker still does if he can get the line cooks to follow my recipe. Hell, I don't know how a business major is gonna run a restaurant without his head cook."

Luke broke eye contact, but that didn't keep him from hearing her gasp.

"She's runnin' the restaurant. Isn't she?"

"Shit," he said softly. While he did enjoy pushing Lily's buttons, it was another thing to actually see hurt in her eyes—and for him to be the one to put it there. "Come on." He hoisted her bag of potatoes onto his good shoulder and started walking. He'd just have to think of a way to distract her.

"You're not supposed to carry heavy things. Are you?" she called after him.

He spun so he was walking backward. "Come on," he said again, and this time she started moving.

He didn't stop until he'd found it—the Cali Corn Queen's Crispy Corn Dogs cart.

He dropped the potatoes to the ground.

"*Hey*!" she said.

He grabbed her other tote and laid it down with the potatoes.

"Two," he said to the vendor. "With mustard."

In a matter of seconds, they were each holding a corn dog that sported a stripe of yellow from root to tip.

"Eat that and tell me it doesn't make you want to say *Fuck you* to all the other bullshit getting in the way."

She looked at the corn dog. Then at him, eyes narrowed.

"It's. A. *Corn* dog."

"Best you'll ever have."

Luke tore a monstrous bite from his, but she still just stood there, probably imagining Sara Sugar in the kitchen where she had worked the past three years. A kitchen he was sure she still thought of as *her* kitchen.

"Hell, that is good." He took another bite. "If you don't move quick, I'm gonna finish this one and go straight for yours."

Her mouth fell open. "You—you are *not*."

He shrugged and lopped off the rest of his, skimming his teeth along the stick. "I bought it. Technically it's mine."

She pointed at him with the delicacy in question. "You are an absolute child."

He made like he was going to take a bite, and she reacted defensively, shoving it into her own mouth.

He watched her close her lips around it, her teeth clamping down, and then he saw it. It was the same face she'd made when she'd sniffed that damn sweet potato.

"Oh my gaw," she said, her mouth full, her eyes fluttering shut for a few quick seconds.

He swallowed the food in his own mouth, pretending not to notice how his throat tightened at the sight of her like this. "See?" he asked. "I know what the hell I'm talking about."

She nodded and took another bite, a glob of mustard catching on the corner of her mouth.

"So good," she said, oblivious. "Your aunt thinks she's a harsh judge of corn bread? I wrote the damned book. And this batter? I've never tasted anything like it."

He could leave that yellow splotch. It wasn't *that* noticeable. If you couldn't see.

Shit. No one would take her seriously with her haggling if she had food all over her face. And while he could get his rocks off watching her give some poor farmer a stern talking-to while looking like the Joker dressed in yellow, he wasn't that much of an asshole. Besides, Jenna would never let him hear the end of it.

He reached forward, his hand cupping her cheek, and let his thumb swipe at the leftover condiment.

Her eyes widened.

"Mustard," he said, his voice low and soft. "You had a little—"

She seemed to be searching for something over his shoulder, so he followed her gaze.

"That the sheriff and that woman?" he asked as the two figures darted behind the tent of another stand.

She nodded, then cleared her throat as he turned back to face her.

He licked his thumb clean and watched her swallow as he did—watched *her* watch him, knowing that whatever she was thinking probably rivaled his own thoughts, and that all of it was a bad, bad idea.

Then he saw that he'd left a tiny yellow speck on the edge of her bottom lip.

And once he was there, touching her again, it was like someone had flipped a switch, and he couldn't flip it back. Because damn if being bad didn't feel so good.

He brushed his thumb over that full bottom lip, one that was always the better half of a pout she seemed to wear just for him.

She swallowed again, the movement slow and visible and somehow hot as hell.

Shit.

He leaned forward, his lips so close to hers he could feel her warm breath tickle his skin. Anyone who saw them would think he was kissing her. And he wanted to. Hell, he wanted to. But before he could finish what they had started last week, she said something that stopped him short.

"Why do you hate me so much?" she asked, a slight tremor in her voice.

His hand still cupped her face. This wasn't the time to lay his cards on the table. He didn't think there'd ever be a time for that.

"Why do you need everyone to like you?"

She blew out a shaky breath. "That's not an answer. Besides, you don't get to ask me those kinds of questions. You haven't earned that right."

"What right is that?" His thumb stroked her cheek. He should pull away. He *needed* to pull away. They were standing out in the open at the goddamn farmers market in front of God and everyone, but he couldn't fucking do it.

"To act like you *know* me," she said. "When all you really know is what Tucker's told you."

He raised a brow, deciding on another tactic to get past

the surface—the only part of her she seemed to let anyone see. "Okay, then. How about you tell me why you hate me."

She opened her mouth, then shook her head and stepped back, breaking their connection.

"This is ridiculous," she said, grabbing her bags and hoisting them over her shoulders again. "We can't do this."

Then she spun on her heel and stormed away.

This time, though, he went after her.

And damn she was fast when she wanted to be. He blamed the broken ribs for not being able to keep up, giving his ego a virtual pat on the back and letting it know they were okay. But when he finally made it to her car, he was hurting enough that he had to brace a hand on the side of the vehicle to counteract the pain.

She dropped the bags next to the driver's-side door and threw her hands in the air. "What are you doing? In case you haven't noticed, I'm not the best chaperone for you. Last week you were hurting minutes after Ava left you with me, and now you're overdoing it for what? To get the last word? Fine, Luke. You win. Okay? Because your aunt is gonna kill me if I don't send you back in one piece, and then I lose my two-for-one discount on the eggs."

He forced a smile and straightened, the pain subsiding. "So the eggs are what's at stake here?" he asked.

"Everything's at stake!" She groaned. "I'm catering my *ex-husband's* wedding. Who is marrying a famous pastry chef. You know you could have told me who she was the other day before I got myself all wrapped up in this mess to begin with."

He gritted his teeth. "I. *Tried.* But you have this habit of steamrolling everything that gets in your way when you want to."

She rolled her eyes. "Whatever. I'm in it now. And if I

mess this up, I'm finished before I start, and I can't fail at this, Luke Everett." She poked him in the chest. "I. Can't. Fail."

He wrapped his hand around her wrist on that last poke, and she didn't pull away.

"You hate me," she said softly.

Hell, if she only knew the depths of his—*hatred*—that it was his only choice. Because the alternative wasn't an option, never had been. Yet here he was.

"You think everything needs to be perfect. That's irritating as hell." And it wasn't a lie. He couldn't measure up with a girl like her. He knew it the day they met just as much as he knew it now. "So it's a good thing you hate me right back."

She shrugged. "You're careless. Reckless. Selfish."

The words pierced his chest. Because standing right here, with his best friend's former girl? It was as selfish as he'd ever been.

He let go of her wrist, ready to walk the hell away. But her fist opened, her palm now splayed against his chest, and some invisible tether held him there despite all the reasons he should leave and never look back.

"Your heart," she whispered. "It's beating so fast. Because I piss you off."

It wasn't a question, but he had an answer.

He licked his lips. "I was just thinking about the night me and Tucker met you at that bar. You danced like you were the most carefree girl in the world."

He squeezed his eyes shut, the memory replaying in his mind. There she was, in a short denim skirt and a sleeveless top the same color as her emerald eyes. The small dance floor was packed, but he'd seen only her—and that smile across her face that was so full of possibility.

She sucked in a breath. "You—watched me dance? You mean, before you came out on the floor to flirt with Dina?"

He opened his eyes, surrendering to the memory, to how close she was right now, and dipped his head so it rested against hers.

What the hell was he doing, letting these tiny truths spill out? This was the exact opposite of walking away.

"I watch a lot of things, sweetheart. And you know I didn't step foot on the dance floor to meet your roommate." He sighed. "Sometimes I wonder if the girl I saw is still in there."

Lily shook her head. "I'm not the girl you think you met that night. I was new in town. I wanted to be someone who—someone—"

"Someone who what, Lily?"

She fisted her hands in his shirt and tilted her head up toward his. "Who could let go and stop weighing her decisions and plans... Who wanted something or some*one* and just—went for it." Then her lips crushed against his, and he was powerless to do anything other than claim her mouth with his own, as if for this small pocket in time she actually belonged to him.

He wasn't lying on a couch like he was last week, and despite any pain he'd felt minutes ago, now his body pinned hers to the side of the car. Her back arched, her pelvis pressing against his, and he could tell by the way she ground along his length that she knew he was hard.

Her lips parted as her arms snaked around his neck, and he lost himself in the taste of her, in her soft moan when he hiked one of her legs up over his hip, urging her to take whatever pleasure she could from him.

"Forget the eggs," she said, and he had to pause for the words to register.

He tilted his head back so their eyes met, and he raised a brow.

"I haven't had sex in almost a year," she admitted, and it didn't take him long to do the math. She and Tucker had been separated for only six months, which meant whatever was going on between them started long before Lily filed for divorce. "Drive me home and—" She bit her lip. "We both know that's all this will be. Just sex. I mean, this is a rebound. And we can't stand each other, right? So let's just do what we both seem to want to do and then call it a day."

He knew if he paused too much longer he'd let logic get the best of him, so he held out his hand. "Give me your keys."

In seconds the car was packed up, and he was in the driver's seat, Lily pulling her seat belt over her shoulder next to him.

She palmed his erection as he sank the key into the ignition and he growled.

"I promise I didn't forget how to do it," she said, her thumb rubbing a firm line up the length of his cock.

Yeah, that wasn't what he was worried about. He was sure she'd get back on the bike without a problem. What he wasn't sure of was the whole *calling it a day*. With any other woman, fine. But this was Lily. If he couldn't walk away before anything even happened, what the hell would he do once it did?

"And we can go right back to not being able to stand each other as soon as it's done," she added, giving him a soft squeeze over his jeans.

He gripped her wrist and placed her hand back into her lap. He needed to drive. He needed to *think,* which was something else he wasn't used to doing in these—situations. Protection, then pleasure. That was the most his brain had to deal with when he took a woman to bed. He was out of his element with *this* woman.

"Right," he said, but his voice sounded distant, even to himself.

"Because this?" She motioned back and forth between the two of them as he tried not to floor the vehicle. "This is oil and water. It doesn't mix." She giggled, and he wasn't sure he'd ever heard her make a sound like that. "Well, except for one way, it seems."

He hated that he knew where she lived, that he'd been there so many times before to pick up Tucker and take him out with the rest of the boys.

He hated that every time he did it, he'd thought about the woman his buddy was leaving behind and how she deserved better.

He hated that he was benched from riding because thoughts of her had creeped into his goddamn head when he should have been focused on the bull.

But mostly he hated that they *did* mix, because he knew this chemistry between them was far more than physical, but the *better* that she deserved? He wasn't it.

"Right," he said again, echoing himself as he pulled onto her street. "Oil and water."

Because Lily demanded perfection. And Luke Everett was *anything* but.

CHAPTER SIX

"What the hell?" she said as her car rolled to a stop behind the silver SUV already taking up space in *her* driveway.

Luke swore under his breath.

"Were you expecting company?" he asked drily.

She groaned. Seeing as how Tucker was not waiting in his vehicle, she assumed he was inside. "I need to change the locks," she grumbled.

She opened the door and climbed out of the car, but Luke didn't move.

"You're not going to just sit there. Are you?" she asked.

The car was off, but his hands still gripped the wheel as he stared straight ahead.

"You got a better idea?"

She grabbed her totes from the backseat, then held one across the center console toward him.

"Here's our story—*not* that Tucker Green deserves one. I bumped into you and your aunt at the market, and Jenna was tired of babysitting you, so she sent you home with me to help me unload, and then I'm taking you back to the ranch so she doesn't have to go out of her way."

He crossed his arms, cocked that brow she did not want to find sexy, and turned to face her.

"You make me sound like I'm so easy to boss around." His tone challenged her.

Something in her belly clenched tight at the thought of doing just that—bossing around the unbossable.

"Look," she said. "It's not like you can take off or anything. You're in *my* car. And nothing happened to violate your bro code or whatever, so just come inside."

He stepped out of the car and looked at her over the top of the vehicle, his eyes narrowing against the sun.

"I guess I am that easy," he said, then reached inside where she'd left him one of the totes, grabbed it, and strode up to her front door like it was the most natural thing in the world for him to do. And because of course Tucker had left the door unlocked, Luke walked right inside.

No, she thought. That was not a man accustomed to doing what he was told. Which meant that despite her perfect cover story, he could be inside right now saying who-knows-what to her ex-husband.

Lily pushed through the front door slowly, exercising caution. She heard Tucker's booming voice and a man's laughter she didn't recognize until she found the two men in the kitchen and realized the unfamiliar sound had come from Luke.

"Lil!" Tucker said, his nickname for her rolling off his tongue like they still saw each other every day. "Figured you were at the market with one of your lists. It is a day that ends in *y*, right?"

That tightening in her belly shifted to something more like anger—coiled and ready to strike. It was one thing for her to be working for Tucker and Sara. But he had no right showing up here unannounced. He had no right to anything from her other than a night of good food and to-die-for cake.

Tucker made like he was going to hug her, but Lily took a step back before he could.

He dropped his arms awkwardly to his sides. "It's good to see you, Lil. And good to know you're helping keep our daredevil here in line."

Lily crossed her arms and swore she saw Luke's jaw clench before he painted on his easy, ever-present grin.

"Come on, Tucker," she said as she absently started emptying her totes onto the kitchen counter. "You know there's no such thing. From what I can tell, all the Everetts are a force of nature. *Kept* isn't in their vocabulary. Everyone in their orbit knows that."

Tucker barked out a laugh. "She sure as shit has you pegged," he said, clapping Luke on the shoulder.

"Sure, asshole," Luke said. "She got me there."

Lily cleared her throat because even though she wasn't quite sure what the elephant in the room was—Tucker's presence, Luke's presence, the fact that mere minutes ago her hand had rested on the impressive bulge in Luke's jeans, or possibly all of the above—the *situation* needed to be addressed.

"What are you doing here, Tucker?" she finally asked.

Her ex-husband let out a long breath, the gesture all at once familiar and exasperating *because* of its familiarity.

"I'm gonna go check on those weeds in the garden you were complaining about," Luke said, not waiting for a response. In seconds he was out her back door, and she and Tucker were alone.

Tucker shook his head. "Ever the wingman," he said under his breath.

Lily crossed her arms. "What are you talking about?"

He laughed, then cleared his throat. The far-off look in his eyes seemed almost wistful, but there was something else hidden there. Something she couldn't quite put her finger on. "Just thinking about that night we met. Everett must have had some sort of sixth sense that I wanted to approach you because he walked right up to you and your friend and pulled you off the dance floor before I had a chance to tell him I couldn't take my eyes off you."

She rolled her eyes. "That's not why you're here, is it? To reminisce about the night we met? Because God, Tucker. That's—that's so—"

"Wrong?" he said. "Not part of your perfect view of our divorce? No matter what happened between us, that was an amazing night. You can't deny *that*." He grinned.

She dropped her hands to her sides, squeezed them into fists. Because of course she couldn't deny it. He was this gorgeous guy—tall with dark brown hair and even darker brown eyes. He'd dazzled her with his talk of wanting to open a restaurant, and when he'd found out she'd just finished culinary school? Well, it was a match made in building-a-successful-future heaven.

There was just one tiny little detail that she'd never admitted out loud. Despite Tucker and her seeming like the perfect fit, *Luke* was the guy she'd been attracted to from the start. It was only when he'd clearly shown his interest was in Dina that she let Tucker take her home.

It wasn't like you fell for a guy in one little encounter at a line dancing bar, so she'd made her peace with the whole Luke situation—especially when Dina didn't make it home until well after noon the next day—and had let herself fall for Tucker.

He *was* the whole package, and he'd managed to sweep her off her feet in the weeks after that night.

"We stopped having amazing nights a long time ago, Tucker. I think it was when you started sleeping with Sara Sugar."

He winced, and so did she. Because if she was being honest, their amazing nights had stopped long before the one when he cheated on her. And none of it was Sara Sugar's fault. She wasn't the problem. *They* were.

"I am sorry," he said softly.

"I know you are," she said.

He pulled out one of the barstools and sat, resting his elbows on the kitchen island.

She sat next to him. "Why are you *here*, Tucker? Why are you letting yourself into my house when you have a pregnant fiancée at home?"

He narrowed his eyes at her. "You're *catering* the wedding."

She nodded. "I guess we haven't exactly discussed that yet. Have we?"

He shook his head.

"Oh God," she said. "Sara's firing me. It's too weird for her, right? I *am* a steamroller. I steamrolled her right into this, and she sent you to get her out of it. It makes sense. I mean, who wants their future husband's ex-wife at her wedding? It's a little crazy, right? I mean, who in their right mind—"

"She's not firing you," Tucker interrupted. "I mean *we're* not firing you. She liked you, and she's got this super Zen sort of outlook on, well, everything. Nothing gets to her. And when I told her what an amazing chef you were, she made me promise not to scare you off."

Heat burned her cheeks, and she wasn't sure if it was because she was flattered or exactly what Tucker seemed to suspect—scared.

"Super Zen, huh?" she asked. "I bet she does yoga and lights a lot of incense."

Tucker laughed. "She actually teaches it," he said, and Lily groaned.

"She's a Food Network star *and* a yoga instructor?" Because at the moment, other than the nest egg from Tucker buying her out of BBQ on the Bluff, she was jobless. Except for the contract to cater his wedding.

He gave her a nervous smile. "She co-owns a studio with her sister in Santa Barbara. When she's on hiatus from shooting the show in L.A., she spends time up there teaching classes."

Of course she did. And she was Zen about *everything*. Unlike Lily, who was wound so tight she almost refused the most delicious corn dog she'd ever eaten.

"I'm *here* because I wanted to make sure you were okay," he said, thankfully keeping her thoughts from traveling down the corn dog path and to the man who'd kissed her up against her car. "And because Luke told me the doctor benched him for four weeks and that Jack has him on wedding detail with you. I guess—considering he was helping you shop today—that you two will be working pretty closely together and I—"

Lily shook her head and let out a bitter laugh. It looked like all roads led to corn dogs.

"God," she said, sliding off the stool. "You really haven't changed, have you? You just want to make sure I haven't ruined your reputation with your friend out there. I told you, Tucker. What happened between us is between *us*."

"And the lawyers," he mumbled.

She groaned, stepping back from the island. "I haven't said anything, okay? And I'm not going to. I'm not even sure why it's such a big deal. Luke is just as much of a good-time-haver as you are—or were, I guess. Is that even a word? *Good-time-haver*? I'm assuming things are going to be different now that you're going to be a father?"

Tucker spun on his barstool to face her, but she took another step back. He held his hands up in surrender. "Don't worry. I'm not gonna try to hug you again. Look—I messed up. I know that. But it's not just my reputation, Lil. Maybe you see me as the guy who was grasping for ways to have that good time, but that's because it wasn't happening at home."

She opened her mouth to protest, but he kept going.

"I'm not blaming you for what I did. But I am blaming *us.*"

She sighed. "We weren't—" She didn't want to say it, didn't want either of them to hurt each other any more than they already had.

"In love like we should have been. We've never really said that out loud, but I'm right, aren't I?"

She nodded. This was the most honest they'd been with each other in a year.

"I tried to fix it," he added. "I mean, I tried to fight for us, but you just left."

Lily shook her head. "Banging on Jack and Ava's door in the middle of the night—*drunk*—isn't fighting or fixing, Tucker. That was just your fear talking."

He winced, and her chest tightened. She might as well have been talking about herself. Lily did leave first, but she'd justified it using Tucker's infidelity. He'd already left her, physically and emotionally, right? She simply walked out the door before he could.

"I don't think what happened defines who I am or who you are for that matter," he said, as if he could read her thoughts. "Sara knows I wasn't a good husband to you."

"But you love her like you're supposed to," Lily said.

"I do. And the thing with Everett? He's more family to me than my own blood. You already know I was a disappointment. I'm doing my best to get it right with Sara. But if Luke ever looked at me like you did the night you walked out? I don't think I could take it, Lil."

Tucker was being Tucker, putting himself first. But she understood. It was why she still hadn't told her mom about the divorce. Lily wasn't supposed to repeat history. She wasn't supposed to mess up. She was supposed to move to California, make a name for herself, and fall in love.

Well, she still lived in California. Those other two items were getting harder and harder, though, to cross off her to-do list.

"Are we good?" Tucker asked. "Not just what I'm asking of you but the wedding—all of it. I mean, this is weird as hell, but if it's what you want and it's what Sara wants, then it's what I want, too. And if you and I could maybe be friends…"

He trailed off, and she knew he was waiting for her to fill in the blank.

"I'm catering your wedding," she said ruefully. "Let's see how that goes. Then we can talk about this friend thing you speak of."

He stood, and this time she didn't retreat as he moved toward her, leaned forward, and kissed her on the cheek.

She felt a weight lift.

"*Oh*," she said, not meaning to speak the word out loud.

His brows drew together. "What?"

She shook her head. "Nothing. Thanks for coming by, Tucker. I'll be in touch so we can set up the menu tasting."

He scratched the back of his neck. A lock of his dark hair fell over his forehead, and he pushed it out of the way. She remembered running her fingers through that hair but for the life of her couldn't drum up any feeling other than the memory.

"I better let Everett off the hook, or he'll be weeding your garden till sundown."

Luke. Luke was still here, and she remembered why he'd come home with her in the first place.

The two of them never quite seemed to mix. Except for when his lips were on hers. When Luke touched her, it was like a chemical reaction. She was permanently altered each time it happened.

Why was she unable to find that with the man she'd married?

Lily said nothing as Tucker made his way to the back door and stepped outside. But even though he closed the door behind him, the kitchen window was open, and she found herself inching closer to it to listen.

"You two clear the air?"

She could hear Luke but could only see Tucker from behind.

"Yeah," Tucker said. "Lil's great. I know you and she never got along, but I'm glad to see you two at least being civil."

Luke didn't respond. Or at least, he didn't say anything she could hear.

"Anyway, man, thanks for being around through all of this. You know you're like a brother to me, right?" Tucker asked. "And I still care about Lily, so thanks for helping her out." He cleared his throat. "I wasn't planning on doing this here, but I guess now's as good a time as any. You'll be my best man, right?"

She sucked in a breath, not exactly sure why this caught her so off guard.

"You're not having second thoughts about doing the big wedding?" Luke asked, and she could have sworn there was an edge to his voice. "You could always elope again."

Tucker laughed. "I'll take that as a yes?"

Luke stepped into her line of sight, and she dropped to a squat, hoping she wasn't in his.

"You were there for me with a lot of the Jack Senior shit," he said. "You know you don't have to ask me twice for anything, except..."

"Uh-oh," Tucker said. "What is it? Tell me anything, Everett. I can take it."

Lily held her breath now. Was he going to tell Tucker what just happened—and what they were about to do?

"The wedding," Luke said. "It's the day before the Anaheim rodeo. If I don't get out there that night, I'll be in shit shape for the ride the next day."

"So you're really going through with it, huh? Another ride after what this one did to you?"

Luke cleared his throat. "I gotta end things on my own terms," he said. "And what happened a week ago was far from it. I'm good enough to get thrown and *not* get injured like that."

"So why did you?" Tucker countered.

There was a long pause, and Lily wished she could see the expressions on both their faces.

"That's between me and myself right now," Luke finally said. "So I'll be your best man..."

"But you can't stay for the whole wedding," Tucker said, finishing his friend's sentence. "If you say you can do this ride and not kill yourself, then I got your back, brother."

That one word sat like an anvil on her chest—*brother*.

Luke laughed. "Thanks for the vote of confidence. I'll make sure I'm there for all the important stuff," he said. "But I won't be able to party like the good old days. Instead I gotta hop in the truck for four hours and get a decent night's sleep."

Tucker snorted. "When did you become the responsible adult in this relationship?"

"You're just sorry I can't drive your drunk ass to your hotel afterward."

Another chuckle from Tucker. "I got a pregnant fiancée to take care of now," he said. "Looks like the good old days are behind me as well."

Tucker wouldn't grow up for her because they didn't love each other like they should have. Lily got that. But it still stung to see someone else getting what she wanted. Maybe she hadn't wanted Tucker himself but the idea of what their marriage could have been.

She didn't hear anything else after that, not until she heard cars starting in the driveway, and she realized Luke must have been moving her car so Tucker could leave. Or maybe he was just going to steal her car and get as far from her as possible. She wouldn't blame him.

But a couple minutes later, she heard her screen door open and then shut. When Luke appeared in her kitchen, towering over the other side of the island, she was still squatting on the floor in front of the sink.

He dropped her keys on the countertop. More like slammed them down, and she finally straightened to a standing position.

"I'm taking off," he said, then turned back toward the door.

Her mouth fell open. "You're what?"

He stopped, ran a hand through his sun-kissed hair, then spun slowly to face her.

"Taking off," he said again, and she could hear the familiar agitation rising. "Leaving. Getting the hell out of Dodge before I do something really stupid, even for me."

She couldn't ignore the sting of his words or how they made her want to sting back.

"You followed me to my car," she said.

"I know."

"You kissed me back, Luke Everett."

He nodded. "And I shouldn't have. You were Tucker's girl once, and he's just as much a brother to me as Jack or Walker. I'm not messing with that just because my dick doesn't realize we can't stand each other."

Okay, scratch what she had said before. That was just the buzzing in her ear before the strike. What he'd just said? *That* was the real sting, and she wasn't prepared for how deep his words could burrow under her skin.

So she just stood there, mouth open, but for once with no retort.

"Fuck," he said under his breath, and then he was out the door.

It took several seconds for logic to return, and when it did she found herself following him out to the quiet neighborhood street.

"You don't have a car," she called after him.

He pivoted so he was walking backward now, but he didn't stop.

"Ranch is only a couple miles." He pressed a hand to his right side, then quickly dropped it. Not quick enough that she didn't notice.

"Those broken ribs all healed after one week?" she asked.

He stopped then, shoved his hands in his front pockets, and considered her for a second more than made her comfortable.

"I'll see ya around, Lily," he said.

And just like that he turned the corner and disappeared from her line of sight.

She wondered why, after years of assuring herself that they hated each other, watching Luke Everett walk away made her stomach sink like a stone.

It had been so easy to blame him for Tucker's less-than-grown-up behavior. The two of them were as tight as brothers, and she'd been so certain she'd chosen the responsible man. The safe man. Surely Tucker's wild tendencies had come from his equally wild friend.

Lily wasn't so sure anymore. Yet regardless of any misconceptions she had about Luke's behavior, an antagonism had always been brewing beneath the surface. She wasn't sure how or when it had started, but once there, she'd bought into it. Fueled it even because somehow it had fueled her both then *and* now.

So much for the chemical reaction she'd been hoping for. "It's more likely we'll explode," she said aloud.

But there it was again, like she'd swallowed something near to a boulder.

Today had just been too much. That's what it was. That damned corn dog, the illogical heat between the two of them, topped off with a surprise visit from her ex-husband. There was also that bullshit line—that Luke had come out on the dance floor that first night to meet her. But that's all it was—a line he fed her to get what he wanted before he walked out the door. Never mind that she had done the exact same thing last week. She was entitled to a double standard after the day she had.

Lily strode back into the house, straight for the kitchen, and scrubbed her hands in the sink. Then she did what she always did when life tried to pull the rug out from under her.

She baked.

CHAPTER SEVEN

Enough. It had been two weeks since Luke lost his focus on that bull, and he was running short on time to train for Anaheim. This was it. He'd get his eight seconds to qualify or die trying because like it or not, the vineyard would produce a crop, and if he knew his big brother—and he did—that crop would yield their first vintage, and everything about his life as a rancher would change.

They'd have two businesses to run. And as much as he liked a good time, Luke knew he'd be putting more hours in at home. Because this was a family business, and family—whether blood or not—was all he had.

He'd promised his brother he'd stay one more night, then finally head back to his own place in the morning. But hell if he could wait a second longer. He said good night to Jack and Ava, waited for them to pull the door to their first-floor bedroom shut, then decided to slip upstairs to grab his few things.

"Where ya headed, cowboy?"

Midway up the stairs, Luke turned to see his younger brother, Walker, silhouetted in the frame of the front door.

"What the hell are you doing here?" he retorted, keeping his voice low so he didn't wake his nephew.

Walker swayed a little where he stood, and Luke rethought his plan, descending the stairs to meet his brother.

"You're half in the bag," he said. Walker didn't argue. "Where's your car?"

His brother shrugged. "All I know is I didn't drive it here. Someone drove *me* here, though." Walker scratched the back of his head. "Shit. I don't live here anymore. Do I?"

"No," Luke said softly. "We moved out." Because Jack and Ava and Owen were a family now—one that didn't need to deal with Luke's late nights or Walker's even later ones. "But it looks like you're crashing here tonight. Let's get you up to bed."

His younger but far from little brother stumbled, and Luke braced a hand on his shoulder.

"This isn't getting old yet?" he asked, but Walker just mumbled something incoherent.

Somehow Luke got him up the wood stairs without the two of them tumbling to the bottom in a broken heap. He squeezed his eyes shut at the memory of a seventeen-year-old Jack doing just that. Though he didn't fall. Their father—in a similar state to Walker—had pushed him.

Walker slumped against his shoulder, which should have brought Luke fully back to the present, but all it did was drum up more memories of Jack Senior, the father that almost killed his oldest son.

"Easy," he whispered, guiding Walker through the door where Luke had been staying.

"This ain't my room," he argued, and Luke slapped a hand over his brother's mouth.

"You don't *have* a room anymore, asshole. Remember? That's Owen's room now. Can I trust you to stay the hell away from Owen's door?" And although there was a master bedroom up there, too, no one used it, not even Jack and

Ava. And they wouldn't until the Callahans gutted it and turned it into something new.

Walker collapsed onto the bed without comment, and Luke took that as a *yes.* He dragged the trash can from the corner of the room to the side of the bed, hoping his brother wouldn't need it. And though he had somewhere to be, he stood there for a good fifteen minutes watching his brother's chest rise and fall, wondering if and when his luck would run out and Walker *wouldn't* make it home after one of his benders.

"Don't fuck up," he said under his breath. "We lost Jack for ten years, Walker. No way in hell we're losing you."

Walker stirred but didn't wake, so Luke ignored the weight pressing down on his chest and backed out of the room.

He couldn't be a prisoner anymore. He couldn't turn off the primal need to test his limits.

He needed to ride.

It was just before dawn when Luke hobbled into the still-under-construction winery. He knew Walker would be passed out in his bed, and Luke was sure that if he tried to reenter the house this early, he would wake the dog—thereby waking the whole house. The last thing he needed was Jack's third degree. The *first* thing he needed, though, was a couple hours of sleep before the crew showed up and he'd have to oversee the day's construction. Plus the horse stalls in the stable were due for a cleaning, and he wasn't sure if their new stable boy was on the schedule for today or tomorrow. He'd have to look into that. There was also that new restaurant owner who'd called late last week about wanting Crossroads Ranch to be part of their farm-to-table menu.

It was gonna be a hell of a Monday.

He made it through the door, locked the place back up, then sucked in a deep breath.

"Shit," he hissed, hand pressed to his side. Maybe he'd ridden an hour too long. And *maybe* hitting the speed bag was overkill for his still healing ribs. But it had been two weeks, and he was feeling—soft.

So, like a rebellious teen he'd snuck out to a buddy's stable and then hit the twenty-four-hour gym.

"And now I'm paying for it," he said softly as he made his way to the office. He'd crash on the couch and then be fine once the crew arrived.

He pushed through the door and was greeted with an earsplitting shriek followed by what he swore was a brick to the side of the head.

"What the fuck!" he yelled, his vision blurred for several seconds.

"Oh my God!" The voice belonged to a woman. "Oh my God, Luke! Are you okay?"

The figure in front of him came into focus—chin-length blond hair, a fitted green T-shirt that matched her eyes, and hip-hugging jeans that would have made him hard in seconds if he didn't want to tear her goddamn head off.

"What the hell are you doing here?" he asked, his teeth clenched and his tone full of vinegar.

She winced and reached for his temple, but he swatted her hand away just in time to feel the small goose egg forming.

"I'm sorry!" she said. "I thought you were a prowler! Did I—re-concuss you?" She worried her bottom lip between her teeth.

He rolled his eyes but at the same time wondered how soon you were supposed to get hit in the head again after having a concussion. He guessed it *wasn't* supposed to happen at all.

Especially not in his case. Not that she knew that. Not that any of them did.

"A prowler? First of all, who the fuck uses that word? And second—*second*—what are you doing in *my* winery, in *my* office, on *my* futon?"

Because Christ, now he had a headache to boot, and he just. Wanted. To sleep.

She reached for his face again, and for reasons unknown to him, he didn't swat her away this time.

"Bumps are good," she said. "Right? Means the swelling is on the outside rather than in... by your brain?" She rubbed a thumb over the small wound, then spun to a bottle of water, wet with condensation, sitting on the small coffee table in front of the futon. *His* futon. Where he wanted to sleep. Had he mentioned sleep?

She grabbed his hand and pulled him toward said futon. "Here," she said. "Sit."

Only because it was what he'd wanted to do all along did he obey. She sat beside him and raised the bottle to his right temple.

He sighed. "Fine," he conceded. "I guess that helps. But let me remind you that I wouldn't *need* the help if you hadn't just clocked me with your crazy bag. What the hell is even in there? And why the hell am I always in worse shape after a run-in with you?"

She gave him a nervous smile. "My planner," she said. "I'm really sorry. I couldn't sleep, and Ava asked me to help her go through paint swatches today. I have a key, so since I was restless at home, I figured I might as well make myself useful here. Plus, the menu sampling is today, and Sara and Tucker wanted to do it here, get a feel for the place. So really, I guess you could say I'm just early for work. What's your excuse?"

He blew out a breath and grabbed the water bottle with his own hand. She scooted back the few inches that she could. But it was a futon. She was as far as she could get yet still close enough to scramble his brain with or without her damned bag.

"You gonna report me to the authorities if I tell you the truth?"

"Your brother?" she asked, and he gave her a single nod. "I guess I sort of owe you one, so no."

He raised a brow.

"Okay, fine," she added. "I guess I owe you more than one after attacking you. But you did scare me, and I was only protecting myself."

The corner of his mouth twitched, but he fought the urge to smile. He didn't want to like anything about this woman, let alone the fact that she kicked ass and took names later. And he sure as shit didn't want her to see that he found anything other than their sexual chemistry appealing. *That* he couldn't hide. But it didn't change the fact that they just didn't mix. That they couldn't mix. Not now. Not ever.

"I was training," he said.

Her eyes widened. "For the rodeo?" she asked.

"No. For the next adult spelling bee." He shook his head. "Christ, yes. For the rodeo. Anaheim is it. My last shot to qualify for the finals." And maybe ever, but he didn't tell her this. It was the one part he hadn't told Jack either.

One more real head injury—not a daily planner–induced goose egg but a real concussion—and he was out for good. Even now the risk was great enough that he was going against his doctor's recommendation. Doc wanted him to retire. Now. But he at least needed to be granted the choice. To do it on his own terms. And he knew if he could just keep his damned head in the game, he'd walk away clean. Then—and only then—could he call it quits.

She opened her mouth to say something, then paused. He waited for the reprimand because if it wasn't his big brother or his aunt trying to parent him, why not her? Never mind that he was a grown man. Everyone seemed to want a hand in telling him how to live his life.

"I get it," she said softly.

"Wait…what?" he asked, assuming he'd misheard her.

She opened her bag—or as he would think of it from here on out, her weapon—and pulled out a sizeable book that must have been the planner. She opened to an interior envelope and pulled from it a piece of paper that she unfolded and smoothed out onto the coffee table.

On it was a sketch of a storefront he could tell was a restaurant. And the sign above it simply read, *Lily's.* The creases in the paper were soft, the pencil faded. She'd had the drawing for quite some time.

He set the water bottle down on the table and ran a hand through his hair.

"I thought you wanted out of the restaurant business," he said. "I thought that's why you let Tucker buy you out of BBQ on the Bluff, so you could do this catering thing."

She shrugged, then let her fingertips trace over the penciled lettering on the drawing.

"Barbecue was his idea. He was the businessman, after all. And he said small town casual barbecue is what would make money over a more eclectic and changing menu…which is what I had suggested." She laughed, but her smile didn't reach her eyes. "He was right, obviously. I mean, the restaurant was in the black almost from the week we opened, and we never looked back. But that was Tucker's dream. Not mine."

Well shit. She did get it. Didn't she?

"The catering gig requires little to no overhead, and you make a name for yourself, which will hopefully turn into your own restaurant someday." It was a statement, not a question. Because he understood her now.

She nodded.

"That's why Tucker's wedding is so important. It won't just put you on the map as a caterer. It can put you on the *map* if his famous wife likes what you do."

She nodded again, and her eyes got all glassy like she might cry. And dammit if he didn't feel the urge to keep that from happening.

"I guess we're both willing to take risks to get what we want," he said.

She reached for his face, ran a thumb over his temple where she'd nailed him with the bag.

"The bump's already gone down." She dropped her hand. "And yes, I'm willing to take risks, but I'm not putting my physical health in danger by doing so. You're walking around with unhealed broken *bones*, Luke. And training barely two weeks after sustaining serious injuries?"

Ah, yes. There it was. The scolding.

He stood quickly. Too quickly, and a quick stab of pain shot through his side. He hissed in a breath before he could stop himself.

Without another word, she stood, too, lifted up his T-shirt, and gasped at the bruises that still hadn't cleared after those two weeks.

"It's nothing new," he insisted, pushing her hand away. "I just overdid it my first night out. Lesson learned, okay? I don't need you to tell me what I already know."

She threw her hands in the air. "You're impossible. You

should be resting, and you're out doing God knows what instead."

So much for her getting it.

"And you're just as irritating as ever. Even more so when you're occupying the space where I planned on *resting*."

"What's wrong with your place?" she asked.

"It's easier for me to crash here, so I'm up when the crew arrives."

"What about your room at the ranch?" she added.

"Walker's been passed out there since he showed up on Jack's doorstep piss drunk last night. You got any more questions that aren't exactly your business you'd like me to answer?"

Christ. He didn't have to defend himself. This was his property. He owned a third of it. So why the hell couldn't he shut up?

She just stood there, fists clenched at her sides. They were at an impasse. If he wanted to catch even a couple hours of shut-eye, he'd have to kick her out of the room. And as much as he wanted to do just that, he knew he'd be sending her back to the place she'd been trying to escape in the first place. If she stayed, that meant the two of them would either continue like this or do what they seemed to keep doing whenever tensions ran high between them. He wasn't sure he'd be able to stop himself from wanting her like that if they kissed again. Because maybe she was right. Maybe he was willing to risk everything for what he wanted, even if that meant the only family he had outside his brothers and his aunt.

Tucker.

She looked at her watch. "Bakery's opening in a few minutes. I'll grab the paint swatches and head there for coffee and a predawn breakfast so you can get some sleep."

She started gathering her things from the table, including the restaurant sketch, which she carefully folded and put back in her planner. "I'm sorry again for—" She hoisted her bag onto her shoulder and patted the so-called assault weapon. "I know it's not my place and that you couldn't care less what I say, but your family cares about you, Luke. And I don't know what it is that makes you do the things you do. That's something you need to figure out, I guess. But putting yourself at risk like you do? It puts them at risk, too. Of losing you. And as much as you pretend like nothing gets to you, I know your family does. Because you care about them, too. And I know Tucker's a part of that."

She kissed him then, on the spot where she'd hit him, and somehow that floored him even more than if she'd pressed her lips to his.

"We may be oil and water," she said. "But that doesn't mean I want to see you hurt."

That was all she said before walking out.

Maybe she didn't understand his need to push himself to the furthest limits, but she got the family bit.

She didn't want to see him hurt in the arena—or come between him and his family.

He lowered himself onto his back on the futon, his legs dangling over the edge, and rested his head on his elbow.

"Well, shit," he said aloud. She wasn't just giving him his space for the rest of the morning. She was backing off from whatever this was simmering between them. And dammit if he didn't like that idea at all.

Not one little bit.

CHAPTER EIGHT

The place was coming along. Not just the public part of the winery but also the production room. Even though they were several months from harvest, the Everetts were well on their way to having a living, breathing winery on their hands. Not to mention the cattle ranch they'd been running since birth. That was a hell of a lot of responsibility for three men under thirty.

Thank the stars for Ava. Born and raised on a vineyard, she knew wine like the brothers knew cattle.

Lily ran her finger along the wood cutout of the circular bar, one she knew would be covered with something beautiful like granite or flagstone. Even though the exterior was all straight lines and right angles, with the bar in place, the interior was a sort of circle, everything revolving around the round, central tasting area. Lily wondered what that would feel like, being the focal point of a room, the center of attention, and let out a sigh.

"Penny for your thoughts?"

She gasped and spun to find Ava standing just inside the doorway.

"Sorry!" Ava added. "I didn't mean to scare you. I just figured you were maybe, probably, on edge a little and might want some moral support?"

Ava's eyes raked over the portable table that was now cloaked with a black tablecloth and set for a party of two, the center lined with silver-domed dishes resting above canned burners. The folding chairs were disguised with white covers, the chair backs tied off with a gold satin bow.

"Oh, Lily," she said, her hand flying to her chest. "It's beautiful."

Lily grinned. "You haven't even seen the food yet." She strode to her friend, who welcomed her with a warm hug. "Thank you for coming," she said. "You *did* scare the crap out of me, but not half as much as this tasting does."

Both women laughed.

Ava stepped back and leveled Lily with her gaze. "Does the fear stem from being in the same room as your ex-husband and his pregnant fiancée or from wondering whether or not you'll please the palate of a Food Network star?"

Lily laughed. "Yes," she confirmed, knowing everything about this day had her on edge. But it was the bruised and battered man who'd knocked off with the crew for lunch who'd kept her there, teetering. "Can I ask you something?" she added.

Ava nodded. "Sure. Anything. I told you—moral support. Think of me like a bra for your well-being, only without the pain-in-the-breast underwire." She raised a brow. "So, how may I morally support you?"

Lily hesitated for a few seconds but decided ripping the Band-Aid off would just get it all out there.

"Do you think I'm a control freak?"

Ava blew out a breath and ran a hand through her thick, red locks. Lily squeezed her eyes shut and her hands into fists, bracing herself for the response.

"Just say it," she said. "I can take it. It's nothing I haven't heard before from Tucker."

And Luke.

It was *his* name she wanted to say. Because it was his perception of her that was burrowing its way under her skin.

"Hey," Ava said, and Lily felt her friend's palm warm on her cheek. "Open your eyes, ya goof."

Lily laughed and did just that. Then the two women took a seat at the makeshift tasting table, both careful not to disrupt the place settings.

"Do you remember when we met?" Ava asked.

"I waited on you, Jack, and Owen at the restaurant. It was the lunch shift. That boy of yours almost ate me out of corn bread."

The other woman laughed. "You didn't even hesitate with that answer."

Lily shrugged. "I don't forget a face. Especially if it's the first time I meet someone. And *especially* if they like my corn bread. But honestly, it's just the way my brain works. I organize, compartmentalize." She let out a bitter laugh. "I am a control freak. Even inside my own head."

Ava rested her hand on Lily's. "*No.* That's not what I was trying to show you. Ugh. Let me do this again." She locked her eyes on Lily's. "When I met you, I was way intimidated." Lily's eyes widened, and Ava gave her head a vigorous shake. "Let me *finish.*" She narrowed her gaze. "There I was—a single mom who'd kept the biggest secret from her son and his father. I loved Owen since the second I knew he existed, but my whole future changed that very same second. And I was lost. For a really long time."

Lily turned her hand so it was palm up and gave Ava a squeeze.

"The day I met you was also the day Jack and Owen officially met. You walked over to our table with this bright, beautiful smile and knew exactly what each of us needed to make *us* smile. You made me feel welcomed when I was in so over my head. You were impossible not to like, even when I thought for a millisecond that you and Jack had a history."

Lily's hand flew to her mouth, and she snorted. "Please. I knew as soon as I walked up to your table that that man was so far gone for you and likely had been for some time. How you didn't know right then and there is beyond me."

Ava's cheeks pinked. "I was way too scared to hope for it then. But I know now. The point is, Lil, that I could see you—this woman who had her head on straight, knew what she wanted, and knew how to get it. If that means wanting things the way you want them, then so be it. Don't let anyone make you doubt how wonderful you are. You're *you*, and that's all that matters."

Lily's breath caught in her throat, but before she could say anything, the winery door flew open, and Tucker Green and Sara Sugar strode in.

Her breath caught a second time at the sight of them, and her heart squeezed inside her chest. Not because she missed him, and not because she was jealous. It was how right the two of them looked, like the last two pieces of a puzzle that made the final image complete.

She didn't miss Tucker. She missed what they'd never had—a perfect fit. Before their marriage fell apart, she'd resigned herself to the fact that maybe there was no such thing. It was easier than the alternative—believing there *was* such a thing but that she'd been unable to find it.

But he proved her wrong. *He* found it. And she couldn't hold that against him. The cheating? Yes. She could hold that against him until the end of time if she wanted. But she wouldn't. No, siree. Instead, she was going to cater his wedding.

"Tucker! Sara!" she said, springing from her seat. "You're right on time. Come. Sit."

She and Ava both stepped back from the table, and Sara's blue eyes brightened.

"Oh, Lily. You've already outdone yourself." She threw her arms around Lily and squeezed. Then she stepped back and clapped her hands. "I can't even tell you how hungry I am right now. I swear, instead of morning sickness, I basically want to eat *all* the time."

Tucker laughed. "It's true. I cannot keep this woman satisfied."

Immediate awkward silence ensued as the four of them stood there, eyes wide.

Finally Tucker cleared his throat. "Wow, Lil. This is—this is amazing." He pulled her into a hug as well. "Thank you," he whispered before releasing her.

"Should we get started?"

Ava pulled out a chair and motioned for Sara to take a seat.

"Oh, you don't need to stay," Lily started. "I'm okay—"

"Bra!" Ava interrupted, and everyone's eyes widened, Lily's included. But then she shrugged and laughed, knowing what her friend meant.

She gripped the back of the second chair and pulled it out for Tucker.

After only six months, she'd grown closer with Ava than friends she'd known for years. Her friends who were married were all moving on to the next phase of parenting. She felt like every time she opened her e-mail there was an Evite for another baby shower. Her single friends were still into late nights of drinking and dancing, a phase she'd grown out of almost as soon as she'd entered it.

She *had* friends. But she'd never thought she needed a

support system. Yet without even asking, Ava had become that.

Her *bra.*

She snorted softly to herself and then cracked open a bottle of sparkling water, filling the crystal goblets at each place setting.

"I realize the irony of sitting in a soon-to-be winery sipping sparkling water, but one—no vintage until next year, and two—well—pregnancy."

She expected her cheeks to flame or her throat to grow tight at the mention of Tucker and Sara's unborn child but was surprised to find the words had no effect at all on her, other than reassuring her she'd made the right choice not to serve wine.

Sara simply beamed. "You're so thoughtful, Lily. Thank you. My midwife said a sip of champagne at the reception is allowable, to toast my marriage. But other than that, Tucker's in charge of what will be served at the bar."

Tucker held up his goblet in Lily's direction. "I defer to the caterer," he said. "She'll know what will go best with the menu."

Lily nudged Ava's shoulder with her own. "And I happen to know the daughter of the couple that runs the Ellis Vineyard. I think we can find you some excellent vintages while the Everetts are still cultivating their own."

Sara and Tucker clinked their glasses and each took a sip. Everyone was all smiles. They hadn't even started with the food, and she already knew the day would be a success. Their *wedding* would be a success. And then Lily would finally have a future to look forward to, one she'd put on hold for far too long.

"Okay," Sara said. "I don't mean to be pushy, but I'm famished. What's first?"

Smiles turned to easy laughter as Lily uncovered the first silver-domed plate to reveal the first item.

"Butternut squash ravioli with garlic brown butter sauce," she said.

Sara's eyes fluttered shut, and she breathed in the escaping aroma. Almost as quickly, she opened them again, picked up her fork, and cut open one of Lily's from-scratch pasta pockets. The three of them watched as the woman who was famous for her own kitchen creations tasted someone else's.

Sara dropped her fork and splayed both of her palms on the table as she closed her mouth and chewed.

Tucker watched his fiancée with a bemused expression.

Ava grabbed Lily's hand.

Lily held her breath.

Sara's head fell back as she swallowed, and for a second Lily thought she'd passed out. Or worse. Maybe she'd choked or something.

But just as she was about to run to Sara's side to make sure she hadn't killed her, the woman's head tilted up to reveal an expression of pure and utter delight.

"*Lily*," the woman said, like she'd just learned some big secret.

"How—was it?" Lily asked.

Sara slapped her palms down on the table, and Tucker crossed his arms and waited, like this was something he was used to.

"How was it?" Sara repeated. "How *was* it? I almost *climaxed*," she said. Then she turned to her husband-to-be. "We're going to have tables of people having foodgasms if we're not careful. Did you taste it yet?"

She skewered another piece, fed it to Tucker, and that was that. Lily had impressed someone she'd thought near to unimpressible.

Next came the shepherd's pie and all the other autumn comfort foods they'd requested for their menu. With each taste Sara commended Lily on her expert cooking. With each taste Lily knew this wedding would be the launch of her new career.

Finally, it was time for the cake. Lily tried to ignore what thoughts of cake tastings made her think of now, but it was too late. Her mind had already conjured the image of Luke Everett sprawled on the couch, her hand resting atop the ice pack that lay on his bare skin.

Her lips on his.

The way he drove her insides so crazy she lost all control of rational thought.

And then the way that—when rational thought returned—she remembered how crazy *angry* he could make her, too.

She lifted the dome from the last plate. Though everything had gone better than she'd imagined, she was now relieved they were at the end. The sooner they gave her the thumbs-up on the cake, the sooner she could clear out of here and get far away from thoughts of the man she vowed to stop thinking about.

"White chocolate raspberry," she said, trying to calm the slight tremor in her voice.

Ava let out a hum of pleasure. "Sorry," she said, hand flying to her mouth. "Involuntary response. I've tasted this one before, and I think I almost climaxed, too."

Lily forced a smile while Sara and Tucker each picked up a fork and dug in.

"Jesus, Lil," Tucker said before he'd even swallowed. "I mean, I knew you could bake, but this? Shit. This is unbelievable."

She couldn't help but feel the swell of pride at his words.

Lily turned her gaze to Sara, expecting a similar reaction, but instead she gasped and shrunk back at the sight.

Sara's eyes were wide as she began to rub and scratch at her neck. Large red bumps appeared there first, then traveling up her face and down her arms.

Hives.

"What's happening?" the usually serene woman shrieked. "Tucker, what's happening?"

Tucker scrambled out of his chair and to Sara's side.

"Can you breathe?" Lily asked, feigning calm. "Sara..."

The woman's horrified gaze locked on Lily's.

"Can you breathe?"

Sara took in a deep breath, as if testing herself and then nodded.

"Does your tongue feel like it's swelling up?" Lily added.

Again, Sara's expression turned to one of quiet examination.

She shook her head. "But it's itchy. Like my skin. Does that mean it might swell? Do you know what's happening to me?"

Lily nodded. "Prior to today, did you have any food allergies?'

"No," Sara said without hesitation. Then she grazed her teeth over her tongue as she continued to claw at her skin. "I work with food for a living. I've tasted everything there is to taste. No allergies."

Lily pulled out her phone and tapped a few buttons, then held it to her ear. "Well, you do now. And because this is your first reaction, we have to act quickly in case you go into anaphylactic shock."

Sara gasped. Tucker held her tight, and Ava just stood there and waited, Lily's underwire of support.

"Nine-one-one, what's your emergency?" Lily heard on the other end of the line.

She started by giving the address of the winery. "I have a woman who's experiencing a severe allergic reaction to raspberries. No, no history, but she is covered in hives, even inside her mouth." Lily swallowed. "And she's pregnant." Lily nodded. "Yes. Still breathing. Still talking. Okay. Yes. Thank you."

She ended the call, pushed back a wave of emotion threatening to surface, and reminded herself that she needed to be calm, to stay in control so Sara and Tucker wouldn't freak out.

"Fire department's closer, so they're sending EMTs from there. They know your situation and should be able to keep you stable until you get to the hospital. If your breathing is okay now, it's likely it will stay that way, but with this being your first reaction—and with the baby—" *Oh God. Please let their baby be okay.* "It's a berry allergy," she told them.

"How do you know?" Sara asked, her voice shaky.

Lily had to force herself not to wince at the sight of the woman she thought so strong and unflappable now so suddenly vulnerable.

"My mom has the same allergy," she said. "We found out with strawberries, though. But it didn't manifest until she was an adult. It was—just the two of us when it happened. I'd saved up, bought some angel food cake, strawberries, and whip cream from the store so I could make her strawberry shortcake. She took one bite, and the hives were instant. But when her tongue started to swell—"

She was interrupted by the sound of sirens. Less than a minute later, the EMTs burst through the door with the rolling stretcher. And only a couple minutes after that, they were rolling Sara out, Tucker trotting beside her with her hand firmly gripped in his.

Then there was nothing but silence, just she and Ava standing in the big empty room.

"Was your mom okay?" Ava said, grabbing Lily's hand.

They both stared toward the empty doorway.

Lily nodded. "I was six," she said. "And I didn't know where her phone was or even how to call nine-one-one. I ran to the neighbor—to the trailer next door—and told them what was happening. I'm still shocked they knew what I was saying through all the tears." She let out a huff of bitter laughter. "Mrs. Wishne's daughter had a peanut allergy. If she hadn't had that EpiPen…"

Ava squeezed her hand tight. "Oh, Lily. Honey. That must have been so scary."

She nodded.

But the fear isn't what she remembered so well. It was the helplessness. Being out of control left her helpless to save her mom. It was only a stroke of luck that she didn't watch her die that day.

Out of nowhere she was awash in a wave of guilt. The woman she'd so desperately not wanted to lose was almost a stranger to her these days.

Maybe she was a control freak, but she'd never put anyone else at risk again since then. Herself included. And today only reaffirmed that it had been the best decision she'd ever made.

CHAPTER NINE

Luke stood with his arms crossed, watching Lily pace the empty ER waiting room. He waited, assuming she'd eventually stop, but when several cycles of the agitated behavior ensued with no end in sight, he reckoned it was time to step in before she wore through the soles of her shoes.

"You know, I don't think you'll get very far if you keep changing directions."

She gasped and stumbled as she forced herself to a stop, and he had to keep himself from rushing to her.

Damn ass-backward instinct.

"What are you doing here?" she asked, and he was unable to glean anything from her surprisingly even tone. It was as if she always spent her early afternoons in the emergency room and wanted to simply inquire if he did the same.

He gestured to the small duffel on his shoulder.

"Tucker called. Wanted me to grab a few of Sara's things from his place to have overnight."

Her eyes widened, and her hand cupped her mouth.

Aw hell.

This time he did rush to her side. He grabbed her by the shoulders, backed her toward an empty chair, and then sat her down.

She dropped her hand. "I almost killed the bride with wedding cake."

Luke tossed the bag on the floor and then lowered himself to squat in front of her, arms resting across his knees. "Yeah, but you didn't."

She hugged her torso, and he realized not only how shaken she was but also that *shaken* had never once been a word he'd have used to describe Lily Green. He guessed almost killing someone with your cooking could do it, though.

"I don't get it," she said. "I *knew* Tucker didn't have any food allergies, but I asked Sara ahead of time. I'm sure of it. I created this food survey for clients to make sure I don't use any known allergens or that I don't use a hated spice or herb. Like cilantro, you know? Some people *hate* cilantro. I'm not one of them, but they're out there, the cilantro haters. And I might have to cook for one of them."

He shook his head, his eyes dipping toward his feet so she couldn't see him bite back a smile.

"What?" she asked.

He guessed he wasn't subtle enough.

He rose long enough to drop into the empty seat beside her, stretching his legs out in front of him.

"Nothing," he said, crossing one boot over the other. "I'm sure there will be plenty of cilantro haters in your future. It's good you're so prepared."

She pouted and backhanded him on the shoulder, but he noted the hint of a smile.

"I wasn't prepared *enough*," she said. "Make fun all you want, but imagine if I didn't check for these things. I could have endangered the baby if I'd served unpasteurized cheese or—" She gasped again. "Is the baby okay? Oh God, no one has told me *anything*. Ava had to go pick up Owen from her parents' house, and Jack is back there making sure Tucker and Sara don't sue, and shit, *Luke*, just tell me Sara and the baby are okay."

Something in his gut twisted at the way she said his name, like it was some sort of a plea, and with zero rational thought before he acted, he draped his arm over her shoulders and pulled her close.

"Hey," he whispered as she didn't even fight it. She just rested her head on his shoulder like it was the most natural thing for her to do. "Sara's *fine*. The baby is fine. Tucker said it's some fluke thing that can happen—allergies emerging during pregnancy that weren't there before. Because Sara's whole life revolves around food, she wants to make sure this doesn't happen again, so they're running some blood tests and keeping her overnight to make sure there's no secondary reaction to the—what kind of cake did you give her?"

Lily let out a long breath that warmed his neck yet somehow made the hair on his arms prickle.

"White chocolate raspberry."

He whistled. "That the one I tried?"

She nodded against him.

"Shit that was good."

She nodded again, and he dipped his head, allowing himself a subtle inhale of her hair. Jesus. She smelled like a goddamn bakery, sweet enough to eat. He closed his eyes and breathed in again, and that's when he heard the sound of a throat clearing.

The two of them bolted upright to see Tucker looming above them, his dark hair falling over his narrowed eyes.

"You two look—cozy," he said, and Luke fought going on the defensive.

He stood and handed his friend the duffel bag. "Hey,

man. No need to be jealous. I'll hold you in my arms next time you accidentally almost kill someone, too."

Tucker grabbed the bag, his jaw ticking once before his expression relaxed into a smile.

"Thanks, asshole," he said to Luke. "For the bag and for taking care of Lily."

Lily shot to her feet. "Tucker, I am *so* sorry. If I'd known pregnancy could trigger allergies, I—I—"

"Lil," he said, pulling her into a hug Luke wasn't expecting. "The EMTs said you were amazing. Because you were so calm and knew exactly what was happening, they got to Sara quickly enough that they were able to stop the reaction with a low dose of antihistamine. Sara doesn't like the idea of taking any medication while pregnant, but they promised it was safe. The hives are gone, and she's totally fine. The baby, too. Thanks to *you*."

He squeezed her tighter, and the sight of the two of them in this intimate moment forced Luke to look away. Yet out of sight did nothing to put the vision out of mind.

Before today, Luke had been the last man to hold Lily Green in his arms. Before today, the only way she'd ended up there was when they were so angry at each other the only choice was to kiss her or explode. But now she needed comfort. She needed someone to tell her everything was going to be okay, but she didn't want that someone to be Luke. And it stung like hell to realize it.

When the two finally broke apart, Lily's shoulders relaxed.

"I'm glad everyone's okay. And I understand if you want to cancel the contract after—"

"Cancel?" Tucker said. "Everything you prepared today was amazing. Cake included. No one could have known this was going to happen, and *no* one could have handled it better than you did. Sara wanted me to tell you that we'll get back to you tomorrow with a list of any other known allergens but that you should go ahead with all menu items other than cake, and we'll figure out an allergen-free choice by the end of the week."

She let out a long exhale. "Wow. Okay. Um. This is...huge." She started backing toward the door. "Everyone's okay, and I'm still catering the wedding, and the menu is a go. I should head home. Time to make a calendar, find a volunteer staff, and get to work. We've got less than two weeks."

Luke watched as she gripped her ever-present shoulder bag, gave them both a nervous, not quite genuine grin, and disappeared through the automatic doors.

The two men stared after her for several long seconds before meeting each other's gaze.

"What's going on, Everett?" Tucker asked, and Luke held his ground.

"Nothing, Green. Just comforting a shaken friend."

Tucker crossed his arms. "I'm married to the girl for three years, and you can't stand her. Now you two are friends?"

"Christ, Tuck. No, we're not friends." It wasn't as if he was lying. They were anything but. "But she was a mess. For fuck's sake, she almost killed her ex-husband's fiancée. With *wedding* cake. I wasn't going to just stand there and watch her punish herself. So I fucking comforted her."

Shit. He was getting too defensive. This shouldn't matter.

Tucker's posture relaxed.

"Look," he said. "I appreciate you stepping in. I just want to make sure that's all it was. I know I wasn't the best husband and that I have zero claim on her. But it still hurt like hell for her to walk out on me, and—I don't know—you're like my brother, Everett. And—"

Luke shook his head. "I get it, man. I get it. I was just

trying to help out." Because Tucker was his brother, too. "I'm just glad Sara's okay."

Then he pivoted and strode out the ER door.

He sat behind the wheel of his truck and debated where to go. When he couldn't come up with a decision, he just got on the road and drove. A good fifteen minutes went by before his phone buzzed in the cup holder beside him. He glanced down to see it was Ava, so he pulled onto the shoulder to make sure everything was okay.

I'm at my parents' with Owen. Jack said he stopped by Lily's to make sure she was okay. Said her car was in the driveway, but she wouldn't answer the door or her phone. I know Sara's fine, but maybe this hit Lil harder than we thought? I'm still an hour away. Can you stop over there if you're in the area? See if she'll answer for you? I'm a little worried.

She was fine. He *knew* she was fine. Maybe even excited to get started on her favorite activity—*planning*—when she'd left.

But what if, for once, the unflappable Lily Green was finally…*flapped*? He knew he wasn't her first choice for comfort. That had already been established at the hospital. And after what Tucker said to him, he figured he should just pretend he missed the text.

He threw his head against the back of his seat and groaned, then started to type.

Yeah. I'll swing by.

Because even if being alone with Lily Green was the worst idea in the world, Luke was a little worried, too. And maybe the reason he'd been driving anywhere but home was because he knew there was somewhere else he'd rather be.

He put the car in drive, pulled off the shoulder, and made a U-turn. He was a man with direction now. The only problem was the imaginary street sign that flashed in his head.

Wrong way.

But these days Luke Everett wasn't great at following the rules.

"Lily, open the door. I know you're in there. Ava's with the kid and can't get here, and she knows you wouldn't open up for Jack. If you don't show some sign of life, she's gonna make me call the police, and you know Sheriff Hawkins is an asshole when he's pulled off his nighttime traffic duty."

It was mostly true. Sheriff Hawkins *was* grumpy as hell if he got pulled from his quiet shoulder of road. Few knew the sheriff actually *liked* sitting in his Tahoe with his radar gun and his German shepherd. But Luke was one of the few. Ava hadn't threatened to call him, though. That was all Luke. Because this *wasn't* like Lily, and he didn't like the sinking feeling he got in his gut each time he rapped on the door to no avail.

He pounded for the third and what he swore was his final time.

"Christ, Lily, just open the goddamn d—"

The door swung open just as his fist was about to make contact again. He stopped short, arm still raised, and felt like *he'd* been socked in the gut instead of almost doing just that to Lily.

She stood there with an afghan wrapped around her shoulders, wearing nothing but a tank top and sweatpants, one hand wrapped around a glass of red wine.

It was her eyes—red rimmed, lashes visibly wet, and no sign of that ever-present spark that usually drove him mad—that threw him off-kilter.

"Sign of life, okay?" she said. "You're now free to go."

She made a move to push the door shut, but he shoved his boot against it, effectively taking an uninvited step inside.

"And you're free to enjoy the pleasure of my company because I don't have anywhere else to be." He pushed past her and strode straight to the kitchen. "Got anything that comes in a can rather than a bottle with a cork?" he called over his shoulder. "Pretty thirsty myself."

He heard her bare feet padding across the wood floor at record speed.

And three. Two. One.

"You can't just barge in here like you own the place. You asked me to answer the door. I answered. Now it's time for you to go."

He didn't answer her right away. First he had to finish rummaging through the fridge to find something suitable to drink.

"Seriously," he said, straightening to meet her death stare. "No Budweiser? Coors? What's a guy supposed to drink around here?"

He winked.

She glared at him, and he noticed the skin under her eyes no longer looked wet.

"You're growing grapes," she informed him.

"So I've been told." He raised his brows.

"So maybe it's time you grew accustomed to your product and learned how to appreciate something that actually tastes good."

He feigned a wince.

"That hurts, Green. You've officially insulted my palate."

Her lip twitched, and he watched her try to fight it. But she failed miserably. And soon enough, there it was—her smile.

He guessed a cabinet, opened it, and withdrew a wineglass. He set it on the counter in front of her.

"Why don't you enlighten my taste buds?" he said, nodding at the bottle. "Ellis Vineyards, huh? You still gonna drink the competition when Crossroads goes live?"

She huffed out a small laugh as she poured him a generous serving.

"Ava *Ellis* is marrying your brother. If anything, her connection will help you guys rather than pose a threat."

He nodded, picked up the glass, and swirled the burgundy liquid. Then he inhaled its fragrance.

"You like the bouquet?" she asked, and he pursed his lips in contemplation.

"It smells like—" He blew out a breath. "It smells like fucking wine. I don't know what the hell a bouquet is."

She laughed again, this time a little louder.

"So you're really not leaving?" she asked, but the anger had ebbed from her voice.

He could walk out right now. He *should* turn and head right for the door. He'd done what Ava asked—gotten Lily to open the door and prove she was okay. And while she was standing before him with no visible injuries—his normal barometer for a person's well-being—she was anything *but* okay.

"I'm not leaving," he said, and waited for her to kick him out.

Instead she grabbed both their glasses and headed around the counter and into the living room. She set her glass on the wooden coffee table—on a coaster, of course—then pulled another coaster from a small stack for his glass.

Without a word she collapsed onto the plush cream-colored couch.

He grabbed the wine bottle, followed, and lowered himself onto the oversize chair perpendicular to her.

"Why are you being so nice to me?" she asked. "First the hospital. Now this."

He shrugged. "Maybe I don't think you should be alone right now."

She nodded slowly, wrapped her afghan tightly around her shoulders, and pulled her knees to her chest.

"Well—maybe I don't want to be alone."

"Then we're in agreement," he said, raising his glass.

She lifted hers as well. "I guess there's a first time for everything."

CHAPTER TEN

Never have I ever planned my life more than an hour in advance," Luke said, staring at her until she lifted her glass and took a sip, but then she gave him an accusatory grin. "What?" he asked. "You're the one who carries around that goddamn dictionary with every minute of your day recorded in it. Not me."

She narrowed her eyes. "Just because you don't write stuff down doesn't mean you don't have a plan. You work the vineyard and the ranch each day. You train for your rodeos. That's not all"—she waved her free hand in the air—"just fly-by-the-seat-of-your-pants kind of stuff. You have to know what your days entail to do your job. You have to *plan* your training so you're ready for the next performance."

He groaned. "It's not a performance. It's a serious competition."

She rolled her eyes. "Whatever. You know what I mean. I'm just making the point that even if you don't want to admit you're a grown-up, you kind of are."

He threw his head back against the soft chair, and she giggled. She didn't know what the hell they were doing, but one thing was sure. Her eyes were dry, and the weight on her chest that had been making it nearly impossible to breathe since the second she dialed 9-1-1? It was lifting. All because she had answered the door.

"Your turn," he said, still staring at the ceiling. He was biting back a smile, which meant his irritation was feigned, maybe for the first time since they'd been in a room together and not been—well—lip-locked. They weren't actively trying to get under each other's skin, which had always been the norm. Right now they were just—being—something they hadn't done before. "Unless you want to throw on your favorite country song and teach me a line dance."

He sat up straight, and her eyes widened.

"You really do remember?" she asked.

He sighed. "The night you and Tucker met?" He dropped his head, shaking it slightly. "I was there, Lily."

She cleared her throat. "I know," she said. "I didn't mean anything by it. I just—wait, do you actually think I don't remember you being there—or my roommate going home with you?"

He lifted his head, and his stubbled jaw tensed. "Forget it," he said. "Your turn."

She nodded and swallowed. She didn't want to fight with him, but this felt different. She wanted to poke and prod but she feared what else Luke might say about that night if she did. Instead she tried to maintain the status quo.

"Never have I ever ridden a bull."

The reaction was immediate, the Luke Everett devil-may-care grin. Because she knew he couldn't stay angry, or bothered, or whatever he was, if she mentioned something he loved.

He downed the rest of the wine in his glass, then filled it again just as quickly.

"What's it like?" she asked.

His grin widened, and she was overcome with the urge to brush her fingers over his smiling lips.

"It's knowing the one thing you can control is whether you hold on to the rope or let go. Sure, there's training and technique, but that's really only there to make sure you don't kill yourself. The rest is just admitting that the bull *will* throw you off. It's just a matter of how long—and whether or not you'll get up to try it again."

An unexpected tear leaked out of the corner of her eye. Without meaning to, Luke had just summed up her life—and the part of it she wasn't sure she could do. Try it again.

His brows drew together. "Shit. What did I say? I swear I didn't mean—"

She shook her head. "Here's the thing," she said. "Never have I ever messed up more than I did today. I mean, I got knocked off the bull in a pretty spectacular way."

"That's not what I was getting at," he interrupted, but she raised her brows.

"I'm not done," she said.

He waited, so she decided to go for broke.

"Never have I ever cried in front of someone else," she added. "Not since I was a kid." She shrugged. "It's probably one of the biggest reasons my marriage didn't work, you know? I don't do vulnerable really well, especially when it means admitting I messed up."

"You're doing good with the vulnerable thing, Lil," he said softly.

Lil. Not *sweetheart.*

"It's because never have I ever heard anyone put into words the reason why. Until now." She laughed. "Not sure you noticed, but I'm a bit of a perfectionist. And lately, my life has been *far* from perfect. But you walked in here and didn't judge. You could have rubbed it in my face or said *I told you so* or any number of things, Luke. But instead you made me feel like—like I *could* try again."

"Lil," he said again, an insistence in his voice that made her heart ache in a way she'd never experienced before.

The tears fell freely now, and the words spilled out of her mouth almost as quickly. It was as if what he'd just said had broken the dam, and she couldn't stop, even if she wanted to.

"One more thing about that night." She sniffled. "Never have I ever admitted out loud that if you had asked me to go home with you, I would have said yes."

And then she saw him as he was three years ago, striding into that bar all confidence and swagger—and *trouble.*

You know I didn't step foot on the dance floor to meet your roommate.

"What happened that night?" she asked him.

He set his glass down slowly, deliberately, the sound of it rousing her from the memory. All the while he held her gaze.

Her heart slammed in her chest, a caged animal threatening to break free.

She was losing it, her control. All he had to say to make her abandon it completely was that he wanted her, too. It wouldn't matter that he hadn't wanted her *then.* Just here. Right now. That's all she needed to do what she'd never been able to—*let go.*

"You left with Tucker that night," he said, voice rough and gravelly. "You left with my best friend. You married him weeks later."

"*You* made that decision for me," she reminded him. "Why?"

She'd never diminish what she and Tucker had, but she'd no longer ignore that the night in question started off on a whole other trajectory.

He let out a bitter laugh. "You chose the better man, Lily. Can't we just leave it at that?"

She bit her lip, setting down her own glass. "But you don't like me," she said, not able to hide the tremor in her voice. "You've *never* liked me," she added, though the more she repeated what she'd always thought to be true, the less she believed it.

Their knees were touching. She'd slid forward without noticing, and now something was happening that was beyond her carefully maintained control.

So she reached out a hand, brushed her thumb over his perfect lips, and he squeezed his eyes shut.

"You *don't* hate me," she said softly.

He opened his eyes, his steely gaze back on hers.

"No," he whispered.

"You—want me?" she asked, a little less sure of herself.

"Fuck," he growled. "You know I do."

She wiped away the last remaining tear.

"Tucker doesn't get to lay claim on me anymore. You think *I'm* the control freak," she said. "But you're the one sitting there holding back from what you want."

He ran a hand through his hair, then stood, pacing a few steps before turning back to face her.

"Jesus, Lily. What the hell else do you want me to do?" he asked, eyes dark with what she hoped was the same heat bubbling inside her.

She stood, too. It didn't matter that he was a head taller than she was. For the first time, she felt like she was on an equal footing with Luke Everett.

For the first time, she was veering from the plan, and it felt—right.

She took a tentative step toward him so there were mere inches between them. "Take it," she said. "Take what you want."

She held her breath and waited a beat, knowing they were either stepping way over the line or retreating permanently.

A beat was all it took before his strong, rough hands were cupping her cheeks, his lips crashing into hers.

Their bodies didn't meet. They collided, two speeding trains not daring to veer off course even if the result would be complete and utter carnage.

She threw her arms around his neck, and he hoisted her up, hooking her thighs onto his hips.

"This doesn't hurt?" she asked, breathless. "I can walk, you know."

He shook his head. "The only thing I feel is you, sweetheart."

"But—" she started.

He cut her off. "Bedroom," he growled, then kissed her harder, deeper, stealing her air, and she gave it to him willingly. "Which door?" His teeth nipped at her bottom lip.

"Second one on the right," she said, legs squeezing around his waist, pressing his erection against her center.

He spun, claiming her mouth again as he carried her to their destination, backing her through the doorway and throwing her onto the four-poster bed.

For a second he paused, taking in his surroundings. This was Tucker's room. Tucker's room *with* Lily. He'd seen it once, maybe twice, but could tell something was different. Was the bed was on a different wall? And he didn't think he remembered the posts. Also the room was as crisp and neat as if he'd just walked into a fancy hotel. The whole space was just so—Lily.

"You make your bed even though you live alone?" he asked.

She rolled her eyes. “Is this *really* a conversation you want to have right now?”

He grinned. *No. No it wasn’t.*

“The bed is new, by the way,” she said. “Tucker and I split up the furniture when he moved out. So—I, uh—I gave him the bed.”

Meaning they’d never slept together in this new one.

“I get it,” he said. “But can we make a rule right now?”

She nodded, waiting for him to continue.

“From here on out, no talking unless it’s me telling you what I’m going to do to you.”

Her legs hung over the side of the bed, and he pushed them open, stepping between them. “Or, vice versa, of course.”

She sucked in a breath, and he pressed his palm against her pelvis.

“Is that a deal?” he asked.

“Yes,” she whispered.

His thumb traced a soft line between her legs, and she whimpered. He massaged the spot over her opening, and she fisted her duvet.

“I’m going to make you lose control, sweetheart. I’m going to show you what it means to let go.”

She reached for him, tugging at the belt loop of his jeans, and he fell over her, his face a breath away from hers.

“And I’ll show you what it means to slow down and savor the moment.”

He raised a brow. “Not as dirty as I’d hoped, but the night is still young.”

She opened her mouth to protest, but he kissed her, his tongue slipping past her parted lips, and she answered him by running her hands up his chest, his neck, and into his hair.

He kicked off his boots and rolled them both to their sides.

She palmed him over his jeans, giving him a firm squeeze that elicited a groan.

"I want you to . . . taste me?"

The statement came out like a question, and he laughed softly. She was trying to dirty talk him, and he didn't know what was hotter—the sweetness of her not being sure how to do it or her knowing *exactly* what he'd been dying to do.

"Better," he said. "But now say it like you mean it."

She grabbed his hand and pressed it to her belly, his fingertips teasing the elastic band of her pants.

Well, shit. Maybe he didn't want her to abandon her control completely because he liked her giving him direction.

"*Taste* me," she commanded this time, and he was more than happy to oblige.

He slid his hand beneath the pants, beneath her panties, and let one finger travel from her clit, down her crease, sinking it deep inside her warm, wet center.

Christ.

He throbbed against his jeans. She had no clue what she was doing to him, that *he* was the one whose sense of control was dangling by a thinning thread.

She cried out as he withdrew just as achingly slow, taking care to circle her clit before his hand emerged. Then he swirled his tongue around the finger that had been inside her, and he thought he might lose his tether right then and there.

"Fucking hell, Lily. Do you know how long I've wanted to do that?"

But he didn't wait for her to respond because he was far too close to revealing more truth than either of them could handle. Instead he lifted her tank over her shoulders, then sucked in a breath as she lay before him, half bare and too beautiful for him to speak.

So he just—stared.

"Say something," she said as he drank her in with his gaze. "You're making me nervous."

She bit her lip and smiled, but he shook his head.

"For some things, sweetheart, there simply aren't words," he admitted. "I mean, there are, but I sure as shit don't have the right ones."

She gave him a teasing grin.

"Not as dirty as I'd hoped," she said. "But the night is still young."

He cupped her breast, pinched her rosy peaked nipple between his thumb and forefinger, and she gasped.

"I just remembered," he said. "I'm more of a doer than a sayer."

He lifted his own shirt over his head. Her eyes widened, and her fingertips explored the dusting of hair on his chest, the trail of it that led to the button of his jeans. But then she detoured, traveling instead over the fading bruises on his side.

"Does it still hurt?" she asked softly, her cheeks turning pink. "I mean, it has to, right? It's only been a couple of weeks. Should you have just carried me? Oh God, did I make it worse?"

"Do you ever get out of that head of yours?" He laughed softly, then kissed her. "And yeah, I guess it still hurts, but only when I think about it. I've been knocked around enough that I think I just get used to the pain. It's the nature of what I do."

She kissed the side of his jaw. "The me that gets stuck in my head would ask why you love something that's also so dangerous—why you put your body through the wringer when you know how high the risks are." She kissed his neck, and he dipped his head, breathing in the sweet vanilla of her hair. "That same me would ask how long you *haven't* hated me." She was kissing his chest now, and he knew in this moment if she asked him any of what she was thinking, he'd answer her. He'd be powerless not to.

She lifted her head, her eyes meeting his. Then she undid the button of his jeans, lowered the zipper, and pressed her palm against his erection.

He hissed in a breath through clenched teeth.

"But that's not who I want to be tonight," she said, rubbing a thumb over his tip, the cotton of his boxer briefs the only thing separating skin from skin.

"Who do you want to be, Lily?"

She slid off the edge of the bed and stood, removing her panties and pants in one quick movement, then pulled his jeans and briefs down his legs until they lay in a pile on her floor.

He rolled to his back, rose up on both elbows, and stared at a woman so beautiful he almost had to look away. But he didn't. He *wouldn't.*

Just like that, there was nothing left between them other than one best friend/ex-husband and years of buried truths he wasn't ready to uncover.

Tucker doesn't get to lay claim on me anymore.

Those were her words, and maybe it was time he believed them. Maybe it was time to let himself want without the guilt.

"I want to be the girl who loses control. Just for tonight. I'm not giving up my dictionary-size planner or anything."

She grinned, then crawled over him, sliding up his length and letting him tease her opening.

"Christ, Lily. What about—"

"I'm on the pill," she said. "Have been for years and never missed a dose. Never even messed up the time of day."

He pressed two fingers to her lips and chuckled.

"Of course you haven't. Okay Lily-who's-letting-go-of-control, don't you at least want to know if I'm free of infection?"

She shrugged. "Are you?"

He knew he was. But he wasn't about to admit *why* that knowledge was a certainty, that since he'd found out about Tucker asking for a divorce, he hadn't been able to sleep with another woman. Yeah, no way in hell he could mention that. So he answered her with the simplest form of the truth.

"Yes."

And just like that, she sank over him, burying him deep inside her, crying out as she did, her back arching and hands raking through her own hair.

A low growl tore from his chest.

He'd been with other women like this. It wasn't anything new. And yet he already knew it was like nothing he'd ever experienced before.

He knew it by the way they fit.

He knew it by the way she trusted him enough to want to let go.

He knew it because it was *her*.

Didn't she know how alike they really were? Despite him living with high risk always in the saddle beside him, Luke Everett controlled the most important part of his life—his heart.

But right now, he was far beyond the strains of his own cultivated control, and he was bound and determined to take her over the edge with him.

He cupped her ass in his palms as they quickly found their rhythm, slow and measured at first, but when she dropped down to kiss him, her soft moans filling the air between them as his tongue slipped past her parted lips, he thrust deeper, faster, wondering how long the two of them could hold out before this lit fuse exploded.

He tested his theory by sliding his hand between the place where they joined, his thumb tracing her wet, swollen center in firm, deliberate circles.

Her breathing hitched, and she kissed him harder.

He felt her start to pulse around him.

Her breaths came in small gasps, and he opened his eyes to find hers locked on him.

Together, he thought. They were going to let go together.

"*Luke*," she said softly, in a short suspended moment before they drove off that cliff.

"I know," he whispered.

And then he cupped her cheeks in his palms, drew her mouth to his, and let go of the wheel.

CHAPTER ELEVEN

Lily woke before the morning light had a chance to filter through her bedroom curtains. No alarm necessary. Her internal clock was forever programmed to *Get up and go before the day gets away from you.* On any given day, she needed to be at the restaurant by 6:00 a.m. to receive the shipment of fresh goods. Plus, she liked it—the routine of it all, the organization it brought to her daily life so much so that her body no longer required an external clock. It just knew.

Much like it knew how to react to the touch of the man sleeping beside her.

She stared at Luke, at how beautiful he was, and wondered how this realization had escaped her before. Yes, the gene pool had certainly been kind to all three of the Everett men, but something had shifted in the way she saw him now.

Could sex do that? Change the way you saw someone?

Fucking hell, Lily. Do you know how long I've wanted to do that?

What had his words meant? Was he talking about just last night? About the past couple of weeks since that crazy first kiss? Or was it something more—something connected to her admitting she had her sights set on him that night in the bar, the night she went home with Tucker Green.

She shook her head, trying to shake away the notion that there was anything more to what happened last night other than them burning off an inexplicable chemistry.

Still, she didn't stop herself from tracing the line of his jaw as he slept, fingertip brushing over the rough stubble that suited his rugged looks.

His brows furrowed, and she frowned in reaction. Sleep was supposed to be where people found peace. But with Luke it seemed to be the other way around.

She smoothed his hair away from his forehead, hoping to smooth away whatever plagued his sleep.

"You gonna kiss me good morning, sweetheart? Or are ya just a tease?"

Lily gasped and snatched her hand away, then backhanded him lightly on the shoulder as he opened his eyes.

"Jesus, you scared me!" Her heart hammered in her chest, but it continued to do so even after she caught her breath. This was—new.

He propped himself up on his elbow, his steely blue stare making her feel naked. She peeked under the sheet. Okay, *more* naked than she already was.

"You didn't answer my question," he said, the corner of his mouth crooking into the patented Luke Everett grin.

"I—"

But he cut her off.

"And you didn't object to *sweetheart*." He leaned closer. "Admit it. The name's growing on you."

"I—" she started again, but this time he did what she'd been too hesitant to do and kissed her.

All the thoughts racing through her head, like *What are we doing?* and *Are we going to do it again?* and *How bad is my morning mouth?* and *Why won't my heart rate slow down?* melted away as *she* melted into him.

She wasn't sure any man had the right to be this delicious first thing in the morning, but it wasn't worth questioning what she should just enjoy.

He nipped at her bottom lip, then parted his own, inviting her inside. She hummed a soft moan as he deepened the kiss, then smiled as she felt him harden against her thigh.

She guessed they were doing it again—a repeat performance of last night. Only this time he took his time with her, and she with him.

She led him to her shower after that. Amid the steam and ceramic tile, he lathered her hair, slid his hands over her slick body.

"If I call in an order for an extra water heater, can we stay in here all day?" she asked as he pressed her naked body to his.

"Don't have any pressing matters until sunrise at least," he said, then kissed her. "You always wake up before the sun?"

She kissed his chest, then looked up at him and nodded.

"One of the perks of working in the restaurant business," she said, smiling at the memory of her former early-morning routine. "My internal clock can't seem to forget, though."

He lifted a lock of wet hair and tucked it behind her ear. "You miss it," he said. "The restaurant. Don't you?"

She nodded again. "Not the actual place itself. But the idea of it. Yeah."

Despite her wish for an eternal shower, the water was already growing cold. So she reached behind Luke and turned it off.

He held her close for several long seconds. The glass shower doors were a bubble protecting them from whatever lay outside, so she took one more leap—one more risk—before retreating to safety again.

"We need to talk about... I mean, when you leave are you..." She groaned. "We have to tell Tucker, right?"

There it was, that tick in his jaw—his tell, she realized. It seemed to be the only sign of true emotion he revealed, yet what it pointed to she had no clue.

"Lily," he said, his forehead dropping against hers, but despite having made love to this man twice in the span of twelve hours, her name sounded like it was falling from a stranger's lips.

"Yeah?" she asked, even though she knew what was coming.

"You know I don't do serious, right? It's why things played out the way they did three years ago."

She slid the shower door open and stepped out. The *This meant nothing* conversation wasn't one she wanted to continue naked.

She pulled a towel from the rack and wrapped it around her body, then yanked off the second one and slapped it against his chest.

She winced slightly, remembering his healing ribs and shoulder, but she'd be damned if she was going to apologize.

"Of course," she said, voice even. "That's why they call rebounds *rebounds*. They don't last. And I don't remember asking you to move in. You'd just made it clear that your loyalty to Tucker was so important that I thought you'd want to come clean with him."

She spun on her heel and strode out of the bathroom, the bedroom, and to the safety of the kitchen, where soon there would be coffee.

She stood staring at the French press, waiting for the kettle to boil, when she heard him approach. She squared her shoulders, turned, and lifted her chin. Then she realized she was dressed in a towel and could only look so proud while *he*—well, he stood there with his damp hair, his stubbled jaw, and wearing his worn rancher's jeans and nothing else.

Dammit. Did this guy ever have an awkward phase, maybe in his teens? Because she'd pay to get her hands on evidence of that, anything that would make it easier to look at him without her own physical need betraying her.

"Lily," he said, a hint of pleading in his voice.

"Luke," she countered, a hint of haughtiness in hers.

He stepped closer, and she was grateful for the breakfast bar between them.

"Look, I think we got our signals crossed. I don't want you to think—"

A crackling sound came from his pocket.

"Hey, asshole. Not sure where you dropped your drawers last night, but Gertie is calving, and we could use your help."

"Christ, Walker," Luke said under his breath, then pulled the phone from his pocket. "I'll be there in about three minutes," he said, speaking into the phone like it was a walkie-talkie, which apparently it was.

He glanced up at her, raising a brow and giving her that irresistible roguish grin.

"You want to see ole Gertie do her job?" he asked. "We need to be out the door in about ninety seconds if you do."

She was so taken aback by the turn of events that the word was out of her mouth before she considered any of the implications.

"Yes." She nodded enthusiastically. "I'd love to."

In exactly ninety seconds she'd turned off the stove, padded back to her room, and thrown on a long-sleeved T-shirt and jeans. Now she was in the passenger seat of Luke's truck, finger combing her still wet hair. And it wasn't until they were well out of her driveway that it hit her. The—implications.

"So we're just going to show up at the ranch at dawn. Together?" she asked.

He nodded, the corner of his mouth turning up.

"You in yesterday's clothes and me—both of us with wet hair?"

He nodded again but kept his eyes on the road.

"Look," he said as they pulled down the road that led to the ranch. "I was trying to tell you something back there, but it came out all wrong." He came to a stop in front of the barn, then turned to face her. "There's something going on here," he said, motioning back and forth between them. "I'm not denying that. But I'm also not denying who I am. I *do* owe Tucker my loyalty. For more reasons than I can explain right now. So yes, he needs to know what happened, and I'll figure out how to tell him. But I also owe you the truth. And the truth is that me and permanency don't mix—except with my family." He forced a smile. "Because they don't have a choice."

She let out a bitter laugh.

What about what I choose? She wanted to say. But instead she said, "Oil and water, huh?"

His smile faded.

"I don't regret last night," he said. "Or this morning." He raised a brow. "That was some fucking chemistry. But—"

She held up her hands, a motion to surrender, because she knew what was coming next. And he was right.

"But we don't mix outside the bedroom. I get it. And I'm not arguing with you. Can we just—can we keep the whole emotional breakdown between us, though? It's bad enough I almost killed my ex-husband's fiancée. I don't want everyone worrying about me or thinking this wedding is too much for me to handle."

He opened his mouth to say something but was interrupted by a fist slamming against the hood of the truck.

They both bolted to attention to find Walker Everett's impatient blue eyes glaring at them.

"Come on, dickhead. You're late. Gertie ain't got all morning."

Luke opened the door and poked his head out. "How long she been in labor?" he asked.

Walker's face was grim. "Too long," was all he said, then started walking again.

So they both hopped out of the vehicle, following Walker as he shoved some sort of device in the back pocket of his jeans and led them out to the pasture where Jack, Ava, and Owen formed an arc around a heifer—presumably Gertie—lying in the grass.

"She's laboring hard," Jack said, dropping to a squat and rubbing Gertie's side. "Harder than I've ever seen from any of the herd, and we're at the tail end of calving season. Something's not right." He wiped his forearm across his brow. "We tried getting her inside the gate, but she just sorta collapsed right here."

Gertie let out some sort of guttural sound that made Lily shiver.

"Ava." Jack looked up at his fiancée and gave her a curt nod. She nodded back, some silent message passing between them, and she put her arm around their son.

"Owen, honey, let's head back to the ranch and get breakfast going. Your dad and uncles are gonna be hungry after this." She turned her gaze to Lily. "You want to come with us?"

No one had even asked Lily why she was there. She

knew that was the furthest thing from anyone's mind. She also knew that Ava was trying to shield her from whatever she was about to witness, just like she was Owen, but Lily shook her head.

"I'm gonna stay and help," Lily said, conviction in her voice.

Ava pressed her lips into a smile. Owen didn't protest as she led him away, and Lily braced herself for what was coming next when Gertie let out a panicked sound again.

Lily gasped.

"We need to get that calf out," Luke said. "She can't do it on her own."

All three brothers were in the grass beside the cow.

"What can I do?" she asked, realizing her presence was probably more trouble than help.

Luke glanced up at her, brushed his hair off his forehead, and nodded toward the barn.

"Walker, you got a bottle ready just in case?" he asked.

Walker nodded.

"Head into the barn," he said to Lily. "There's a supply area at the far end with a few shelves lining the wall. Grab what looks like an oversize baby bottle. You can't miss it."

She nodded and took off for the barn, heart racing. She found what she was looking for easily, grabbed the bottle, and sprinted back to the field. When she got there, Jack and Walker had seemingly pulled the calf free, and she smiled with relief—until she found Luke, still crouched by Gertie, rubbing the heifer's side as she wheezed out a breath. She watched him, transfixed by his gentleness, his care. He seemed to be whispering something to the cow, something she couldn't hear over the commotion of Jack and Walker hooting and hollering as the calf bleated its first cry.

Up and down went Gertie's side, Luke stroking her hide with each breath she took until, after several seconds, she was still.

Lily's breath caught in her throat, and she started forward, the urge to go to Luke compelling her toward him.

But he rose quickly, brushed his hands on his jeans, and strode to her instead. He didn't say anything, just grabbed the bottle, and stepped past her and to his brothers.

"We lost her," he said, his voice flat, and thrust the bottle into Walker's chest. "You know what to do." Walker nodded. "All right then. I'll go call someone to pick her up."

Then he kept on walking, past his truck and up toward the ranch. And Lily just stood there, death and life on either side of her, and the man who said he didn't believe in permanency clearly shaken by what he'd just seen.

"I don't get it," she said out loud, and Jack backed away and let Walker feed the calf. "You raise them for food, right?"

Jack nodded. "It's a huge contradiction. I know. But it's a whole other thing to watch the life go out of another living creature before her time."

She nodded, then glanced back toward the ranch.

"Just give him a few," Jack said. "It's nothing he hasn't seen before."

Maybe so, but Lily hadn't seen anything like this before—not what had just happened to Gertie and not what had just happened to Luke. This Luke Everett was someone Lily had never seen.

All these years she thought she'd had him pegged, right down to knowing in her bones that despite what happened between them last night—and this morning—that he was right. They were oil and water. No chance of anything real other than their chemistry.

"Hey," Jack said. "What are you two doing together at the crack of dawn anyway?"

He raised a brow.

"I'm not sure," she admitted. But she made a mental note to find out just what ingredient she needed to see if maybe, possibly, oil and water could attempt to be mixed.

CHAPTER TWELVE

Luke had finished cleaning himself up and was pouring a much needed cup of coffee when he heard the front door open and then close again. He braced himself, expecting Ava, Owen, and their dog, Scully, who always managed to make a frenzied entrance. But they'd barely been gone five minutes, and he knew Scully never cut a good walk short.

He shook his head as silence instead of paws clicking against the wood floor stretched out before him. He'd thought he wanted to be alone. But instead he welcomed her because being alone meant thinking, and things never turned out well when he let himself do that.

"Drank the last of the pot," he called over his shoulder, not yet ready to turn and face her. "But I can put more on."

He'd already guessed it was Lily. No Everett entered a house without anything less than a holler. Even his stoic, reserved older brother, Jack, still announced himself when he walked through the front door.

"Hey." Lily spoke softly, tentatively, approaching in just the same manner.

"Hey yourself," he said, not sure if he wanted to be alone with her. He was too tired to put his guard up, and he was afraid of what he might say to her with it down.

She took a step closer, but there was still a kitchen table between them, a barrier of safety.

"I wanted to see if you were okay after—you know…" But she trailed off, not finishing the thought. "Also," she added, "you're sort of my ride home, so I wanted to check and see if that was still the case or if I should ask Walker or Jack. I don't think Jack would mind." She squinted out the window just past his shoulder and over the sink. "Though it is a beautiful morning. I'd actually enjoy the walk. There's plenty I should get done today."

He shook his head, the ghost of a smile spreading across his lips. "Do you ever just slow down and shut the hell up?" he asked.

She crossed her arms and gave him an indignant scoff. Then she opened her mouth to say something else but must have thought better of it just as quickly because she slammed her lips shut.

"Oh, come on, sweetheart. I didn't mean it like that. You're always just go-go-goin', though. Don't you sometimes want to—I don't know—just have fun?"

Because he could use a distraction right now.

She clamped her jaw shut and narrowed her eyes at him. "Are you saying I'm *not* any fun? Because if I remember correctly, you had a good time at my place and—"

He threw back his head and laughed, and damn if the release wasn't exactly what he needed.

"Yes," he said. "I sure did *enjoy* myself, but believe it or not, I'm talking about something other than sex."

She raised a brow.

"Yes, ma'am, I *do* find other ways to enjoy myself outside a woman's bed. I'd never see the outdoors, otherwise."

He scratched the back of his neck. She did need a ride home, and he'd most likely be the one to give it to her.

"You ever ride a horse?"

She snorted. "Yeah, when I was, like, seven years old. But I'm guessing that doesn't count in your book."

He shook his head. "I bet Owen could school your ass, and he's only ten."

Her cheeks flamed, and he didn't hide his amusement at getting under her skin so easily.

"Let me guess," he said. "You don't like people being better than you at something. I knew you liked to argue, but are you holding out on me, sweetheart? Because no one likes some good competition more than me."

Lily huffed out a breath. "I am totally fine being bested. Just not by someone a third my age. How long has Owen been riding?"

"Six months."

She shrugged. "Well, being older, wiser, and trained in the fine art of observation, I should be able to pick it up pretty quickly, right?"

He laughed, tension releasing from his shoulders.

"Guess we won't know till we put you to the test, huh? How about a proposition?" he asked, and she pursed her lips, regarding him with those knowing green eyes.

"I'm listening," she said with mild hesitation.

"I'll take you riding"—he paused, making sure they were still alone—"as long as you keep our little outing between us."

She threw her hands in the air. "I don't want to be some dirty little secret, Luke Everett. I'm not asking for promises or commitment or anything of the sort, but I sure as hell won't be your secret shame."

His secret shame? He couldn't help but laugh, which made Lily clench her jaw and narrow her eyes. Hell, he was just trying to think of a way to spend the day with her without admitting he wanted to spend the day with her. He wasn't ready for admitting and hoping and—shit. He just wanted the two of them to *be*. Like last night.

He strode toward her, cupped her face in his palms, and dipped his head toward hers so they were close enough to kiss. But all he did was speak.

"*You* are not my dirty little secret," he said, his voice low and insistent. "Far from it, Lil. But I—as you remember—am supposed to be benched for two more weeks. So I'm going to take you riding at my buddy's ranch. And you're going to keep quiet about it so Jack doesn't go all fatherly on me and put me on house arrest again. Can you handle *that*?"

He watched her throat bob as she swallowed. He remembered the taste of her skin on his lips and stepped back, hoping she couldn't smell the desire he was still powerless to quell.

"But if you get hurt again, on my watch—" she started, and he knew she was just looking for excuses now. She wanted to say yes. He could feel it. And he wanted to share something important with her, even if it was under the guise of training.

"You'll be there to protect me," he teased.

She rolled her eyes.

"I'm riding today with or with you. So the only question you have to answer is whether or not you're joining me—and whether you think you're good enough to stay in the saddle."

She groaned, and he knew he'd closed the deal.

"No tricks or anything like that," she said. "Not on my watch. You can ride, but you need to be careful."

He tucked her damp hair behind her ear, trying to ignore the way her breathing hitched as he did.

"Don't you know?" he asked. "Careful's my middle name."

It was the biggest lie he'd ever spoken. The one he never gave voice to, though? The reason why today was more dangerous than she could ever fathom? Well, he knew better than to say that one out loud. Because that would make it all too real, and Luke Everett didn't do real.

She let out a shaky breath. "Why do I get the feeling you're more trouble than I realize?"

The corner of his mouth quirked up. "Lily Green—you have *no* idea."

She eyed him warily when they got out of the truck thirty minutes later. "Callahan Brothers Contracting?" she said. "You're going to teach me how to ride a horse with the guys who are building your wine tasting room?"

Luke shook his head and grinned. "They board a few horses on the side, too. It was their father's business before he got sick last year, and, well, they just haven't had the heart to sell it."

"Oh," Lily said. "Is he—still around? Their dad, I mean."

He grabbed his training hat out of the back of the cab, then placed his hand on the small of her back, urging her away from the car and toward the stables, but he couldn't deny the way she fit against him, even in something as simple as this.

"He was diagnosed with early-onset Alzheimer's. He still lives in the house."

She let him lead her, and he felt her muscles move against his palm as they walked.

"He's got round-the-clock care, but that's why Sam and Ben have their office space here. To keep an eye on him."

The corners of her mouth turned up, but he could tell it was a sad smile.

"What is it?" he asked as they came to a stop at the stable doors.

She wrapped her arms around her torso and shrugged.

"It's just nice. I mean—not their dad being sick. But seeing family take care of each other. *Having* family to take care of each other. I see you and your brothers do it. Your friends apparently do it. It's just...different from what I grew up with. That's all."

He was ready to ask her how—realizing he didn't know this woman other than what he'd gleaned these past few years. And after that first night in the bar, *most* of what he'd learned had been with her as Tucker's girlfriend. Then fiancée. And then wife.

This was new ground.

But either Lily wasn't too keen on sharing her childhood memories, *or* she was super eager to ride. Whatever the reason, she didn't give him a chance to ask questions. She was already pushing through the doors.

"Explain to me," she started as she walked cautiously between the stalls. "How it is that you get to come here and ride other people's horses, especially when your buddies aren't even home?"

There were only three horses boarding right now, and all three took notice of the beautiful woman disrupting their morning. Not surprisingly, none of them seemed to mind.

He stopped at the second stall to pet Ace's black nose. The horse greeted him with an appraising whinny, and he grinned.

"Part of boarding 'em is exercising 'em. And when they get an Appaloosa like Ace, they always add me to the contract to work the horse out. Gives me a place to train away from home, and it gives the horse what he needs, too."

Luke opened the stall and stepped right inside, rubbing a hand along Ace's black-and-white-spotted coat. "Atta boy," he said softly. "You want to meet my friend Lily?"

He glanced over his shoulder to find her standing outside the stall, peering in.

"You're really good with him," she said. "And that expert opinion comes from the fact that he hasn't kicked or bitten your face off yet."

He chuckled. "If that's the extent of your horse knowledge, then what the hell made you want to ride one?"

She gave him a nervous smile. "Because I need to step outside my safety zone," she said, a slight tremor in her voice.

He kept one hand on Ace's flank and rested the other on the stall door.

"You're scared," he said matter-of-factly.

She nodded slowly.

"We can start slow," he said. "I can work him out, do a little training, and you can watch and see how safe it is. Plus, I heard I'm quite entertaining." He waggled his brows.

"You're impossible," she said.

"So you've told me on several occasions. Doesn't change the fact that if you'd like to start by sitting back and enjoying the show, I can arrange that easily."

She groaned. "I *want* to ride, you egomaniac. I can be scared and still want to do it."

Now that was something he could get behind. It was how he lived his life—with the rush of fear and doing whatever came next anyway.

Except he called the shots—chose the origin of the fear.

Trick riding, barrel racing, getting thrown from the bull time and time again.

Each time his heart raced with the type of adrenaline that only came with the fight-or-flight response. And when it came to the rodeo arena, he always fought.

But right now his heart rate was speeding up, a response so similar and yet entirely different. Because when it came to Lily, he *should* run. But despite his body's physiological response, he couldn't bring himself to do it.

"Let's go, then," he said.

He tried not to grin as she watched him affix the pad and saddle, but it was hard to keep his expression impassive when he could *feel* her appraising him.

"I'm gonna take him for a couple of laps around the arena to get him warmed up, and then it's all you, okay?"

She bit her lip and nodded.

He lifted his hat, wiped the sweat from his brow with his forearm, and then dropped it back on his head before hooking his boot into the stirrup and hopping into the saddle.

He winced, only slightly, but it wasn't slight enough for Lily to miss.

"Luke Everett," she said, "if you hurt yourself…"

But he didn't wait for her to say more, just tipped his cowboy hat and tapped his stirrups against Ace's flanks.

He could spout his bullshit about permanency all he wanted, but it didn't matter. He might have been safe up on a horse, but he was never truly safe from loss. Maybe he tricked Lily into staying with him today, or maybe she was right there with him—not wanting to let him go but not ready to admit the truth. Right now all that mattered was that she was his—at least for the day.

"Ya!" he called out, and Ace took off for the far end of the arena.

He knew his brother would have his ass if Jack found out what he was doing. But somehow, having Lily here made it all seem okay. And as much as he knew every part of what he felt about this moment was wrong on *various* levels, he couldn't suppress his ridiculous grin.

CHAPTER THIRTEEN

Lily swallowed hard and dared to let her eyes dip toward the ground—the ground that seemed so, so far away.

Was Ace this tall when Luke was riding him? She knew horses matured faster than humans did, but she wasn't so sure they could grow several feet in a matter of minutes. Then again, food was her forte, *not* growth patterns of the equine species.

Lily wasn't sure why she felt the need to prove herself to Luke. Maybe it was that part of her that wanted to believe they could connect on more than a physical level—that this chemistry between them went beyond skin deep.

No. It was bigger than that. If she could do this—look one tiny fear in the eye and say *Not today*—she might gain the confidence to face something even bigger.

"You all right there, sweetheart?" Luke asked from miles below her where he stood.

She nodded a little too enthusiastically and forced her gaze to where she swore she could see the horizon over the ocean if she just squinted hard enough.

"Lily?"

Luke's hat cast a shadow over his usually certain blue eyes, and she really wanted to see that certainty right now.

"Yeah?" she answered.

"You afraid of heights?" he asked.

Okay, so maybe this was more than a tiny fear.

She nodded again, this time without the same enthusiasm, and before she knew what was happening, Luke hooked his foot in the stirrup and hopped up onto Ace's back behind her.

His torso pressed against her back, and his legs outlined the shape of her own. Every inch of her was touching every inch of him, and her already shallow breathing now lacked any depth at all.

"Careful there, my little equestrian," he hummed into her ear as his hands grabbed her hips to right her as she swayed.

She cleared her throat. "Sorry. I got a little light-headed, I guess."

He grabbed the reins from in front of her, and she marveled at how the horse stayed so still, as if he and Luke spoke some silent language she couldn't understand. Because she had nothing of her own to grip for purchase, she unapologetically wrapped her hands around his wrists that rested in her lap.

"You should have told me about the heights thing," he said.

She let out a nervous laugh. "It's kind of a combination. I mean, the fear of heights is real, but it might be compounded by the fact that I'm perched this high on a wild animal that basically has my life in its hands."

He sighed. "You wanna get down? There's no rule that says you have to ride at all today. I wouldn't have goaded you into it if I'd known you were scared."

She shook her head and steeled her resolve.

"There is a rule, though," she insisted.

His breath was warm on her neck. "Oh yeah? What's that?"

She blew out a long breath. "The one that tells me that being careful is what got me where I am in my life right now. I thought I was making safe choices, following a prescribed plan for my relationship and my career. Maybe you were right. Maybe I need to let go...in more ways than...you know."

She wasn't sure what to call what they did last night—and again this morning. Was it lovemaking? Just plain old sex? What would he call it when he told Tucker? Or would he fall back on his whole philosophy of impermanence and call it a mistake not worth mentioning once he had time to think about it?

And jeez, could she get over herself and cool it with the overanalyzing?

"You want to be a little reckless?" he whispered, and a shiver traveled from her neck all the way down to her core, where it melted into liquid heat.

She nodded.

"Hold on, then, sweetheart. Because here we go."

She barely had time to clamp her death grip onto his wrists before his strong forearms jerked Ace out of his stillness while his heels knocked against the horse's sides.

And then they were off.

Lily yelped as Ace lurched from a complete standstill to an all-out gallop. Her nails were surely breaking Luke's skin, but she couldn't ease her grip. It didn't seem to faze him as they took the turn without so much as slowing down, and Luke whooped and hollered in what could only be described as pure, unfettered glee.

"You feel that?" he called as the wind whipped her hair against her cheeks. "That's how you let go...in more ways than one!"

She laughed at him echoing her phrase but realized he said nothing about the act being reckless.

Because riding like this…with him? It was exhilarating *and* terrifying. But she knew as long as Luke Everett was in the saddle behind her, riding was the furthest thing from reckless she could get.

It was the racing of her heart that started the second he hopped onto the horse. It was the way she leaned into him as he leaned forward into her, like they were the sole forces holding the other one up.

It was letting him into her bed when she knew he wasn't suited for what she wanted—*and* needed. She could pretend all she wanted from Luke was a rebound, that his being against permanent didn't matter. But she was lying to herself. And to him.

Fear had kept her trapped in these invisible parameters that were supposed to keep her safe from the heartache her mother went through—the heartache she herself endured when her father left them both. It was why she let herself fall for Tucker, the man she thought was the safe choice. It was also why she ran when he strayed—leaving before he could. But her connection with Luke was different, the thought of what she could lose exponentially more terrifying.

Oil and water, she thought. They didn't stand a freaking chance, and yet she hoped for a night like last night again.

Lily hoped for *more.*

And that—beyond her imminent, physical danger—was where she was careless. Hasty. And oh…so…*reckless.*

After several laps around the arena, too many to count in her current state of perplexed fear, Ace slowed to a trot and then to a walk before he stopped completely.

Luke hopped down, then reached a hand for her and helped her slide to solid ground.

"What'd you think?" he asked.

She laughed, and her knees wobbled. "I think Owen would ride circles around me," she admitted.

He laughed, his eyes crinkling at the corners. "And there you have it, folks. Lily Green humbled by a ten-year-old."

She backhanded him on the shoulder, and he held up his hands in mock surrender.

"All right. All right. Remember I'm still an injured man, here. You don't want to further damage the goods."

She crossed her arms and scoffed. "*You* put yourself in danger of damaging the goods every time someone's not looking."

He reached for the hat on his head and transferred it to hers instead.

"How about a small gift to buy your silence?" His brows pulled together.

"What?" she asked, her voice as unsteady as her legs.

His jaw tightened, and the stubble on his chin shone gold in the late morning sun.

"That hat," he said, his tone unreadable. "It—suits you."

She chewed on her bottom lip. "Um...okay? I mean, thanks for the gift."

He was still holding Ace's reins, but the horse seemed to pay them no attention, as he was more concerned with the trough of water up against the arena fence than with anything they were talking about.

"It also makes me want to kiss you," he said without warning, and in a strange moment of boldness, she answered him back.

"Then what are you waiting for?" she asked. "I've got a mile-long list of what I need to do today. I suggest you get to it."

So he kissed her, his mouth firm and insistent, and she parted her lips so he could taste his fill.

And for the first time in the history of Lily Green's planned-out life, she ignored whatever was on that to-do list and made a new one that had only a single bullet point—Luke Everett.

The ride to her place, while only about twelve miles, was wrought with more tension than waiting for a soufflé to rise. After that kiss—good Lord, that kiss—Luke hadn't said another word... at least to her.

He'd had a full-on conversation with Ace, the lovely horse who hadn't killed her, as he led the Appaloosa back to the stable and into his stall. But to Lily, there had been no more words—not even a request for her to return his hat as he squinted into the sun the entire drive back. And she? Well, she could have broken the silence, but with what?

He stopped in her driveway, but he didn't kill the engine. And Lily had finally had enough.

"What?" She threw her hands in the air. "What *now*? Because I get that what happened this morning with losing Gertie was hard, but it's part of the job, right? And—and you looked like you were having fun out there today with Ace." She groaned. "No," she said, more to herself than to him. "I'm owning this." Then her eyes bore into him again, regardless of him staring straight out the windshield. "*We* had fun out there today. Maybe I didn't master the whole riding thing like I'd anticipated, but I enjoyed myself, Luke. I enjoyed myself with you. So tell me what the hell has you shutting down now?"

He let his head thud against the back of the seat. But he didn't turn her way, didn't look at her.

"Can you at least acknowledge that we are good together in more ways than one?" she asked.

He sighed and closed his eyes, so Lily threw open the car door. "You're impossible, you know? All I want is something genuine from you, Luke. When you're ready for that, please let me know."

She stormed out of the truck and up the walkway to her front porch. Then she marched straight through to the kitchen where she grabbed her gloves and then continued out the back door. That's where he found her, several minutes later, knees in the dirt with three ripe tomatoes in her lap.

"What the hell are you doing?" he asked, arms crossed over his chest as he stared down at her.

She gave him a cursory glance, then went back to work. "I think it's more than obvious," she said. "But if you need me to spell it out for you, I'm gardening."

He didn't respond. He'd followed her back here, which meant he wanted to give her an explanation, right? Yet he just stood there, waiting, his silence more maddening than if he'd just answered her tirade with one of his own. Of course she ignored the voice inside that told her to keep gardening, that told her not to react to this man who'd always driven her mad—mainly because he was such a jerk. But these days he was driving her crazy for entirely different reasons.

She sighed and looked up.

"Why do you always look at me like that?" she asked when she saw his clenched jaw and his piercing blue eyes. "I get the whole oil-and-water thing and that we don't get along, but Jesus, Luke. I can't piss you off *that* much. Not when we can have a night like we did last night and a day like today. It makes no sense, especially when I don't even know what the hell I did." She let the tomatoes tumble into the dirt, careful not to bruise them, and stood to face him. "So either say something or go. Because I don't have the energy for you right now."

He took a step toward her, but she retreated, shaking her head.

"This isn't the farmers market, or me having a breakdown about almost killing Tucker's fiancée, or you being all cowboy in shining armor on that horse. You don't just get to kiss me to shut me up."

The words flew out of her even as she silently begged him to kiss her anyway. Because as much as she knew this thing between them was only physical, she couldn't help wanting to slip past those concrete barriers Luke put up between himself and the rest of the world. Even if it was only for the briefest moment, she wanted to be able to communicate through more than just the heat refusing to simmer between them.

"Christ, Lily," he growled, then ran a hand through his blond hair. "What the hell do you want from me? I thought I was your rebound. This wasn't supposed to mean anything."

She scoffed out a laugh. Because the truth was, he was right. This wasn't supposed to mean anything, but somehow, against her will, it did. She had no idea what she wanted from him, only that it had to be more than this.

"I want you to admit that whatever this was or wasn't supposed to be, it's taken on a life of its own. I mean, we haven't even fought since last night when you threatened to call Sheriff Hawkins on me. Not that I believe you were truly angry. Frustrated, maybe. But not angry."

He grunted. "You *do* frustrate me."

She rolled her eyes. "I mean, thanks for the words instead of trying to solve whatever's going on with just sex."

He raised his brows. "Okay, I didn't mean to insinuate that sex between us was *just* sex because yes. It was good. Real goddamn good. But you're missing the point."

He shoved his hands into the pockets of his jeans, but he

made no motion to move closer to her again. And though the air outside was clear and crisp, the space between them was thick with a tension she didn't recognize. This was different from all the times before, because she was stepping beyond the boundaries they'd set for themselves and each other. Maybe he was a rebound, but it felt like more. And maybe he did shy away from permanence, but he wasn't exactly shying away from her today.

"What's the point, then, sweetheart?" he asked, but there was no mocking in his tone.

"Why did you come over yesterday, after the hospital?" she asked, dipping her toe into the shallow part of the ocean between them.

He stood firm, boots planted in the dirt. "Because Jack and Ava would have had my ass if I didn't make sure you were okay. I can handle my brother," he said with a half grin. "But I sure as shit ain't crossing my almost sister."

She knew he was trying to make light, but her heart squeezed at the way he referred to Ava as his sister. He wasn't kidding when he spoke about family and permanency. And that one little statement was enough to show her how fierce his loyalty was.

"Why'd you stay?" She waded in deeper, forcing her voice to stay even. "Was it just in the hopes of having sex with me?"

"Jesus, Lily," he said under his breath, but she had both feet in now. What difference did it make to go further?

"You can just answer yes or no," she said. "That would be enough."

The muscle in his jaw ticked, but he answered. "No."

"Why take me with you this morning—and spend the day with me—if all you were going to do was continue this silly dance? This blowing hot and cold whenever it suits you?"

He shook his head and let out a bitter laugh. "I thought you said *yes* or *no* would be enough."

She narrowed her gaze. "It was…for *that* question. But the way I see it, Luke, you're looking for reasons to keep your distance. And I get that the whole Tucker thing is weird and that this rodeo coming up is a big deal and that you don't do permanent." She laughed. "And I know what I said about this being a rebound. Is there another way to define it? Because I haven't been with anyone since…" She shook her head. "That's not the point either. The point is, I got jerked around once already, by the guy who was supposed to be the safe, reliable choice. So—so, either be honest about what you want or don't want from me, or let's just go back to whatever we were before. No hard feelings. Okay?"

She rested her hands on her hips, held her breath, and waited for his response. Because no matter what came next, she'd just let the tide carry her away. Either he'd pull her back to shore, or she'd be a goner.

He stood there, unreadable, for longer than she could keep from breathing. Finally he nodded toward her hands.

"Can you at least take off those ridiculous gloves? I feel like I'm talking to goddamn Mickey Mouse."

Lily glanced down and saw she was still wearing her white gardening gloves, the ones with the puffy cuffs, and she couldn't help it. She burst out laughing.

She peeled off one glove and then the next. After that she chucked each one, playfully, at Luke's chest.

He caught them both, dropped them to the ground, and then finally took that step to close the distance between them.

This time, she did not retreat.

He wasn't touching her, but he was close. So close that the air warmed between them when he spoke.

"I came by yesterday because Ava told me to—because she said you wouldn't open the door for Jack, and that it wasn't like you to retreat like that. I stayed because you asked me to...and because once I saw how upset you were...maybe I didn't want you to be alone."

He took a long, steadying breath, and Lily readied herself for the letdown, for the reason why he couldn't stay *now.*

"And I asked you to come with me riding today because I wasn't prepared for how hard the situation this morning hit me. I don't know if you've noticed, but I don't do unsettled."

She snorted. "Unless I'm the one unsettling you." But then she threw a hand over her mouth. "I'm sorry. I didn't mean to make light—"

He pulled her hand away, then snaked his fingers into the hair at the nape of her neck, his thumb brushing over her parted lips.

"You're right," he said. "The oil-and-water thing is bullshit. At least, it is now." He urged her closer to him, dipping his head so they were millimeters apart. "I asked you to come with me today because something about being around you after what happened *settled* me. And selfish prick that I am, I wanted more of that."

She licked her bottom lip. "Was that so hard to say?" she asked.

He nodded. "Very."

"I already told you," she said. "I'm not looking to jump into anything either. But I'm also not looking for you seeming interested one minute and totally detached the next."

Because as perfect as they might have looked on the outside, that was exactly what she and Tucker were beneath the surface. Detached. And neither was willing to admit it.

Maybe for Tucker it was simply about pride. But Lily knew why she swept her unhappiness under the rug—and why she was willing to do the same as far as keeping Tucker's infidelity a secret.

He hadn't loved her enough to stay. She was a hypocrite to even think it because she'd been more in love with the idea of the life she and Tucker could have had than with the man himself. She was far from innocent in the emotional breakdown of their marriage, and she owned that.

That was why she couldn't bear to watch Luke shut down like she had. Shutting down meant he was pulling away—detaching himself from the situation when it was too late for her. For better or worse, the attachment was there, and she couldn't turn it off. What did it mean if Luke could?

"You're right," he whispered. "You deserve more than that."

His blue eyes darkened with something she knew was still left unsaid.

"Then...I want more," she admitted. "Not forever. Just—more."

His lips brushed against hers, not a purposeful kiss but something that told her he was considering her request.

"More," he said, his voice rough, and she swallowed hard. "Count me in, sweetheart."

She raised herself up on her toes and sealed the deal, pressing her mouth to his.

This kiss wasn't like any of the others—not like anything they had shared last night. He was slow as he carefully explored her lips with his, as his fingertips traced the outline of her face, causing goose bumps to pepper her skin.

"No more shutting down," she said against his mouth.

"All I need from you is the truth. No matter what it is. But if you shut down again like you did today, then I'm out. Okay?"

He nodded but kept kissing her, lips moving to her jaw, her neck, her collarbone. Her whole body tingled. She loved how well he seemed to know her physically, but she knew to really get past those walls of his, she'd have to part with one or two of her own.

She cleared her throat. "You said that I settled you." He nodded. "Well, then I guess you…unwind me." She smiled. "I've lived a long time in fear of losing what's important to me. With you I can somehow be scared but still feel safe. Does that make sense?" she asked, hoping he'd give her a small piece of him as well.

"You don't want to know those other parts of me," he said, as if reading her mind.

"How do you know if you don't give me a chance?" she asked. "I'm not asking for everything. Just some small bit of good faith that shows me that whatever this is—for now—that it's…*more.*"

He blew out a breath and swallowed. He dipped his gaze toward the ground, then back at her, and she could already feel the pain in the words that hadn't yet come.

"I don't know how much Tucker told you about me and my brothers. I'm guessing not much, which is how I like things. I like people knowing the me I show them—not the me that made me who I am."

She shook her head. "I don't get it. You're not making any sense."

"Our mama died young, and Jack Senior—our father—never recovered. He drank. And he blamed us, somehow. For still being alive? I don't know. What I do know is that the drinking changed him. And he started taking it out on

Jack. Before long Jack would provoke him, just to keep him from laying a hand on me or Walker."

"Oh, Luke..." She reached a hand for his face, but he backed away.

"I don't deserve your sympathy. That's not why I'm telling you this. Walker and I—we let Jack protect us, and he almost got himself killed because of it. So if it looks to you like I don't take my life seriously, just know that you're way off there. I live by *my* terms. If I break a bone or bleed—it's because I allowed it to happen. I call the shots, even if that means taking risks. Now you know why."

Her heart broke for the man she'd always thought cared about nothing other than having a good time.

"You deserve a lot more than you give yourself credit for," was all she said. Then she pulled him close, kissed him, and whispered in his ear. "Now take me inside and let me cook you dinner."

His eyes widened. "Let you—you want to cook for me?"

She nodded.

"But it's, like, three o'clock."

She laughed. "I'm not going to just throw something in the microwave, Luke Everett. I'm a professionally trained chef. I don't even own a microwave." She raised her brows.

"Yes, you do."

"Fine, I do, but I've made my point. I'm sure you can find something to keep you busy while I prepare something special for you."

He grinned at this, the guilt in his eyes melting away to be replaced by something playful and wicked.

She knew what she'd done—allowing him to close the door he'd just opened. But she also knew he couldn't take back what he'd shared, and even if she wasn't able to put words to whatever this thing was between them, she'd show him that he deserved someone who cared—that he was worthy of more than he was willing to recognize.

So she threaded her fingers through his and led him back to where they'd found themselves that morning, the one place where Lily felt truly herself.

The kitchen.

CHAPTER FOURTEEN

He'd thought she was going to lead him to the bedroom. That would have been a great way to keep him busy for a while. After all, that was how they communicated best, and after the bomb he'd unwittingly dropped—telling her about his father—he was counting on not having to say much more tonight.

Instead she'd handed him a beer and told him to go relax. But he wanted to watch her work.

What he wasn't counting on was how goddamn sexy she was when she cooked. Or how out of his element he was watching someone go to that much effort for *him.*

"What can I do to help?" he asked, too restless to simply sit or stand.

She handed him the bottle of zinfandel. "Here. Open this."

He did as he was told, watching with quiet appreciation as she chopped carrots and onions, readied the cuts of chicken, and pulled from the fridge what looked like homemade tomato sauce.

He handed her the opened bottle when she had a free hand.

"Is anything in this place store-bought?" he asked.

She laughed. "Everything tastes better when it's homemade," she said. She poured herself a glass of wine, then dumped the better contents of the bottle into a glass bowl with other various ingredients. "Even this," she said, holding up her glass. "When you and your brothers sip that first vintage that you'll have created with your own bare hands, you'll see what I mean."

She clinked her glass against his bottle, and they both took a sip.

He leaned against the counter. "What, exactly, are you preparing for us tonight, sweetheart?"

He'd wanted the nickname to sound teasing, but instead it had come out soft and warm, like *sweetheart* was a word he could use and really mean. Like she'd *believe* that he meant it.

She must not have noticed the change in tone because she just kept working as she spoke.

"Coq au vin."

He raised a brow. "Cock oh what? Why, Lily Green, are you coming on to me?"

She snorted and threw a dish towel at him. "It's French, you adolescent. For chicken and wine."

She shook her head and laughed some more, and he looked on as she continued her well-choreographed dance that had her spinning from the counter to the stove and back again.

"And you just happened to have all these ingredients lying around for such a fancy meal?"

She covered the wine-soaked chicken and vegetables on the stove and wiped her hands on a towel she'd tucked into the top of her jeans. Then she gave him something between a wince and a smile.

"Wait," he said. "You have a weekly meal calendar. Don't you?"

She lifted her wineglass to her perfect pink lips. "Maybe?" she said.

He laughed until he conjured the image of her toiling away in this kitchen by herself—of her sitting alone while she ate. It wasn't much different from what he was used to—a couple of beers and a frozen pizza—the single guy's *home-cooked* meal. But at least it took zero effort to provide himself with sustenance. What Lily was creating was art. How had Tucker missed that?

"I love what I do, Luke. So stop feeling sorry for me."

He snapped himself out of his daze, his eyes meeting hers.

"I wasn't—" he said. "I mean, I didn't—"

She sipped her wine and laughed softly. "I know it seems silly for me to plan out my weekly meals or to go to so much trouble when it's just me, but this is what makes me happy."

She spun toward the stove, turned the heat to a simmer, and then tossed her towel on the counter.

"We've got about fifteen minutes," she said. "Let's sit."

They took their drinks to the couch, to where just last night he'd crossed over the line between what he wanted and what he knew was the right decision. But maybe the definition of *right* had changed. Tucker had moved on. Like Lily said, he had no claim on her anymore. He'd understand if something unexpectedly sparked between her and Luke.

But would he forgive Luke if *his* spark had burned a bit longer than Lily's?

"What's that for?" she asked as they both collapsed onto the couch.

"What's—?"

She brushed her thumb over the crease between his eyebrows, and his shoulders relaxed at her touch.

"You look worried about something. And the Luke Everett I've come to know doesn't worry."

She set her glass on the coffee table. She took his bottle from his hand and did the same. Then she proceeded to crawl into his lap, straddling him as she cupped his face in her hands.

"I know what you told me outside was hard. And I also know that you don't want to talk about it further. But I think it's important that *you* know there's nothing you could say that would make me not want you like this."

He wrapped his arms around her waist and let his head fall onto her chest.

You're going to ruin me, he thought. But those weren't the words that came out of his mouth. Instead he said, "Goddamn you smell good."

She laughed. "I call it garlic and thyme. You think I should bottle and sell it?"

He lifted his head. There was a flicker of something in her green eyes that he didn't understand. All he knew was that he wanted to kiss her—*needed* to kiss her—now.

"What you got, sweetheart? There's no way to contain that in a bottle."

And just as her breath hitched in response, his lips claimed hers, consuming her with a need he'd pushed so far down, he hadn't thought it possible to resurface. But here it was, making his chest ache and his heart race.

She parted her lips, and he could taste it, that emotion he couldn't quite name, the one he'd forced himself to believe he was content without. That he could have been content without *her*.

Because the only thing he'd ever truly hated about Lily Green was that she chose Tucker. But that didn't change the fact that he'd already fallen for her years ago—her strength and determination to succeed, that she knew what she wanted and went for it. Even that she'd call him on his bullshit instead of just walking away because God knew he did enough to push her. It might have been her blond pixie cut and short skirt that caught his attention three years ago, but it had been everything else that had made it impossible for him to truly walk away. Once he cleared everything up with Tucker, then maybe he'd actually have a shot at getting her to fall for him right back.

She ground her pelvis against his, and he growled her name.

"*Lily.*"

She gasped and pulled away. "Did I hurt you? Shit, I keep forgetting that you're sitting there all broken inside. I'm sorry." A timer went off in the kitchen, and she sucked in another sharp breath. "The chicken! I'll be right back!" She gave him a quick kiss. "Actually, no. I need you at the table." She was a frenzy of movement now. "But I promise to be more careful with you later!" she teased as she raced into the kitchen.

He just laughed, his physical injuries the furthest thing from his mind.

He *was* all broken inside. She hadn't gotten that part wrong. But for the first time in years he was starting to believe those pieces might be ready to be put back together.

"So?" Lily asked, pouring him a glass of wine. "What did you think?"

He leaned back in his chair, swirling the wine in the goblet.

"On a scale of one to ten?" he asked, not yet giving her the satisfaction of a grin.

"Sure," she said, eyes bright, hopeful, earnest.

Had they always been like that?

"Come *on*, Luke! You're killing me."

She snapped him out of his head.

He cleared his throat. "Come on, *Lily*," he said, mimicking her. "You know you're a goddamn artist in the kitchen. What you just *threw* together? I'm going out on a limb and saying it's the best damn meal I've ever had. You tell my aunt Jenna I said that, though, and I'll call you a liar." She laughed. "But a guy sure could get used to that kind of treatment."

He winced a little at his own statement, thinking about how Tucker had been the one on the receiving end of such treatment for the better part of three years.

She leaned forward, her elbows on the table. "What is it?" she asked. "It doesn't do much for my ego if you compliment my cooking and then grimace."

He forced a laugh. "The food was outstanding. It's just little reminders, you know? Of you and—"

"Tucker," she said, finishing his sentence. "I get that he's been in your life a hell of a lot longer than me. Bros before hos and all."

He shook his head. "God I hate that phrase."

She laughed. "Good. Me, too." But then her face grew serious again. "But it doesn't make it not true. Your loyalties lie with him first. He's your family. Blah-blah. If this is too weird, then just say so."

He shook his head again and pulled out his phone. "I just need to tell him. Get it out in the open."

What the hell he was going to say was another thing entirely. Were they dating now? Just sleeping together and agreeing they didn't hate each other? How far into the truth did he get with Tucker? With Lily? Because honesty *was* important. And the way he saw it, that started now, right? With Tucker and with Lily.

"Speak of the devil," he said. "Looks like he texted me an hour ago. Must have missed it." His brows pulled together. "You're on the thread, too."

She scooted her chair next to his, and they read the message together.

> Hey guys. Guess the whole allergic reaction thing yesterday threw Sara for a loop. She wants to get away and "recenter." Headed to Grass Valley for a two-week yoga/meditation retreat at this ashram Sara loves. Wish me luck. No cell phones allowed. Don't worry, Lil. I got the restaurant covered. But if you happen to check in and see all hell has broken loose? Well, don't call. I won't get the message. Be back in time for final walk-through of the venue. Sent Jack what we'd like to do for tables already. Lil, we trust you on the menu. Yesterday was a fluke. Luke, just—keep an eye on everything for me, yeah? Thanks, man.

He quickly hit the call back button, realizing his only shot at coming clean was now.

"Tuck!" he said, grateful his friend was able to pick up. "You're still there!"

Lily's eyes widened.

"Just about to power down, actually," Tucker said. "You literally caught me with my thumb on the power button. Sara's gonna kill me if I don't drop my phone in this confiscation basket in the next thirty seconds." He laughed.

Luke's palms were sweating, and he thought he might drop his own phone. Christ, he could sit on the back of a bull but was losing his shit trying to tell Tucker...*Shit*, what was he actually going to say?

"Look, man," he said. "I need to tell you something

before you go dark. It's about Lily, and it's something I probably should have told you—"

"I've got fi...een...econds..."

Shit. He was cutting out.

"Tuck," he said again. "You're breaking up. I need to tell you about *Lily.* Lily and *me.*"

"Sorry, Everett. Reception is crap. Guess that's how they kee...us...cheating..."

And then the call ended.

"Dammit!" He slammed his phone down onto the table. "*Shit,*" he hissed, checking to make sure the thing was still in one piece.

Lily's hand was on his. "Hey," she said, her voice gentle and soothing. "You tried. It's not your fault he left town."

He blew out a breath, and with it, as much of the tension as he could.

"You're right," he said. "I just wish I could have said—"

"What?" Lily blurted. "What exactly would you have said? I mean, I know what you need to tell him, but I guess I was just curious about how you would word it because...like...am *I* supposed to tell people? Do you want to stop having sex until Tucker gets back? Because I've gone longer than two weeks before, but then I hadn't known what sex was like with..." Her cheeks reddened. "Should we—"

He kissed her, slid his fingers into her hair at the nape of her neck, and grinned as she sighed against him, kissing him back.

"It's killing you not to have a plan. Isn't it?"

"Slowly and painfully," she said with something between a laugh and a whimper. "But I meant what I said, that I'm not looking for anything past the here and now, which means I don't need a label."

He kissed her again.

"I'd like to label that as delicious, though," she told him. "Your mouth and that stubble. Don't ever shave that stubble or whatever we're doing here is over."

He chuckled, a deep throaty sound. He didn't laugh like this with anyone else. True, he was always the first to note the humor in any situation or to fall back on it when things got too serious. But laughing with Lily was effortless. She brought out of him what he had to force with so many others.

"Ava's birthday is next weekend," he said. "Jack's just doing something small—Ava's parents, Owen, Jenna, us, and maybe a few friends from her art program. You should come."

She skimmed her teeth over her bottom lip. "I'm—already on the guest list. I'm baking the cake, actually."

Luke groaned. "I'm not asking if you want a ride. I'm asking you to come with *me.* Like we show up together—and leave together."

She raised her brows. "So this isn't a secret?"

He shook his head.

"And you don't want to put it on hold until Tucker gets back?"

He had contemplated that. But he'd also rationalized what Lily had already said. Tucker didn't get a say in Lily's love life, especially now that he'd moved on. And if Lily chose Luke now—even if he technically was her second choice—then he had just as much right to choose her back.

He shook his head again.

She rested a hand on his thigh, her palm noticeably warm, even through his jeans.

"So, if we leave together... from the party, what will we do—*after*?"

He slid a hand up *her* thigh, stopping when his thumb reached the bottom of her zipper. He stroked up the seam, and she sucked in a breath.

"Maybe we need a little preview," he started, but then she jumped up from the chair.

"Dessert!" she said. "I forgot dessert!" She bolted for the fridge, throwing the door open, and when she turned back to the table with a glass bowl in her hand, he was standing right behind her, waiting.

"Lily?" he said.

"Luke?"

"Are you nervous?" he asked.

She nodded slowly.

"But we've already done this. *Twice*." Though he knew this time would be different. They could chalk up yesterday and this morning to the heat of the moment, to an unexpected encounter culminating after a couple weeks of brewing tension. But now they'd made a decision. And although they'd agreed this wasn't serious or permanent, it was *something*. Something that he was suggesting they put out there for everyone to see.

"Whatcha got there?" he asked, glancing down at the glass bowl in her arms.

She cleared her throat. "Homemade white chocolate mousse with raspberry swirl."

He laughed. "That you just happen to have lying around."

She shrugged and gave him a beautiful yet sheepish grin.

He dipped his finger into the mousse and spread it across her bottom lip.

"Oh," she said, her voice almost a whisper.

And then he licked the decadent confection away.

"*Oh*," she said again, this time breathier than the last.

"We're just eating dessert, sweetheart. Nothing to be nervous about."

He took the bowl from her hands, set it on the counter, and then lifted her up so she was sitting beside it. Wordlessly, he pulled her shirt over her head, unclasped her bra. Then he painted each breast, each rosy peaked nipple, until soft, delicious whimpers fell from her lips.

He dipped his head, but then looked up through a hooded gaze.

"Just so you know," he said. "Dessert's my favorite part of the meal."

CHAPTER FIFTEEN

She dipped her own finger into the bowl, then pressed it to his lips. His tongue swirled over her flesh, and she held her breath—waiting, wondering.

She knew this thing with Luke could end as quickly and unexpectedly as it had begun. Still, she couldn't help but think of how dinner with Tucker had never been like this—an experience so sensual and intimate that it changed their whole dynamic.

She bit her lip to keep from crying out as he painted her breasts again. She'd thought it was wrong to compare, that Luke wasn't Tucker and vice versa. But God she'd never felt so—so Lily. Did it even make sense, that she could feel more herself with a man who was so beyond her comfort zone that she could no longer find said zone even if she had a map?

Maybe there was no stability with Luke, but there was this. His igniting in her what she didn't even know was there. The thought of ever dousing the flame made her chest ache, so instead she focused on the here and now.

"I like dessert, too," she said, her voice punctuated by tiny gasps as he licked and nipped at her tight peaks. And when he carried her off to the bedroom—God she loved how he did that—it was without the mousse. Because the only thing he seemed hungry for—was *her*.

He laid her down on the bed, then silently eased her out of her jeans and what she knew were decidedly unsexy cotton bikini briefs, but he still looked at her with a reverence she wasn't used to.

His jaw tightened, but he still didn't speak—just removed his own clothing in the same soundless manner, an undeniable look of appreciation in those blue eyes that always wore a mask of amusement that she now knew was an act.

But he was no longer acting for her.

She stared at the beautiful man bared before her, wondering if her eyes told a similar story. That this was different. That *he* was different. Just weeks ago she'd thought they couldn't last more than a few minutes in the same room without tearing each other's heads off. Now she wanted him with a hunger that felt insatiable and couldn't fathom how they'd gotten from there to here.

"Luke," she started, but she didn't know what came next.

He lowered himself over her in response, nudging her opening, testing to see if she was ready.

She nodded, answering his unasked question, and he sank in slowly, deliberately, until he filled her so completely she wasn't sure she'd survive him pulling out.

He said nothing as he moved within her, as he rolled them to their sides so he could kiss her, the stubble she'd warned him not to shave grazing her skin, leaving her raw.

He pivoted again so she now straddled him, and gripped her thighs in his rough palms. His blue eyes were open and clear, locked on her as he simply watched their bodies move. She'd never felt more exposed—and never wanted to reveal herself to anyone else like she did now.

She tilted her hips and sank over him again, so close but wanting to prolong the moment of teetering on the edge. It was everything like the night before yet so entirely different.

"Luke," she said again as she slid down his length, her aching core burning from kindling to an unstoppable wildfire.

"You're safe with me, sweetheart," was all he said, but it was enough to give her permission to come undone, and come undone she did.

Wholly and completely until her muscles and bones no longer had the ability to hold her up, and she collapsed in a heap beside him, their bodies still joined.

He lifted a lock of hair, damp with sweat, from her cheek and tucked it behind her ear.

"Best dessert I ever had," he said with a grin, and she watched him retreat back behind the mask, taking comfort in knowing that she had the power to see beneath it, if only for brief periods of time.

She kissed him, and her chest tightened as he pulled her close.

"Duly noted," she said. "I'll add it to my list of treats to always have on hand."

He nipped at her bottom lip. "You and your lists."

She huffed out a breath, a failed attempt at haughtiness considering the position they were in.

"Yeah, well, if it weren't for my extremely organized lists, you'd have eaten Kraft macaroni and cheese for dinner followed by a Hostess cupcake."

He laughed, then kissed the side of her jaw. "I'm willing to bet you don't even own a boxed version of mac and cheese—*which* I do eat on a regular basis along with the occasional cupcake."

She rolled her eyes. "Of course I don't own instant mac and cheese. What do you think I am, a monster? Anyway, say what you want, but I stand by my meal planning lists. And you said yourself it's the best meal you've ever had, so—you're welcome."

They both laughed, and for a long while they lay there like that—teasing and kissing like there was nothing else they'd rather do. And as far as Lily was concerned, it was true.

Later, when they'd finally resigned themselves to going to sleep, she curled into him, kissing his bare chest, her fingers tracing the still visible bruises over his ribs.

She waited for his breathing to slow, not yet letting the rise and fall of his torso lull her to sleep.

"Luke," she whispered, testing her assumption.

He didn't stir.

She lifted her head, her chest aching as she watched him sleep.

"I'm not really, am I?" she said, recognizing the realization in her tone. "Safe with you."

Because as much as she could let go in the bedroom, trusting him not to let her fall, it was all the moments before—witnessing both birth and death with him at the ranch, riding Ace with him this afternoon, and cooking a meal with something else in her heart other than a simple love of the food she prepared.

Lying beside her was a man she'd sworn was as close as a person like her could get to having an enemy.

She laughed, even as her throat tightened, the threat of tears ready to choke her.

Lying beside her was a man with whom she might be safe in bed, but what about her heart?

It was twenty to six when she heard his truck roll into the driveway the following Saturday evening. Lily's heart sped up, but she told herself it was because he was ten minutes early and she still had to write *Happy Birthday Ava* on the cake and not because they'd gone the whole week without seeing each other.

He knocked twice on the screen door, a courtesy, really, since she'd left the front door open.

"Come in!" she called, trying to concentrate on the triple chocolate cake in front of her.

But when she heard the door open and shut, she couldn't help but freeze where she stood.

How would he greet her? Or should she be greeting him, since it was her house? He and Walker were gone for the better part of the week making deliveries to several restaurants up north, so this wouldn't just be the first time they'd seen each other since—since white chocolate mousse. It would be the first time they'd even spoken.

"Well doesn't that just look good enough to eat." His voice rasped in her ear, and she sucked in a breath.

"It's chocolate cake with dark chocolate chunks and chocolate fudge frosting," she said. "I call it my triple threat cake."

He brushed a soft kiss on her neck and spun her to face him.

"I wasn't talking about the cake."

He looked her up and down, from the fitted bodice of her dress to where it flared out at her knees to the peep-toe red wedges on her feet.

He whistled. "Are those cherries?" he asked.

She nodded as she glanced down at the images of the red fruit speckled all over the black fabric. "I like dressing up when the occasion calls for it." She smiled, then finally drank him in, all the way from his fitted, faded denim shirt to his khaki pants, to the dirty work boots that were just so Luke.

He winked at her. "So do I."

She laughed. "Really?" And he shook his head.

"God, no. These were my only clean pants. I didn't even know I owned them. Plus, something told me you'd like a man who could clean up good every now and then."

She toed one of his boots with her sandal.

You could take the man off the ranch…

She reached for his cheek, her breath catching in her throat. "You dressed up—for me?"

He shrugged, and she ran her thumb across his stubbled jaw. "And you didn't shave," she added. A statement and not a question.

He shook his head slowly. "This beautiful woman who, by the way, tends to drive me up the goddamn wall, told me if I shaved she'd end things between us. I figured seeing as how we're just getting started, that'd be a shame."

She narrowed her eyes at him. "Who tends to drive you up the goddamn wall?"

He raised a brow. "Did you miss the beautiful part?"

She huffed out a breath. "No, but has anyone ever taught you how to give a compliment without wrapping it up in an insult? Because if you're looking for a short tutorial—"

"Lily?" he said softly.

"Yeah?"

"I'm gonna kiss you now, okay?"

She nodded. "Yeah, okay."

And then his mouth was on hers, his palm at the nape of her neck, fingertips hidden in her hair. God she loved how he did that—just put her at ease before her verbal tirade got the best of her.

She parted her lips, inviting him in, and oh the taste of Luke Everett on her tongue was everything. She wrapped her arms around his waist, then slid them up his back, fingers trailing the tight muscle beneath the fabric of his shirt.

"How much time do we have," he said against her lips, his voice rough.

"Not enough," she admitted. "Plus I still have to write the message on the cake."

He groaned, releasing her after one more kiss, and her body protested, aching at the space growing between them.

She smoothed out her dress, then pressed a finger to her lips.

"I think you're wearing more of my Sinful Cerise than I am now. I'll have to reapply."

One corner of his mouth rose into a crooked devilish grin. He ran his thumb across his lips, wiping away the stain she'd left.

"I plan on wearing more of that later," he told her, his voice the devil itself.

"O-okay," she said, a tremor in her response as she spun back toward the cake, her knees wobbly just at the thought of *later*.

"Come home with me tonight," he said from behind her as she started writing the word *Happy*.

She held her breath, concentrating until, in perfect pink script, she'd finished the words *Birthday* and *Ava*. Then she lined the perimeter of the round layer cake with the same color pink roses. Only when she'd finished did she exhale and face him again.

"Okay," she said again, her vocabulary reduced to that one word for the time being.

He grinned. "I almost forgot." Then he reached for a basket on the opposite counter, one she hadn't noticed a second ago. "I brought you these."

He handed her the basket, which was lined with a red-and-white-checked towel. Inside it was loaded with a variety of—seeds. Or, packets of seeds to be exact.

"Winter vegetables," he said. "Looked like you were almost done with your fall harvest. Figured the garden was ready for its winter crop."

She swallowed back the knot in her throat. Some men on a first date—if that's what this was—might bring flowers. But not him.

"Luke Everett," she said, shaking her head. "You brought me vegetables."

He tipped a nonexistent hat and gave her a cocky grin, one that said nothing got past him. At least, that's what it would have said to anyone else in the room had there *been* anyone other than her. But what Lily saw was that this man, who for years treated her with nothing more affectionate than indifference, had just given her the most thoughtful gift she'd received in longer than she could imagine.

She set down the basket and then turned to fasten the lid that also acted as the carrying case for the cake.

"Thank you," she said, leaning up to kiss him again.

Then she had the nerve to hope he'd still be around in the coming weeks to help her plant the seeds.

CHAPTER SIXTEEN

There were already cars in Jack and Ava's driveway when they arrived, and Luke just shook his head with a laugh.

"What?" Lily asked.

She'd reapplied that red lipstick when she'd gotten into the car so that every time he so much as glanced in her direction, the first thing he saw were those full, perfect lips. Lips meant to be kissed by him. Lips that *needed* to be kissed by him soon.

"Luke?" she asked, and he realized he'd been staring.

"Huh?" Shit, he was like a goddamn deer in the headlights all of a sudden. This did not bode well for the rest of the evening, especially for the immediate future.

"You were laughing to yourself just a second ago," Lily said. "And then I think you went mildly catatonic." She raised a brow. "Are you okay?"

He blew out a breath, then ran a hand through his hair.

"I told Ava we were coming together," he admitted. "And believe me, she could not have been happier."

She laughed softly. "I know. Ava called me soon after you told her."

Her cheeks flushed, and he was still floored that he had the ability to affect her like that.

"The point is," he continued, "that while my brothers know I'm bringing you *with* me tonight—"

"They haven't had a chance to give you hell face-to-face yet?"

"Exactly," he said. "We may be grown men, but that doesn't mean we act like it on a regular basis."

She narrowed her eyes, then leaned over the protected cake in her lap and kissed him softly on the cheek. "I, for one, appreciate the grown man side of you *very* much."

He chuckled, the tension leaving his shoulders. "And here I thought you were going to make a joke about me being an irresponsible boy hiding in the body of a man."

"Luke Everett," she said, her breath warm against his ear, "I do not joke about your manhood."

He grazed her cheek with his stubbled jaw, and she sucked in a sharp breath.

"We don't *need* to go inside. Do we?" he asked.

But because they weren't irresponsible teens who could run off and later be forgiven, she pulled away, patting the plastic dome covering the cake.

"They would notice if the birthday cake was missing," she said.

She yelped as a palm came down hard on the windshield with a double tap.

"Christ," he said, staring at Walker where he gave them a knowing grin through the glass.

"Come on, asshole," his younger brother said, raising a bottle of beer, as if to toast them both. "Party's in back."

Luke mouthed *Fuck you* to his brother and pulled the keys from the ignition.

"And so it begins," he said, and they both exited the truck.

"Where did he even come from?" she asked.

He shrugged. "Walker's got a small workshop at the far

end of the stable. He makes furniture, like wooden tables and shit. It's sort of a side job—when he's sober. I just hope he wasn't doing anything stupid like operating machinery with a beer in his hand."

Lily's eyes widened. "Oh—um—I'm going to head into the kitchen," she said, crossing toward the front porch while he headed for the back deck. "I want to make sure the cake is somewhere safe first."

He started to follow her lead. "I'll come with you," he said.

She shook her head. "You go. Grab a drink. I'll be out in a few." Then she spun toward the house and was up the steps and inside before he could say another word.

Great. He'd managed to start the evening with a glimpse of the darker side of the Everett clan before they'd even made it to the house. No wonder she'd wanted a minute or two inside. He was pretty sure she was in there rethinking saying yes to coming home with him tonight.

And why shouldn't she? He *was* the irresponsible boy hiding in the body of a man. He didn't blame her for choosing Tucker that first night, and he wouldn't blame her for jumping ship now.

Okay, so that was a balls-out lie—the part about not blaming her for choosing Tucker. Not that she'd ever know that. Because he'd been blaming her for three years when really, the only person responsible for what happened—or what never did—was himself.

He made his way to the back of the ranch, each step bringing him closer to admitting that what was going on between him and Lily was bigger than he'd anticipated, and he didn't know what the hell to do with that.

He was barely up the steps to the deck before Jack slapped a cold, perspiring longneck into his palm.

"You look like you could use one of these," his older brother said.

Luke let out a mirthless laugh. "Is it that obvious?"

Jack's laugh was genuine. "Shit. When Ava told me—I didn't realize how deep you were already in it." He clinked his bottle with Luke's. "I need to go say hi to Ava's parents."

That was it? That was all the ribbing he was going to get? "Hey!" he called to Jack, but his back was already turned as he approached his soon-to-be in-laws.

How deep he was already in it?

What the hell did that mean?

"Hey, Uncle Luke!"

He turned to see Owen in the yard to the side of the deck throwing a Frisbee for his dog, Scully, to chase.

"What's up, Shortstop?" Luke said, heading back down the stairs and to the safety of semi-anonymity with his nephew.

Owen rolled his eyes. "I still don't play shortstop."

Luke shrugged. "It's still your nickname. So deal with it."

He ruffled the kid's hair, and Owen swatted his hand away. At ten years old, he already seemed miles ahead of Luke as far as emotional maturity. But he guessed his nephew's stable home life had something to do with that. Even before Jack came into his son's life, Owen and Ava had a good thing going. Now that good thing was better.

Luke could barely remember *good.*

"Did you bring my mom a present?" Owen asked.

Luke took a swig of his beer. "I brought the woman who made your mom's fantastic birthday cake, so I think that counts."

Scully bounded up to them with the Frisbee in his mouth, and Luke dropped down to take it from him and throw it again.

"Besides," he said after the dog was off and running once more. "Your mom said *no* presents. And when your mom tells me what to do, I listen."

Owen laughed. "I guess that's pretty smart. Still, I got her a weekend alone with Dad. Well, me and my grandparents did. She's been so busy with school that we're sending them away for a few days when she has a break."

Something in his chest ached every time he heard Owen refer to his brother as *Dad.* He'd only come into Owen's life less than a year ago, yet already Jack was everything their own father had never been. Maybe Luke wasn't the best at saying things out loud, but he was damn proud of his brother.

This time Scully didn't bring the Frisbee all the way back. Instead he stopped in front of a blonde with full red lips and a dress covered in cherries. The dog wasn't stupid. He dropped his toy at her feet then wagged his tail with what Luke swore was a goddamn grin.

"Hey, Lily!" Owen waved as he ran over to retrieve his chocolate Lab and the canine's weapon of mass flirtation.

She dropped to a squat, balancing on those sandals that made her at least two inches taller, and gave Scully a pat on the head and a much wanted under-the-chin massage.

"How's my Mr. Scully?" she asked in the type of voice reserved only for speaking to animals. Scully dropped to his back, and she rubbed his belly like it had been her intent in coming here—to simply put this dog into a state of complete and utter bliss.

Luke approached, Owen already in the grass joining in on the animal pampering.

"Shameless flirt," Luke mused, staring down at the dog with one brow cocked in accusation.

Lily rested her arms on her knees and looked up at him.

"I wonder who taught him," she said. "Every time I'm here it's like he knows exactly what to do to make me putty in his hands." Scully gave a soft howl, and she went back to rubbing his belly. "You're right," she said. "*Shameless.*"

Luke studied her a moment before he spoke again.

"*Every* time you're here?" he asked. "I'm here nearly every day," he said. "Unless I'm training. But I'd swear the first time I saw you here was the morning you unwittingly decided to cater your ex-husband's wedding."

He hadn't meant the comment to sound so harsh, but it was too late. She stood, narrowing her gaze at him, then glanced back down at his nephew and dog. "I'll be back for more snuggles in a bit, Mr. Scully. You'll keep him busy until then, Owen?"

The dog was licking Owen's face, the boy giggling uncontrollably.

"Sure, Lily," he said between laughs, and she started sauntering away—*without* Luke.

"Hey," he called after her. He'd just been a dick, but he didn't think it warranted her walking away. "Hey," he said again, catching up to her before she made it up the steps and to the deck. "Jesus, Lily. I'm sorry."

She spun to face him, her green eyes unreadable.

"You were an asshole," she said softly. "And I didn't want to swear in front of Owen. He makes Ava pay actual money when she does."

He huffed out a laugh. "Oh I know about the swear jar, and as far as being an asshole, you beat me to it. I *was*."

She shook her head. "Not just now. I mean, yeah, just now, too. But that's not what I was talking about."

"I don't follow," he said.

She rolled her eyes and groaned. "It's just—I already knew that Walker makes furniture. And that Scully loves to be massaged under his chin and definitely on his belly. I knew the perfect spot on the counter to hide the cake from prying doggie noses, and I knew if I let you go out back first that Jack would probably hand you a beer and put you at ease. Luke, I know your whole family. They welcomed me into their home and gave me some much needed friendship at a really lonely point in my life. I've been coming to see your brother for help with the divorce since he got out of the hospital after the car accident. Then Ava and I started getting close, which made meeting with your brother when you weren't around all that much easier."

"I wasn't easy to be around, huh?" he said.

She shook her head slowly. "Which never made any sense to me, because you had this reputation of being the life of the party, the guy everyone wanted to be around. I swear that's the guy I met that night in the bar, but then everything changed. Why?" she asked.

He blew out a breath, deciding it was time for a little honesty.

"'Bring him home in one piece, Luke,'" he said.

Her brows furrowed.

"'He's got a meeting with investors tomorrow, Luke. Don't mess this up for him.'"

She chewed on her bottom lip.

"And one of my personal favorites," he added. "'Tucker's a grown-up. Try to remember he's got a wife to come home to and a restaurant to run.'"

She winced at that one.

"I said all those things?" she asked.

He gave her a slow nod. "Maybe not all at one time. But I've compiled a nice list over the years." He forced a smile.

Her eyes widened. "You didn't make him think I was a controlling shrew," she said, recognition in her tone. "I *was* a controlling shrew. But not with him." She stood silent for several seconds. "I blamed every one of Tucker's indiscretions—partying too much, staying out too late—on you." She shook her head, like she was trying to shake the realization. "I wanted so badly for our problems to be something outside of us, you know? So I could manage it and fix."

"Control it," Luke said.

"Yeah," she admitted. "Control it. I'm—sorry, Luke. I was terrible to you."

His chest tightened. "It's not like I did a whole lot to change your opinion of me. I let you assume those things about me because it made it easier."

"Made *what* easier?" she asked, her words slow and careful.

He'd been mostly telling the truth about why she wasn't easy to be around. Her assumptions about him stung. That wasn't a lie. But 100 percent honesty with Lily Green? God, how the hell did he just come out and say it was easier to let her think those things so he had a reason to dislike her—so he wouldn't have to admit to wanting what Tucker had.

Not many things scared Luke Everett, yet somehow being completely honest with Lily topped the list.

He shrugged. "Easier for Tucker, I guess. Figured if I could take the brunt of your disapproval, you'd have less for him."

She gave him a mournful smile.

Shit, he was even more of an asshole than she knew. He held out his hand. She hesitated, and he wondered if he'd read the moment wrong. Maybe Tucker wasn't the real reason he was holding back anymore. *Maybe* what they'd assumed about each other these last few years was too ingrained for them to get past it. But then she slid her fingers through his and gave his hand a reassuring squeeze, and he led her up the steps to the party.

He wasn't good with words, so he kissed her, right there in front of anyone who cared to look, and she laughed softly against his assertive mouth.

"Now that's what I call an entrance," she said when he tilted his head back to look at her.

"Can we put the past in the past?" he asked, and those cherry red lips parted into a gorgeous smile. "Start fresh?"

She nodded. "Yes please. As long as the offer still stands."

He took a swig of his beer and crossed his arms. "Offer?"

And damn if that smile didn't transform into something a little wicked.

"For you to wear more of my Sinful Cerise later."

He brushed two fingertips against his lips. "And here I thought I'd already fulfilled my bargain."

She backhanded him on the shoulder, and he leaned down, kissing her right next to her ear.

"Later," he said, "I'm going to kiss every damn drop of color from your lips. And then I'm going to kiss you some more."

She sucked in a shaky breath. "Is it time for cake, yet?" she asked, echoing his earlier sentiment of skipping the party entirely.

He chuckled. "Soon, sweetheart. For now we have to play nice and"—he feigned a gasp—"mingle."

CHAPTER SEVENTEEN

Ava was in the kitchen, licking a candle clean of its frosting, when Lily found her friend. Ava playfully slapped Jack's hand as he pulled the final blown-out candle from the cake, then teasingly held it over the garbage can.

"Don't you *dare*," she warned her fiancé, then laughed softly as he handed it to her and held his hands up in surrender.

"I'm going to bring this back outside to cut," he said. "I don't trust you to share otherwise."

Ava narrowed her eyes. "It's my birthday," she said haughtily. "I can eat the whole cake if I want."

"Or," Lily interjected, "I could always bake you another one."

And with that Jack escaped out the back door.

"Sorry," Lily said. "But I'm on his side when it comes to spreading the love for my triple threat cake. Everyone out there is a potential client, you know."

Ava sighed. "Fine. Only because I want your catering business to be a huge success. But all the leftovers are *mine*."

Lily laughed. Tonight was—good. Luke had a family, and it was nice to be a part of it sometimes.

Ava was giving her a look, that kind of look that said she

wanted to ask Lily something but was waiting for the right moment.

"Come on," Lily said. "Just say it."

Ava grinned—a big, goofy dopey grin. "You came here tonight with Luke. That means something, right? Please tell me that means something. Because I would love it if it meant something."

Lily raised brow. "It sounds like you want it to mean something."

She laughed then, maybe a little too hard, and maybe a little too forced. Because it wasn't just Ava who was looking for meaning. Lily was, too. And she wasn't a fan of looking for things that weren't there. Certainty was more her style, and she'd been pretty lousy at finding herself some good old certainty these days.

"I don't know," she finally said. "Maybe it does mean something. Maybe it doesn't. All I know is that I'm enjoying myself. I like being around him. I like being with him. And it feels so weird to say that."

"I thought you two couldn't stand each other," Ava said. "Not that I mind seeing you guys like this. I like it, actually. And Jack's pretty happy about it, too. But what happened? What changed?"

Wasn't that the million-dollar question? Maybe it was the sex. Good sex could connect two people who didn't connect before, right? But then there was the fact that he had her come with him for Gertie's delivery, that he'd spent the day with her afterward—after losing the cow. And now this. Tonight. With his family.

Lily shrugged. "In some ways nothing. But then in some ways everything. I honestly don't know what to think. He said he doesn't do permanent." Yet at the same time he'd agreed to wanting more.

Ava raised a brow. "People say a lot of things. The question is, what do you read between the lines? What does he say without the words?"

Lily snorted. "Since when are you so poetic?" she asked.

Ava hooked her arm in Lily's and led her toward the open back door to where they both knew there was cake.

"I'm an art student," she said with a grin. "Maybe I have an artistic way with words, too." Her smile faded. "I don't want to say the *T* word, but it'll be the elephant in the room at some point if I don't. Does Tucker know?"

She shook her head. "And I think it's sort of eating Luke up that he hasn't told him. He wants to. He tried. But he caught him just as he got to this no-phones-allowed yoga retreat with Sara, and the call cut out before he could tell him everything."

Ava bit back a grin.

"It's fine," Lily said. "I'm over it now. *Almost.*"

Ava let a small bubble of laughter escape. "Over almost killing your ex's pregnant fiancée?"

Lily shook her head. She didn't know whether to laugh or cry. Instead she settled on gratitude.

"Thank you," she said to Ava. "For sending Luke over that night. I mean, I was pissed as hell—"

"Because you don't like people seeing you upset."

Lily's eyes widened. "You knew that?"

Ava nudged Lily's shoulder with her own, then nodded toward Jack slicing and setting out pieces of cake on the deck table. "Sure as I know I'm going to marry that man," she said. "Look, I know it's hard not having family close by, but *we're* family, Lil. Okay? No matter what happens, I'm here."

Lily's heart squeezed. Ava *was* the closest thing she'd ever had to a sibling. And she was here for her now. But what about when things with Luke went south? How much did she truly stand to lose?

Jack held out a slice of cake toward each of them.

"Marry him quick," Lily said. "He's got connections to a really great baker."

Each woman reached for her slice of cake, but Lily waited for Ava to take the first bite. If there was one thing she loved, it was watching others react to her food.

First Ava's eyes fluttered. Then she made something akin to a soft moan. And then she *definitely* made a loud moan.

And Lily was satisfied.

"Come with me."

Luke's voice sounded to her left, and then his hand rested gently on the small of her back.

"Can I bring my cake?" she asked.

He chuckled. "Sweetheart, you can bring anything you want as long as you're with me."

Warmth flowed through her like the richest hot fudge, melting any and all of her defenses. Was she supposed to read between the lines?

"Luke Everett, you are going to have a hard time getting rid of me if you keep saying things like that," she said, testing the waters.

He led her off the deck and out into the grass toward the barn. But he stopped when she said this. "What makes you think I want to get rid of you?"

She dug her fork into her cake, then licked it clean.

"I like what we're doing," she admitted to him. "I like being with you. And maybe, on a really great night like tonight, I just don't want to think about it eventually ending. Not yet."

He shrugged. "Then don't."

So he wouldn't know he'd stunned her into silence, she kept at the cake for the rest of the walk to the barn.

"I want you to meet someone," he said. "The newest member of the Everett family."

He opened the door and ushered her inside. Right there, in the first stall, was a beautiful black-and-white-spotted calf.

Lily sucked in a short breath.

"That's...her?" she asked, setting down her fork and her almost empty plate on the first shelf she could find. "I mean, is it a her or a him? Those are udders, right? That makes her a *her*?"

He laughed and crossed his arms. "Is it me, or did you take a biology class or two when you were in school?"

She rolled her eyes. "Funny. You're really funny."

He raised a brow. "I've elicited a smile or two."

And wasn't that just the thing? It seemed all this man did lately was elicit smiles from her, and she'd even done the same with him.

"Want to feed her?" he asked

Lily's eyes widened. "Really? I can do that?"

He nodded. No smart remark. Just a simple nod with a simple grin that could very well melt her heart.

He strode to the other side of the barn and a couple minutes later came back with a large bottle in his hand, the same one she'd grabbed the day the calf was born.

He freed the wood slat of the barn door from its fastening and pulled it open.

The calf was lounging, chewing on some hay. Her head rose to greet them.

Luke squatted just as the calf stood. He held out the bottle for her to see, and her big black eyes perked with recognition.

"Just like this," he said, holding the large bottle with two hands. The calf latched on in a matter of seconds, and the sheer force of her hunger knocked him right onto his ass. Lily snorted.

"She's a bit greedy sometimes if she's really hungry," he said, not even fazed. "Worst that can happen is she tugs the thing away from you, and you fall down, or she rips the nipple off and you're covered in milk."

Lily eased herself down slowly then asked with a raise of her brows if she could take over.

"You know the risks," he said. "You sure you're ready?"

Butterflies danced in her belly. She knew he was asking only about the cow. But everything she was doing—not just tonight and not just with Luke but everything, from catering this wedding to answering a question that went much deeper for her—was a risk.

She was risking her career.

She was risking Luke's friendship with Tucker.

She was risking her heart. And maybe—just maybe—she was risking his, too.

She held the skirt of her dress over the back of her thighs and lowered herself onto her butt as well. "Maybe I'm done playing it safe," she told him.

The corner of his mouth turned up. "Does that mean you're tossing the paperweight planner?"

She scoffed. "I said I was maybe done playing it safe. I didn't say I'd lost my mind."

She chuckled and nodded toward the bottle. As soon as her hands were on it, he let go, but he didn't stand up, just crossed his forearms over his knees and stared at her.

"Oh my God!" she said as the calf tugged on the nipple and drank. "I'm doing it!"

He nodded. "You sure are," he said. "You could do just about anything if you wanted to, Lily."

Then he placed his palm on the small of her back, his thumb stroking the ridges of her spine as she continued to feed the calf. And they just sat there, the three of them, in comfortable silence.

"What's her name?" she finally asked and saw him shrug out of the corner of her eye.

"She doesn't have one yet. You wanna do the honors?"

Her breath caught in her throat, and she turned to face him, his ocean blue eyes ready and waiting for her to sink to the very bottom.

"But I'm not—this is *your* family's business. I'm just—I'm your brother's client."

"You're Ava's friend, too," he reminded her.

She waved a hand in the air and almost lost the bottle to a hungry tug. "By-product of being your brother's client. I got lucky there."

And wasn't that the truth? She'd cut herself off from any sort of social life once she and Tucker had gotten married and opened BBQ on the Bluff. It was just the nature of the restaurant business—up and out early, home late, and then do it all over again. It had been hard to maintain anything more than making sure she got enough sleep to not fall over the next day. Ava had come into her life just as it seemed everything was unraveling.

Yet here she was, not yet fully unraveled and somehow finding time for more than just what *had* to be done.

"You were there," he said. "You were a part of something big in our world, and I want—we *all* thought we'd let you put your stamp on it."

"What?" she asked, her voice suddenly shaking. "But I thought—I mean, you made it clear you don't—" She didn't want to say the word because that would mean admitting she wanted what he clearly didn't. Instead she handed him the bottle, then stood and brushed the hay and dirt from her skirt. "I need some air." Then she hightailed it out of the barn to where she could finally breathe.

She was part of something big in his world.

He wanted her to name a freaking cow, but names were permanent. She and Luke were not. And eventually, when the calf had served her purpose, she wouldn't be either.

"Hey, Lily."

She'd barely had two minutes to collect herself, and there he was, *Hey Lily-ing* her. God that was so like him. Well, if she couldn't control what she wanted from Luke, she could at least control the whole *Hey-you-wanna-name-my-cow?* situation.

"How much?" she asked.

His brows drew together. "How much what?"

"How much for me to *buy* her," she clarified.

"The calf?"

She nodded. "The calf."

"She's not for sale. Not yet, at least."

"Well, I'm not naming her if I can't take her home with me."

He raised his brows, then chuckled. "Even if I did sell her to you, where the hell would you put her? In your backyard garden? And unless you're raising her for the same reason we are, isn't it just a little hypocritical? I mean, last time I checked you weren't a vegetarian chef. Or a vegetarian for that matter."

She groaned. He was right. She sounded ridiculous. And yet she couldn't back down.

"That's not it." Whatever the future held, she wanted to remember what it was like to be a part of something that mattered to him. And if that meant a pet cow, then so be it. "Look, I know it sounds insane, and no. I don't have anyplace to put her just yet. But maybe, if this catering thing takes off, I can sell the house and get something with more land. Right now, though, I'm just looking to buy a calf."

He shook his head and blew out a long breath. "She'd be like Gertie," he said. "Used for breeding. She wouldn't—I mean it'd be a long time before—"

"How *much*?" she interrupted.

"A thousand dollars."

She opened her mouth, then closed it. Well, at least he didn't try shutting her up with a kiss this time. Instead he went for shock value, and it worked.

He took a step closer, and she crossed her arms, holding her ground, one small little act of defiance, though she wasn't sure *what* she was defying.

"Give her a name, and she's yours whenever you get the money—and land. You cannot put livestock in your backyard."

Lily pouted. "She'd probably eat my garden."

"She'd *definitely* eat your garden."

He placed his palm hesitantly on her cheek, but she stayed where she was, even leaning into it.

"What I said before, about you being a part of something big in our world? I didn't mean that."

Her eyes widened, but he just laughed, his other palm cupping the other side of her face.

"That was a cop-out," he added. "Me being too chickenshit to tell you the truth."

Something squeezed inside her chest, and she held her breath, waiting for him to say more.

"You're a part of something big in *my* world, Lily." She sucked in a sharp breath, and he laughed again. "You weren't supposed to fit," he said.

She rolled her eyes. "If you're going to give me that oil-and-water crap again..."

"If someone had said to you a month ago that we'd be standing here right now, like this, what would your reaction have been?"

She chewed on her upper lip. His hands were on her face, and he was so close to kissing her. But she wasn't going to lie just to prove a point. Or to get his mouth on hers any faster.

"I would have said you were an overconfident jackass who was too attractive for his own good."

He raised a brow. "As much as you tried to insult me, I can't help noting how attractive you think I am."

"*Too* attractive," she reminded him. "It's like you use those eyes and that scruff and the whole cowboy thing as a distraction for the overconfident jackass part."

He huffed out a laugh. "Is it working?"

"That depends," she said. "Are you going to kiss me?"

"Yep."

And just like that, his lips were on hers, his tongue slipping past her parted lips.

"You taste like chocolate," he rasped, and she hummed against him.

"You taste like—you," she said, and he nipped at her bottom lip, eliciting a small gasp.

"Is that a good thing?" he asked.

She nodded as his kisses trailed the line of her jaw, as he moved farther south into the sensitive crook of her neck.

"The best thing," she squeaked. "The best thing I've ever tasted."

He tilted his head up. "Seeing as how you're a chef and all, that says a lot."

He went back to kissing her, moving from her collarbone

to the swell of her breast just above the line of her dress, his teeth grazing the delicate flesh.

"Luke?" she asked, barely able to find enough breath to make the word.

He tipped his head up, whispering in her ear.

"Lily?" Then he tugged her earlobe between his teeth, and her knees buckled.

He caught her, of course. He'd never let her fall, would he?

"About going home with you tonight?" she managed to ask.

He continued to pepper any skin he could find with soft, tingly kisses. "What about it?" he asked.

She pressed her palms to his cheeks, urging his head up to where she could look him in the deep ocean of his eyes.

"Is it time to go home yet?"

Like a switch had been flipped, he grabbed her hand, lacing his fingers through hers, and led her to his truck.

She giggled as she almost ran to keep up. "Don't we have to go say good-bye to Ava and Jack or something?"

Luke nodded to her purse on the passenger-seat floor of his truck. "Text her. She'll understand."

Lily scrambled into her seat, pulling out her phone and typing in Ava's name.

Happy birthday! Talk tomorrow... I'm reading between the lines.

She finished typing, hit send, and then dropped her phone back into her purse all in the time it took Luke to make it to his side of the truck and climb in.

"Lucky," she said when he pulled the door shut and slid the key into the ignition.

"What?" he asked.

"The calf," she reminded him. "I'm gonna name her Lucky."

And then she let him drive, wondering how long her own luck would last, *hoping* that it never had to run out.

CHAPTER EIGHTEEN

Luke's jaw, shoulders—hell, just about everything—tensed as they pulled up in front of the small, ramshackle green house. Two windows, a door, and a porch light stared back at them as he rolled up the driveway that might have had more weeds than concrete.

Shit. What the hell was he thinking, bringing her back here when they could be in her nice little suburban two-bedroom with that fenced-in yard and granite counters and...

"It's a fixer-upper," he said before she had a chance to speak first.

She rested a hand on his knee and squeezed. "You bought the land," she said, staring off into the hills.

And because she got it—because she fucking got *him*—he kissed her. She hummed a soft moan as he did.

"Mmm," she said when he pulled away. "What was that for? Not, by the way, that I'm complaining. Feel free to do that again."

He chuckled, then skimmed his fingers across her forehead, tucking her overgrown bangs behind her ear.

"I want to show you something," he said, then kissed her again softly before pulling away and hopping out of the truck.

She was already out by the time he got to her side, and he simply took her hand, leading her through the overgrown wild grass of his front lawn and around to the back of the two-bedroom house.

It was nearly dark, but there was still enough light in the pink-and-orange-streaked sky for her to see.

She stopped short, hand on her chest. "It's just sky and hills. For as far as you can see."

He squinted into the waning rays of sunshine. "Just to be clear, it's not *all* mine," he said. "But there was enough payout from the life insurance to help make sure we didn't lose the vineyard and to put a down payment on a couple of acres."

Her eyes widened, and he crossed his arms, brows raised as he took her in.

"You're surprised," he said. A statement—not a question.

Her mouth hung open for a second. "No... I just..." she stammered.

"You didn't think I gave a shit about anything other than *fun*."

He said the word like it was a curse and wondered if that's exactly what it was. He'd done so well at cultivating the persona of the guy who was always up for a good time that he'd grown to believe it, too. It didn't stop him from going back to the night they met, how he could have sworn she saw through his bravado. What's more was that he'd wanted her to, but as soon as Tucker swooped in, it didn't matter. He couldn't compete, and he hadn't wanted to. Not when Tucker had needed a win—and not when Lily had so clearly preferred a guy who could give her the world to a guy who had no more than himself to offer.

She crossed her arms right back at him, then shivered.

He stepped closer to her, the movement as natural and

instinctual as breathing, and rubbed his hands up and down her shoulders.

She cleared her throat. "You're making it very difficult for me to chastise you."

The corner of his mouth quirked up. "I didn't realize I was in need of chastisement." He rubbed more warmth into her goose bumps–covered skin.

She narrowed her eyes at him. "I don't think you give a shit about nothing other than fun. Not anymore."

He pulled her closer, pressing his torso to hers, and she sighed. "Are you saying you misjudged me?"

She splayed her palms against his chest. "I've always known you gave a shit about your brothers. And your aunt."

"They're blood," he said. "Doesn't count. I have no choice. You gotta give me something better than that."

His tone was playful, and yet he hung on to the edge of the silence between his request and her response. Because he wasn't sure who he was trying to convince more—her or himself.

"You *do* have a choice, though. Who or what you give a shit about, I mean." She placed a hand on his cheek. "You aren't the man I thought I knew," she said. "When I made any assumptions about you—whatever I said before..." She shook her head. "I was wrong."

His jaw tightened, and he closed his eyes as he breathed in deep, filling himself with the scent of earth, and salt, and *her*.

"And I was wrong about something else, too."

Her voice trembled, and he opened his eyes to find her emerald pools glassy in the waning light. She let out a shaky breath.

"I didn't plan on doing this tonight, but it's all just sort of hitting me, you know?"

She wasn't smiling, and her eyes seemed to fill with something he couldn't put his finger on—something like sadness or regret, and it suddenly felt like the ground was opening beneath him, ready to swallow him whole.

He shook his head. "No, Lily. I don't know." His teeth ground together. Because even though they never promised each other anything, was she going to walk away tonight? Just like that?

She backed away, rubbing her bare arms with her palms, and he froze.

"I thought I'd be okay with this no permanence stuff because I was convinced this was a rebound—that all I needed was to get you out of my system. But—I'm not okay, Luke. Not anymore."

He scrubbed a hand across his jaw. "Lily—are you ending this?"

His back porch light went on, spotlighting the moment, the timer right on cue.

"I thought we hated each other, you know? I thought whatever this was that it was just two people burning away this sudden fire, that when the time came it would be easy to walk away. But—you tried to save me from getting mixed up in Tucker and Sara's wedding. Then you came over that night after the hospital when I needed a friend. And then there was Gertie, and riding Ace, and Lucky my new calf..."

The corner of his mouth twitched, but he fought the urge to grin. Because if this was it, there'd be nothing to grin about. And he'd have no one to blame but himself.

"I don't know how to walk away," she said, and there went a tear. "Even knowing you'll leave, eventually, that you'll have to, because this isn't what you do, I don't know how to do it myself. Because you're *not* out of my system,

Luke. You're so goddamn far from being out, I don't know what the hell to do."

He closed the distance between them, palms on her tear-streaked cheeks.

"You were right, about me having a choice," he said, kissing her wet lashes and tasting the salt on his tongue. "About who or what I care about. I thought if I chose not to care about the things that could really get to me—about the people who could hurt me—that I'd be invincible."

"But the rodeo," she said. "You were hurt so badly last time."

"Broken bones heal." He took her palm and placed it on his chest, right above his heart. "But I don't know the first thing about fixing this part. Forget what you think you know about me. You said it's my choice, and Jesus, Lily—I choose *you.*"

He kissed her as they backed toward the door, as he fumbled for his keys, clumsily unlocking it by touch alone.

His lips never left hers as they passed through the kitchen and small living room to his bedroom on the other side.

Only after he'd undressed her—after she'd done the same to him—did he finally find the words.

"I don't want to walk away," he admitted. "Not from you. But I don't know what the hell I'm doing here, Lily. I don't know how to do right by you."

She sat on the edge of his bed and held out a hand for him. He took it.

"Don't break my heart," she said matter-of-factly, then pulled him over her.

For so many years he'd thought he had life figured out. He loved what he did—the riding, competing—more than he loved anything else. And even if it broke him, it could only break him so deep.

That's why when he and Tucker walked into that bar three years ago and the prettiest, funniest, smartest girl there went home with his best friend, he'd stepped back. Hell, he'd stepped back before that, hadn't he? Because he'd gone and assumed a girl like her would see nothing more than a guy who liked to have fun. And when that's how she *did* see him, he blamed her for it.

Even as he fought with her, pressed her buttons, and made sure she never saw past the facade, he used it as ammunition to blame her—because that was easier than admitting the truth. Every day she'd grown closer to Tucker, Luke had fallen harder. Hating her had been the only way to survive, even if he'd always known it was a lie.

Don't break my heart. That was all she'd asked.

So what did it mean that she'd already obliterated his time and time again?

He nudged her opening, coating himself in her warmth. There would be no foreplay tonight. He needed to bury himself in her—bury himself and never fucking come up for air.

"I won't," he said, brushing his lips over hers. "Break your heart, I mean."

She ran the tips of her fingers over his bottom lip and gave him the most beautiful, radiant, red-lipped smile. And he remembered his promise to kiss that cherry-red right off her lips.

"Famous last words," she said.

He'd be a man of his word, in more ways than one if he could help it.

She kissed him then, snaking her arms around his neck, and he sank down inside her, right to the very root.

She cried out, her fingers fisting in his hair.

This woman was going to wreck him—utterly and completely—and there wasn't a goddamn thing he could do but let it happen.

It was just like riding that bull. Eventually he'd get thrown off balance, and something would break. He just wasn't sure he'd be able to get back up when it did.

He slid out slowly, his chest aching with every inch because it hurt—physically fucking hurt—to put even the slightest distance between them.

"Jesus, Lily." She tensed around him as he sheathed himself once again in her warmth.

"Kiss me," she said, voice hitching. "No talking. Just—"

She gasped as he pulsed inside her, and he claimed her mouth with his own. Her lips parted, his tongue sweeping inside to tangle with hers.

No talking. That was sure as hell fine with him. Because something was shifting tonight. A silent admission that he wanted more with this woman, even though he had no idea what that meant or how to do it.

He rolled onto his back, the two of them still joined, then eased onto his elbows, urging her onto his lap. Soon they were both sitting, her knees bent beneath her, her eyes meeting his.

He slid a hand up her side, cupping her breast before pinching the hard, peaked nipple between his thumb and forefinger.

She sucked in a sharp breath, then rose and fell over him. So he took her into his mouth, teeth teasing as his fingers had, and he swore nothing she cooked—and she was a goddamn artist—tasted as good as her skin on his tongue.

"*Luke*," she said, arching her back, head tipped toward the ceiling as he licked and nipped, all the while anchored to him, her every movement threatening to send him straight off the edge.

"Are we talking now, sweetheart?" he teased, because the alternative was acknowledging not only the plea in that one word—his name—but how much he thought *he* might need *her*.

Her knees clamped against his thighs, and inside she tightened around him.

He kissed her hard, then lowered his hands to her hips as she moved in a slow rhythm, writhing against him.

Then she rose and fell. Rose and fell. And slow was a thing of the past.

His fingertips pressed into her skin, thumbs against her hip bones as he guided her down again and again.

"Let go for me, Lily," he said, sliding one hand between them. "Let go all the way."

He pressed his thumb into her crease, rubbing slow circles around her swollen center, and she cried out so hard one could have mistaken the pleasure for pain—sweet, aching, tear-you-in-half pain.

That's when he realized she hadn't let go alone.

Something feral tore from his chest, and he was all at once grateful for his lack of neighbors and fucking terrified that whatever he'd just ripped apart was unfixable.

Not his ribs.

Not a dislocated shoulder.

Not a goddamn concussion.

They collapsed together, him still inside her, sweat glistening between her breasts.

She brushed her thumb over an old scar on his cheek—his memory of his first time on a bull.

He kissed her palm.

"That was—" she said, then kissed him softly, her teeth

tugging playfully at his lip. "I mean, I've never—" she added, but she wasn't able to fill the rest of it in.

All he could say was, "I know."

And then, because this was real life and not some movie where sex—even mind-bending sex like that—was some sort of magic pill, he pulled out, let her clean herself up first, and then indulged in a long, cold shower.

"Lily?" he whispered when he came back into the room in nothing but a towel. "You awake?"

She hummed softly, her face buried in one of his pillows, his sheet pulled up over her still naked form.

He dropped the towel and climbed in beside her, and she stirred enough to burrow into him, head resting against his bare chest.

"I guess I wore you out, huh?" he mused, then planted a kiss on her forehead. This time she didn't make a sound. So he sucked in a deep breath, then blew it out, long and slow.

They needed to have a little chat—only one where she wouldn't really remember in the morning.

"I don't know how to do this," he admitted. "Broken bones heal. And I got scars on my skin that prove you *can* put a man back together again. But this?" There it was again, that weight on his chest that made him sure he was being torn apart from the inside out. "I could fall all the way for you," he said. "But if you knew me—knew *all* of me—then you'd know the truth."

He waited for her to respond, for some sign that she was with him, because maybe it was time he just put it all out there, all his fucking cards on the table.

But when she inhaled with a sweet snore, he huffed out a nervous laugh, and he lost his nerve. He couldn't lay it all out there if she couldn't even hear him. He was at least a better man than that. But he could tell her enough—admit to himself how he knew this would all go down.

He tucked her hair behind her ear, felt the warmth of her breath against his chest. He spoke just above a whisper.

"I want permanence in my life, Lily. I want it with you. But I don't deserve what happened tonight. I don't deserve what you're willing to give me, not when there's something else I need to do first. I need to come clean—to Tucker. To you. In that order. And if he doesn't kick my ass first, well, then you get to do the honors. But right now the weight of it is driving me goddamn crazy."

This was why it was torture being benched. There was nowhere to go—nothing he could do to keep his shit together if he wasn't on the back of a horse.

He checked his phone on the nightstand. It was barely ten o'clock. Someone would be up and around the Callahan place. They never let their old man spend a night alone. And Ace could always use a little workout.

He slid out from under her, making sure he slipped the pillow beneath her head before it hit the mattress.

She barely stirred.

He threw on a pair of jeans and a long-sleeved T-shirt, stepped into his boots, and kissed her warm cheek.

"Back in a bit, sweetheart. I gotta go see a man about a horse."

He laughed at his own joke, then strode out of the room and straight through the front door to his truck.

One quick ride was all he needed to get back in control. Tucker would be back next week. He'd tell Tucker about him and Lily, and then he'd tell Lily everything—that he'd been such an ass all these years to serve his own selfish needs. Because how do you watch the only woman you've ever loved fall for another man and make it out alive?

He didn't have the answer. He was so close to what he'd always wanted, but he'd gotten here by lying to the people he loved most.

He needed to work off a little steam, clear his head.

He pressed a hand to his side, his ribs still tender to the touch, but they were healing. *He* was healing, which meant he could push himself tonight. He still needed at least a week to get on the back of a training bull, even though he knew that was cutting it close. He was ready to ride tonight, and he'd be ready for what lay ahead soon.

He idled out of the driveway, not really hitting the gas until he was a good distance from the house. Lily should sleep. He could work this all out and get back before she even knew he was gone.

It wasn't until he saw the sign on the truck that read *Callahan Brothers Contracting* that he reached for his phone in the cup holder and realized it wasn't there.

"Shit," he hissed, then threw his head against the back of his seat.

Just one quick ride. She was out like a light. And if he didn't get whatever was building up *out*, he was going to explode. There were no two ways about it.

One ride tonight—and then eight little seconds a week from now.

He'd prove that he could take it—prove that he was worth it.

That he was worthy of whatever she felt for him.

Or he'd crash and burn. Whichever came first.

CHAPTER NINETEEN

Lily opened her eyes as soon as she heard the truck pull away. It was only then that she allowed herself to gasp for a much needed breath of air, yet it did nothing to clear her thoughts.

I don't know how to do this.

I could fall all the way for you.

He could fall for her? He damn well better have been falling because what the hell was she doing?

But there he'd gone, getting all cryptic on her when she knew there was something holding him back. Why make love to her like that? Why tell her he wanted to try permanent when deep down he thought he wasn't capable?

At least that's what it had sounded like.

She was pacing now, wrapped in Luke's bedsheet. She should have let him know she was awake and made him say what he was afraid to say, but he was a man of such few words—at least when it came to the ones that counted—that she needed to listen. And hope that he just might be ready to let her in.

Instead he clammed up even further—and then left.

Every step forward with this guy came with one that put them right back where they started. She wasn't asking for much. Not yet, at least. Just something to hold on to so she knew she wasn't going to get clobbered. Of course she wanted permanent with Luke. What they had was beyond what she'd thought possible. But he kept disappearing—emotionally and physically—when things got too close to real. What happened if she admitted she'd fallen, too? She hadn't been enough for her father or her husband. Even if she and Tucker weren't in love like they should have been, it still hurt like hell when he found comfort in another woman's bed.

What if Luke disappeared for good this time when all she'd asked of him was not to break her heart?

Her throat tightened, and she braced herself for the tears. But they didn't come. She wasn't sad. She was angry.

She didn't know whether to storm out of his place or wait up for him just to tell him off to his face.

"You don't have a car, genius," she said aloud. "Remember? Tonight was your first public outing as a couple."

She dug her phone out of her purse. It still had a few bars of battery—enough to give Luke Everett a piece of her mind.

Except when she pressed send, she startled when she heard the sound of metal vibrating against wood.

She spun to find Luke's phone on the nightstand and groaned.

So she was stuck—no car, no way to get in touch with him, and no way for him to get in touch with her—if he even wanted to.

She stormed into the kitchen, letting the sheet fall, and flipped on the light switch before throwing open his fridge.

"Typical," she muttered when she saw the carton of eggs, a six-pack of beer, and various to-go containers.

She checked the date on the eggs and nodded her approval when she found they weren't actually expired. Then she rummaged through cabinets until she found an unopened bag of flour and various other baking sundries.

"I bet your aunt Jenna set you up real nice when you moved in here," she said, crediting the woman with stocking his cabinets and maybe at one point his fridge. Certainly not the latter anymore.

In the absence of a mixer, she settled on a spatula and a giant metal spoon. Then, after preheating the oven, she got to work.

It was after midnight when a car rolled into the driveway and Lily was pulling the last tray of cookies from the oven. She froze, tray in oven-mitt-covered hand.

The door creaked open, and she heard Luke kick off his boots.

"Lil?" he said softly, obviously seeing the light in the kitchen. "You up?"

She didn't have to answer because he materialized seconds later.

"What the—" he started.

But Lily interrupted him. "Oh my God. You're *bleeding*!"

She let the tray of cookies clatter onto the counter as she went to him, her hands inspecting the butterfly bandage over his eyebrow where dried blood stuck to his skin.

"And you're *naked*," he said with a chuckle. "Baking cookies."

She crossed her arms over her breasts and pursed her lips, not caring that she was doing exactly as he said. "You know, you make it really hard to be pissed at you when you walk in here all beat-up like you are."

"I'm *not* beat up. Ace got spooked by a damn firefly is all. Knocked me off. Thankfully the fence post of the arena broke my fall."

She grabbed his hand, led him to the kitchen table, and pushed him down in a chair.

"Did you even clean it off?" she asked.

He grinned. "Now why would I do that when I can come home to my naked girl and have her do it for me?"

She groaned and strode into the bathroom, rummaging through his medicine cabinet until she found the hydrogen peroxide and a fresh bandage. On her way back, she also snagged a T-shirt of his that lay at the foot of the bed, trying hard to ignore the scent that lingered on the fabric.

She would clean him up—and then let him have it.

He'd somehow snagged a cookie and made it back to the chair. Before he could take a bite, though, she grabbed it from his hand.

"Seriously?" he said, his eyes raking over her. "You take away my naked girl *and* my cookie?"

She dropped the cookie onto the other side of the table, then set down her supplies. "You need to *earn* it."

He chuckled, glancing at the plate stacked high with snickerdoodles and at the fresh tray still cooling on the counter.

"I don't think we're going to run out," he teased. "Or were you planning on taking the whole lot home with you? I should probably remind you that I'm your ride, and I take gas payment in the form of baked goods—or you giving me permission to explore what you're hiding under that Fruit of the Loom tee. I wore it the whole ride home in the truck with Walker the other day. I'll bet it still smells nice and ripe."

He laughed, and she rolled her eyes.

The truth was, it smelled like *him.* All man. All Luke. And she could live in that T-shirt if he'd let her.

Lily huffed out a breath but didn't respond. Instead she just got to work.

She peeled off the bandage, the adhesive sticking to the dried blood and part of his eyebrow. But he didn't flinch as she pulled it free, didn't even make a sound.

So this was how he was going to play it after all his teasing—Mr. Stoic?

She poured hydrogen peroxide on a cotton ball and cleaned the cut. It wasn't as bad as it looked once the blood was washed away, but it wasn't *nothing* either.

She scrubbed at the stubborn flecks, the slight tensing of his jaw the only hint that it hurt at all.

"Why are you so impossible?" she asked, affixing the new bandage.

"Why do you have such a rough bedside manner?" he countered. "Not that I don't like it a little rough—"

"Ugh!" she cried through gritted teeth, then headed for the counter, where she emptied the last tray of cookies onto the plate with all the rest.

He was up and behind her just as quickly, snagging a snickerdoodle from the top of the plate.

"Decided I wanted a warm one instead," he said, his stubble scratching against the side of her face. "I think I earned it after being such a good patient."

She wasn't going to let his charm get to her, not when he was sitting there *bleeding*. Didn't he get how much worse it could have been—how much worse it would be if he let a bull get the best of him again?

Even though she wasn't there those few weeks ago when he got thrown, Lily imagined it now—Luke lying in the dirt. Broken. She could barely breathe.

She spun to face him. "How about explaining why it's so hard for you to just admit you're in pain—*any* kind of pain? How about you stop punishing yourself physically for something you had no control over when you were a kid? You have broken bones, Luke. And a concussion. When is it enough?" He opened his mouth to say something, but she wasn't done. "And how dare you tell me you're falling for me and then sneak out the door? If you can face me and deal with all of that, *then* you'll earn your damn cookie."

She didn't need to snatch this one away because it crumbled to near dust in his rough, calloused hand as he backed away and, as seemed to be the theme of the night, strode right out the back door.

"*Shit*," she hissed. She padded into the bedroom, wrapped herself in his comforter, then followed him outside.

The back light was on, but it did nothing to drown out the blanket of stars speckling the sky.

His back was to her, but he hadn't gone far. She tiptoed into the grass, stopping just before she was even with where he stood.

"You're probably starting to notice a pattern with my verbal vomit," she said. "But you said all those things while I was asleep and then left me here to—to bake, and then you come back laughing and teasing like there isn't some big elephant in the room we need to address."

"You weren't asleep," he said, an edge to his tone.

She cleared her throat. "No. I wasn't," she admitted. "I was dozing off, though. But then you started talking—and saying these important things that you wouldn't have said if you didn't think I was unconscious."

He crossed his arms but kept staring straight ahead. "Maybe I'm not ready to say everything yet," he said. "There are things I have to do first. I know it doesn't make sense, Lily. But I did this all wrong. And I have to make it right. With everyone involved."

She took the few steps around him so she wasn't having

a conversation with his back. He continued staring into the distance at first, but she held her ground. Finally, he let out a long breath and dipped his head to meet her gaze.

"What does that even mean?" she asked. "If there's a certain way this was supposed to happen, then why did you let it happen at all?"

He ran a hand through his hair, then shoved both into the front pockets of his jeans.

"This *wasn't* supposed to happen," he said. "You were Tucker's girl. And as far as I should be concerned, you still are. Bro code and all."

Lily scoffed. "Screw bro code."

He laughed, but his smile didn't reach his eyes. "I have messed up in so many ways, Lily. With you. With Tucker. My brothers. The only thing I seem to be able to get right is what I do in the arena."

She laughed this time, the sound bitter and resigned. "That's what you call a dislocated shoulder, cracked ribs, and a concussion? Not to mention getting up close and personal with a fence post tonight?"

He shrugged. "It's all expected going in. I know what I'm up against."

"What if you get hurt again? I've watched a medical show or two. I'm pretty sure more than one concussion isn't a good thing."

"Dammit, Lily." His tone was strained, and she knew she'd hit a nerve.

A chill rocked through her, and she pulled the blanket tighter around her nearly naked form. The question she wanted to ask was simple enough, but for some reason she dreaded the answer.

"What happens if you get another one?" she asked. "Tell me *one* true thing, Luke. Straight to my face."

The muscle in his jaw ticked.

"Possible brain damage," he said, his voice tight. "It's not a guarantee, but it's a risk. I mean, you clocked me in the head with your death planner, and I was fine, right?"

Her breath caught in her throat, and her eyes burned. How could he joke about this?

"Don't ride," she told him. No—*begged* him. He had to hear her plea.

"Lily—"

"*Don't* ride that stupid bull. You don't have to. You actually have a choice here, and didn't you say that's what's important to you—being able to make your own choice?"

He shook his head and reached for her cheek, his palm rough after having ridden Ace.

"I choose to ride," he said flatly. "I know you think I've got some sort of guilt vendetta here, and maybe that is part of it, but it's also something I've been working toward since I first climbed on a horse and knew I was good. I am the best version of myself in that arena. And I know—Jesus I know the risks. But I also know this will be my last ride. My last shot. Cancer took my mother and turned my father into a monster. I had to sit by and watch while Jack bore the brunt of the fallout for five damn years. I have lived my entire life on other people's terms, Lily. This time it's *my* say. I screwed up last time, let my thoughts get to me. But I won't fall this time, not if I keep my damned head in the game."

His thumb swiped at the tear that fell from the corner of her eye, but more just came in its wake.

"Maybe my situation is different, but that doesn't mean I don't understand loss. My dad left me and my mom when I was twelve, and Tucker—well, you know how that turned out. I get what it's like not to have a say, but you're knowingly putting yourself at risk."

Her lip was starting to tremble, but she had to steady herself—to get out the words.

"You said you wouldn't break my heart," she reminded him. "And if anything happens to you..." But the rest of her words failed her.

He nodded. "I also said I wouldn't walk away from you, so I need to make something clear. Me getting on that *stupid* bull is not the same as me walking away. But if you can't handle it—if you want to walk away from me, you can."

She pressed her palm against his hand. "You are such an asshole."

He nodded. "There's another truth for you."

She shook her head. "You're about to risk the rest of your life for eight seconds of glory, and that scares the hell out of me. Have you considered what that would mean if I'm falling for you right back?"

"Lily," he said softly.

"Do your brothers know? Does Jenna? Because they'd all tell you—"

He stepped back from her, his hand dropping to a fist at his side. "Dammit, Lily. No one's going to tell me what I can do or how much is too much. It's more than eight seconds of glory. I thought you might understand that."

"What about their support?" she added. "Maybe you don't want anyone telling you what to do, but what about them being there for you? Or their understanding at least? I want to understand, Luke. I really do, but I can't get past the risk."

"And I can't get past why you, Jack, or anyone I give a damn about doesn't seem to have faith in my word."

He paced now, back and forth while she waited, letting him work through whatever it was he wanted to say next.

She knew that feeling, that one where the right words

wouldn't come, when she just had to *do* something. That's why there were piles of snickerdoodles in the kitchen.

When he finally stopped, he stood right in front of her again, chest heaving, the muscles in his neck and shoulders tensing.

"Why are you catering this wedding?" he asked softly.

Her brows drew together. "What does that have to do with anything?"

"Just answer the question. Why, even after finding out that you were catering your ex-husband's marriage to a new woman, did you insist on keeping the job?"

She opened her mouth to answer, then thought better of it. He was playing their old game, backing her into a corner and trying to outsmart her, and she was not about to walk into his trap. Didn't he get the memo? She was supposed to be interrogating him, not the other way around.

"Come on, Lil. You know you want to tell me off right now."

She pouted. "I do not."

The corner of his mouth turned up. She didn't know what was worse, the fact that he had the nerve to smile or that she found his audacity even the slightest bit charming.

"Just say it," he said. "You know this isn't going to end until you do." Then he leaned in close, putting those warm rough lips right next to her ear. "Tell me why you didn't back out of the catering contract."

His breath was warm, but she shivered despite being wrapped in his comforter.

She gritted her teeth. "I couldn't," she said, her words soft but certainly not gentle.

"Why?"

This time his lips brushed against her earlobe, and shivers turned to freckles of goose bumps all over her skin.

"Because."

"Because *why*?"

She groaned. He was going to win, and he knew it. She might as well throw in the towel.

"Because I don't quit. And because I need to prove to myself I can do this whole business thing on my own, that even though I got knocked down, I didn't stay there."

He grinned. And shit, it was so unfair. Because that smile of his—the one she felt like only she got to see—had turned her insides straight to goo.

He surprised her by threading his hands in her hair and kissing her. And she surprised herself by melting into it—into him.

His lips were warm, insistent, like he was trying to make her understand something, but he needed to understand too.

"Wait," she said, dipping her head to break the kiss. "Just—wait."

He stopped but didn't back away, keeping his forehead pressed against hers.

"I get it," she admitted, wrapping her arms—and therefore his comforter—around his torso. "I've got something to prove to myself, and so do you."

He buried his face in her hair. "Knew you'd catch on, sweetheart."

"But there's one difference," she said, knowing there'd be no going back after this. "If you asked me not to do this wedding—if it in any way could hurt you for me to do it—I wouldn't."

If she could have convinced her father to stay or done something to make her and Tucker as perfect in real life as they were on paper, she would have. Now here was this man who—like it or not—already had her heart, and he couldn't promise her he'd stay. Maybe he wasn't technically walking away, but it was close enough.

"Lily."

There was accusation in his tone. She hadn't meant to, but she'd hurt him.

"You're wrong," he added, and the strain in his voice made her grateful she couldn't see those blue eyes right now. "There are *two* differences." He kissed the top of her head. "I would never ask you to give up your dream."

And then, just like that, he spun toward the house and walked away without another word.

The thing was, though, her dream wouldn't kill her—not in the physical sense, at least. His? His actually could. And even if the worst-case scenario was what another concussion could do to him—it still meant the same thing.

It meant him leaving her.

She made her way back into the house, grabbed two cookies, and tiptoed toward the bedroom. Luke was in the bed, shirtless with his jeans still on, his arm bent under his head as he stared at the ceiling.

She held out a cookie. "You—you earned it," she said. "So I'm making good on my offer."

She sucked in a breath, prepared to hold it until he gave her some sort of response, but he reached for the cookie immediately, his head tilting toward her.

He took a bite, then patted the empty spot on the mattress next to him.

Her throat tightened, but she kept it together as she crawled in next to him with her own cookie, trying not to think about sleeping with crumbs.

"You still mad at me?" she asked.

He nodded. "You still pissed at me?"

She nodded right back. "I do have faith in you. So does your family. But this whole situation is bigger than that, you know?"

He didn't say anything, just stroked her hair.

So they lay there, eating snickerdoodles. And with every rise and fall of her head on his chest, she fell harder for the man who made her absolutely crazy.

Luke needed his support system, but Lily realized she needed hers, too. She needed the one person she'd been afraid to face for more than six months.

She needed to go home.

CHAPTER TWENTY

Luke woke with a knot in his bad shoulder and an empty space in the bed next to him. He paused for several seconds, hoping the scent of bacon or something would come wafting into the room. *Not* that he expected her to cook for him. It would just be a sign that she was still there. But Luke Everett didn't believe in signs, and he knew that last night was both a breakthrough and a damned setback.

He pushed himself onto his side and reached for his phone on the nightstand, letting out a breath when he saw the waiting text. At least she hadn't just disappeared without a word.

Had a friend pick me up. Don't worry. I didn't get all dramatic and walk home.

He laughed. God he'd been such an asshole—too many times to count. But he must have done something right to wind up where they'd been last night before he went and messed it all back up.

I could fall in love with you, Luke Everett. But I can't watch you risk your life just so I can lose you. I know this is selfish, and you can hate me for it. For what I have to do. But I'm leaving first this time. It's the only thing I can control. Figure you can understand that part.

How about that? She went and used his idea of doing things on his own terms to walk right out the door.

Muscles stiff, he padded into the bathroom where he took a long, hard look at the man staring back at him from the mirror. She'd done a good job cleaning up his cut, and when he peeled off the bandage, it stayed closed. No more bleeding. While the fading bruises on his torso would be easily hidden under his shirt, there was no hiding a fresh injury to his face. He'd have to explain himself to Jack when he got to the ranch.

When he'd dressed and made it into the kitchen, he found the place cleaner than he'd left it before she'd miraculously found ingredients to bake. And the cookies were piled high on a plate, covered in plastic wrap.

At least he had proof that it hadn't been a dream. She had been here. *They* were real. She could fall in love with him. *Could* fall. But what? She got scared and stopped herself? That was bullshit. He'd tried *not* loving her for three years, and look where that had gotten him. But he couldn't give up what he'd worked for. He wasn't calling it quits on someone else's terms—only his own. And if she couldn't stick around for that, then he'd live with it. He'd already planned on living with much less.

He lifted the plastic wrap, snagged four cookies, and decided to grab coffee at the ranch before popping into the winery to help with the drywall. He had to hand it to the Callahans. They were fast and efficient, but they didn't cut any corners.

Luke expected his brother to give him the third degree about the cut above his eye. He *expected* to have to appease Jack, assure him that he wasn't doing anything dangerous, that Ace just got spooked.

What he wasn't prepared for was his older brother waiting for him on the porch steps, which meant Luke wouldn't even get a sip of coffee before he had to play defense.

"Morning," Luke said with a grin as he strode toward the porch.

"Morning," Jack said, his tone unrecognizable. He could be tired or pissed, but Luke couldn't decipher.

Maybe he'd judged too quickly. *Maybe* his brother was just enjoying a bit of fresh air before doing whatever it was needed doing by a lawyer/rancher before 9:00 a.m.

But when Luke tried to pass where his brother sat on the steps, Jack stopped him with a single word.

"Sit," he said.

Scully, Owen's chocolate lab, came bounding from somewhere on the side of the house, stopping at Jack's feet and doing exactly what the man had said.

Luke didn't let his smile falter when he said, "I'll assume you were calling the dog, then? Because I'm light on sleep and could really stand to be heavy on caffeine."

Jack absently scratched the dog behind his ear before saying, "Scully, *get*!" And the dog scampered off again. "You know I mean you," he continued, eyes narrowed at Luke.

"Whatever it is can wait until I get a goddamn cup of coffee."

Luke strode past his brother and up the stairs. He almost made it inside, even had the storm door open when Jack let him have it.

"Tell me about the concussions."

"You know about every concussion I've ever had," Luke said, his jaw tightening.

Jack blew out a breath. "Tell me about the risks. Tell me what the goddamn doctor said could happen if you get another one."

Luke's hand squeezed the door handle so hard he thought it might snap off.

You can hate me for it. For what I have to do.

He'd thought Lily meant leaving, and he'd already forgiven her for that.

"Shit," he hissed. "She had *no* right."

"She had *every* right," Jack snapped.

Luke let the door go and turned. He wouldn't do this from up here, so he took the steps two at a time, stopping right where he'd started, face-to-face with his brother.

Jack was standing now, arms crossed, his blue eyes boring into Luke's.

Luke ran a hand through his hair and let out a bitter laugh. "I'm a grown fucking man, and you still want to make decisions for me. When are you going to let go?"

"Maybe when you start acting like one." Jack's voice was low and controlled, which Luke knew meant a quiet fury brewed underneath. "How about we start with you telling me how you got that cut above your eye?"

Luke gritted his teeth but didn't respond.

A slow clap came from just behind the storm door, and both men turned to see Walker taunting them from where he stood.

He pushed through the door, wearing nothing but a pair of jeans and the same week-old beard as Luke after their time on the road together. He dropped onto the top step, letting his elbows rest on his knees. His little brother somehow looked older and more spent. And he wondered if the guy ever slept.

"Come on, Big Jack," Walker said, and Luke swore he could smell the liquor on his breath even from four steps below. "How about you make him?"

"Fuck you," Jack said, and he started pacing. Seemed that was the way of the Everett men these days, either taunting or pacing.

"Looks like for once we're in agreement," Luke added, then tilted his head toward Walker. "Fuck you," he said.

Walker just laughed. "See, I knew this happy-all-the-time, I'm-just-enjoying-life stuff was bullshit. You're just as fucked as the rest of us."

Luke crossed his own arms, hiding his clenched fists. "At least I'm not halfway to a liver transplant."

Walker leaned back on his elbows. "Just some possible brain damage," he said, then winked. "See? Just as fucked."

Luke and Jack were chest to chest, only a few inches between them. He'd always thought it would be Walker and one of them that would come blows. Wasn't Walker the volatile one? Not Jack. Not *him.*

"Is she here?" he asked Jack. "Is she at the winery?" Not that he'd know what the hell to say when he saw her. Just the other night he'd told her how well she fit into their world. Into *his* world. Now all he could think was that she'd overstepped—crossed a line she didn't have the right to cross. And he wanted to hear her admit why.

"No," Jack said, his voice softening just a bit, like he was about to give *worse* news than Lily betraying his trust.

"What do you mean *No*? Would you care to expand on that?"

"This should be good," Walker said.

Jack broke eye contact for a second and cleared his throat. "She left. Went back to Phoenix."

Something in Luke's gut twisted, then dropped.

"She's got the menu set for the wedding. Said her mom's not too bad of a cook and that she would help her shop, prep, and freeze everything she needs so she can bring it back for the reception."

"Fuck," Luke said, pacing. "*Fuck.*" He stopped in front of his brother. "What the hell did you say to her?"

Jack pressed a palm to Luke's heaving chest. "Come on, man. You know this isn't about me. I think maybe you just need to take a breather. Why don't you go check on the drywall."

The storm door opened and then slammed shut. All three men turned to find Ava staring at them, her eyes narrowed, with a bucket of paint supplies at her feet.

Luke stepped back from his brother's outstretched arm, and Jack clenched and opened his fist before dropping his hand altogether.

"Hey, Red," he said.

Ava picked up the bucket and took two steps toward Walker. She dropped a paint roller onto the porch next to him. Then she hopped down the few steps, approached Luke, and lifted his arm by the wrist before slapping a heavy paintbrush into his hand. He figured he had no choice but to grab it.

She spun toward her fiancé and pressed a roll of blue tape to his chest, breaking character for a few short seconds to give him a quick kiss.

Then she stepped back, crossed her arms, and grinned.

"I thought we agreed on the design being lots of wood and shit. What the hell is there to paint? They can't be done hanging the drywall already," Walker protested.

Ava nodded. "Sam and Ben and their crew stayed till near sundown yesterday to get it done early. Said they had a family thing come up, so they're taking the day off."

Luke swallowed, his anger ebbing. "Their dad okay?"

"I think so," Ava said. But Luke wasn't convinced. He'd have to check in on them later.

"Anyway," she continued, "remember how we decided on that little corner for folks to sit, where we'd maybe serve cheese trays and other snacks? *That* area we're keeping light and bright, which means *you* boys get to paint."

All three of the men started grumbling.

"Christ. She's headed to Arizona. I need to—" Luke started, but Ava shook her head.

"You don't need to anything," she said, her voice softening. "She needs some time to think. And so do you. Plus, we got the ranch hands tending to the herd, and judging by the new injury on that pretty face of yours, you could stand a few hours indoors."

Jack was next to open his mouth, but she was even quicker to cut him off. "I checked your calendar, and you don't have any client meetings until after lunch. Consider this brotherly bonding time a rare gift."

He rolled his eyes, and Luke was tempted to do the same.

"And *you*," she said, raising her brows at a pouting Walker. "I just love a good excuse for your brothers to keep an eye on you—and you on them."

She dusted off her hands, even though they were clean, and let out a breath. "Owen's at school and going to help out on your aunt's farm after. I'm headed inside to finish my project for class, since it's due in about three hours, but don't think I won't check on you."

She made sure to look each of them in the eye to gauge their understanding. All three of them nodded, and Luke was sure each of his brothers was as reluctant as he was to do so. But none of them seemed to be able to say no to Ava.

She kissed Jack one more time. "Paint's already there. All you have to do is tape and get to work."

Then she hopped up the stairs and back into the house.

"What about coffee?" Walker asked.

Jack shrugged. "We'll drive over and pick some up at the bakery." He turned to Luke. "Are we good?" he asked.

Luke's jaw tightened. "You still want to run the show?" he asked.

Jack blew out a breath. "That's not how it is. You know it isn't."

"I guess we'll just have to agree to disagree for now."

Walker stood, grabbing his paint roller. "You assholes are cute. But can we just get this over with?"

"I'm with him," Luke said, nodding toward his younger brother. "I'll drive myself over."

"Fine," Jack said. "Let's go."

Jack and Walker headed to Jack's truck and Luke to his. And despite his anger, every step he took beat in time with words looping in his head.

Lily's gone.

Lily's gone.

Lily's gone.

The floor had already been covered, thanks to the contracting crew. So Jack climbed the ladder to tape the seam at the ceiling. Walker took the edge against the molding on the floor. And Luke got to opening and stirring the first can of paint before pouring some into a tray. None of them spoke. If it wasn't for the open windows, the sounds of the outdoors, it would have been a goddamn tomb.

But they worked, Luke edging in once Walker and Jack had finished and moved on to the next wall. Soon all three were painting. Ava had left extra brushes and rollers so that once they each had their own wall, they wouldn't have to deal with one another much...if at all. And for upward of thirty minutes, they didn't. Not until Luke went for the ladder.

"I'll get the high spots," Jack grunted from his corner of the room.

Luke let out a bitter laugh. "The hell you will," he said.

Walker groaned. "When the hell is this place gonna actually have some booze? Because you two boys could use a drink."

Luke pointed his brush at his older brother. "What kind of problem do you have with me on a ladder?"

Jack motioned right back at him with his roller. "This," he said. "You've been broken and bloodied too many times for me to count, and that's just in the half a year I've been back. I'm sure there's plenty that went on while I was gone that you didn't bother telling me."

Luke shrugged, hooked the ladder over his shoulder, and carried it back toward his wall.

"And look," he said, dropping it in the spot he needed. "I'm still here to tell the tale. You let go for ten fucking years," he said. "Why can't you do it now?"

Jack gripped his roller, knuckles turning white, and strolled to the ladder. He climbed to the top and began filling in the upper quarter of the wall.

"Dick," Luke mumbled, not wanting to waste the energy on engaging.

He turned toward the paint tray and squatted to lay his brush for the time being. He guessed now was as good a time as any for a break if Jack was so hell-bent on keeping him out of the imminent danger of a six-foot ladder. But before he could straighten, something wet and cold dripped onto the back of his neck.

He looked up, and there was his brother quietly concentrating, the edge of his roller dripping down the wall.

"Hey, asshole," Luke said, dipping his brush in the tray and deciding he wasn't exactly done with painting after all. When Jack tilted his head down in response, Luke flicked his wrist, and his newly dipped brush sent a splatter of paint right across his big brother's face.

"You're kidding, right?" Jack asked, his expression deadpan, his voice a mask of calm.

Luke scratched his chin. "See that's the funny thing," he said. "Because I sure as hell like to kid. But I couldn't be more serious right now."

Jack blew out a breath and descended the ladder, roller still in hand. He said nothing. Just shook out his dripping roller over the tray—and then painted a fat ivory stripe up Luke's T-shirt.

"I'm *always* serious," Jack said.

Luke clenched his jaw.

Walker whistled, then asked, "Do I need to call in some sort of referee, or am I good to just sit here and wait for Ava to come kick *both* your asses?"

Jack raised a brow, and Luke suddenly relaxed. For once he and his brother seemed to have a common goal.

"On three," he whispered, then mouthed the numbers to his brother.

One. Two. Three.

The two of them charged Walker, and the youngest Everett brother wasn't fast enough to dodge their blows.

Luke's brush stroked across Walker's face while Jack's roller made sure the front of Walker's black T-shirt wasn't so black anymore.

Walker stood there, stock-still for several long seconds as he took his brothers' torment without a complaint. But

Luke could see it—the slow heave of his chest and the eerie calm in his eyes. Walker Everett would *not* go down quietly.

Before Jack had a chance to react, Walker's boot swiped his oldest brother's foot out from under him, and the man was flat on his back in seconds.

"Shit!" Luke swore. "Are you goddamn crazy?" he asked a chuckling Walker.

"What?" He shrugged. "I made sure to kick his good leg out from under him. I'm not a fucking monster."

It was then that they heard the laughter—Jack's laughter—coming at them from the floor below. Their mistake was looking down. Jack still had his brush in hand and had managed to reach into the paint tray to *reload.*

When their heads dipped, a spray of wet paint hit them both—first Walker and then Luke—straight in the face.

"What in the hell is going on in here?"

All three of them spun to where the small alcove opened into the rest of the winery. Luke squinted through only one open eye, the other squeezed shut to ward off the dripping paint.

There Ava stood, hands on hips, with a bakery bag on the floor at her feet.

She raised a brow. "I picked you up some cookies and muffins, figuring you'd want to break for a snack." She pointed toward her fiancé, who still lay on the floor with his paint-filled brush pointed at his brothers. "While I was hoping for some sort of brotherly bonding, I expected *you* to be the voice of reason."

Luke swiped his forearm across his face, then slowly blinked open his closed eye, grateful the paint hadn't sealed it shut *or* blinded him.

Jack tried to school his features into that of the calm,

controlled patriarch, the role he'd inserted himself into the second their father had sought solace at the bottom of a whiskey bottle. But for the first time in years, Luke saw the big brother he remembered from before their mother had died—before they lost Jack Senior to his abusive grief.

Jack dropped his head back to the floor and laughed hard. Luke spared a glance at Walker who, although a mess of splattered paint, was not the mess he always saw him as. He knew Jack worried too about Walker sharing too much of their father's DNA—mainly the tendency toward the bottle. But this morning he was simply their asshole little brother. And despite everything—especially the shit they were certainly in with Ava—the corners of Luke's mouth turned up, and he laughed.

Soon all three of them were a chorus of laughter. And possibly a few snorts. When he snuck a glance at Ava, who hadn't said another word, all he saw was her shaking her head—and fighting her own smile.

Since they weren't allowed back in the ranch until the paint dried, they'd each cleaned up the best they could with the icy water from the hose out back. They repurposed a couple of crates and buckets into chairs and tore into the bag of pastries, the three of them quiet for several minutes as they ate and let the sun warm where the cold water and paint had soaked their clothes. Their only view was the budding vineyard, lush and green where it once had been a tangled mess of brown.

"You think we're really gonna do this? Make wine… raise cattle? It's a hell of a lot," Luke finally said. "But it'll all keep me busy after—I mean, once I retire from the rodeo circuit."

Jack's head snapped up while Walker feigned disinterest

as he reached into the bakery bag for something more. But Luke could tell he was still listening.

"So you're *not* going to ride?" Jack asked, and Luke could hear that glimmer of hope in his brother's voice.

"No, I'm riding," Luke assured him. "But I'm not an idiot. I know this is my last one."

Jack's jaw tightened. "Why?" he asked, his voice low and his control ebbing. "You've won every other event at one time or another. Why this? Why now, when you know the risk?"

Luke stretched his legs out in front of him, crossing one ankle over the other.

"I think it goes back to Mom—losing her. And then losing Jack Senior to his grief. I will never forget what you did for us—what you sacrificed to keep Walker and me safe."

Luke glanced toward his younger brother, who picked at some drying paint on his jeans. He knew Walker still had miles to go before letting go of their past. But he hoped—goddamn he hoped he was getting there in his own way.

"But it still messed me up, man. Watching you put yourself at risk for us—watching you push Jack Senior over the edge just so you could be sure he'd come after you instead of us." He shook his head. "The horses…the bull riding? I love it all. I really do. But it's more than that."

Jack crossed his arms, but he didn't speak. He just kept his eyes focused on Luke's.

"You were able to control what happened in that house until he almost killed you. I had no choice but to sit back and watch that happen. The rodeo—getting knocked down again and again but always getting the fuck back up? It's *my* control. I need to walk in there *knowing* it's my last ride. It needs to be my choice."

Jack nodded again. "I guess I can understand a thing or two about choice."

Luke wondered if he meant leaving Oak Bluff once he turned eighteen, promising only to return once Jack Senior was six feet under—or the choice he never got to make with Ava. With her having his son. Either way, Jack got it. Luke knew he did. And he knew that's why Jack wasn't yet a fury of protest. But he was sure it was coming.

"You put your life on the line for us," Luke said. "And I know it sounds crazy as shit, but I'm putting mine on the line for me."

"Right," Walker drawled, breaking his silence. "You're not doing it as some sort of penance for what big brother here did for us. I'm calling bullshit."

Luke blew out a breath. "Fine," he said. "Maybe that was part of it for a while. I controlled when and how I got hurt. I always figured if you could take what you did for us when you were just a fucking kid—I could deal with a few stitches. A broken bone here or there. But it was also because I was good at it. You had a baseball scholarship, law school. None of that was for me. But damn I can ride a horse. Why not a bull?" He gave his brothers a half smile. "I don't have a death wish, but I need to finish what I started while it's still my choice to do so."

Jack leaned forward, resting his elbows on his knees. "I can't stop you," he said, resignation in his tone.

Luke shook his head. "I don't need to win. But I do need to see this through. I swear I know what the hell I'm doing. I've trained twice on the bull already this week, and look—nothing new is broken. You have to trust that I know what the hell I'm doing."

"Jesus." Jack shook his head. "And Lily?" he asked.

Luke's jaw clenched. "She only sees the risk. The worst-case scenario is the only one she can imagine, even though I promised her I'll be okay. As far as she's concerned, me riding is me leaving her." He gave Jack a halfhearted shrug. "I can't put her first until I do this," he said. "And maybe that sounds selfish, but I don't want to regret not trying. And I sure as hell don't want to resent her if I decided to back down."

Jack's eyes narrowed. "You're in love with her. *Aren't* you?"

Walker huffed out a laugh. "He's had a thing for her longer than I bet he'll admit—to her *or* that ex-husband."

Jack raised his brows.

"Stay the hell out of it, Walker," Luke warned. "It's my damned mess."

Walker popped a piece of blueberry muffin into his mouth. "I wouldn't touch your mess with a cattle prod. I'll leave you to clean that up all by yourself."

But the corner of his little brother's mouth turned up, and even if he wouldn't admit it out loud, Luke figured that was the closest he'd get to support—for this one last ride and whatever happened with Lily after.

If there *was* an after.

He left his brothers and decided to wander into the vineyard—their father's legacy and, if all went according to plan, the future of the Crossroads Ranch.

He pulled his phone out of his pocket, surprised it wasn't covered in paint, and pulled up Lily's number, immediately hitting CALL.

It went straight to voice mail.

"Hey, sweetheart," he said without hesitation. "Just letting you know I still haven't walked away."

He just kept reminding himself that this was his choice, and he *chose* to get things right, with whatever happened on the back of that bull—and Lily, too.

CHAPTER TWENTY-ONE

Lily was sure she had the address wrong. Because when her mom had told her she'd moved, Lily had assumed that meant moved the mobile home to a different park. But she wasn't parked in front of a trailer. Instead she idled at the base of a small driveway that led to a small but cute white stucco cottage. She picked up her phone, ready to text her mom to double-check the street name and number when the front door flew open, and the woman herself bounded onto the walkway.

Lily's heart rose in her throat, and she wasn't sure if it was the relief at seeing her mother's radiant smile or at the prospect of telling her why she was here. Because there was no simple way to lay it all out there—her marriage ending, Tucker's wedding, or falling for Luke only to find out she could lose him in a way she hadn't anticipated. Brain damage. What did that even mean? There were so many possibilities, and all of them scared the crap out of her. Why couldn't he see that?

She pulled forward, parking along the curb, then tried unsuccessfully to steady her breathing before her mom threw open the driver's-side door and pulled Lily out, scooping her into a hug.

This—*this* was what she needed, the support of the one person who loved her without question, who was always there, even when Lily was too afraid to tell her the truth.

"Oh, sweetheart," the woman said. "It's been too long." She squeezed Lily tight for several long seconds before stepping back, hands still on her daughter's shoulders. "Let me look at you!" And she did just that, eyes roaming from Lily's head to her toes, then back up again. Except for her mom's longer blond hair pulled back into a messy bun, it was like looking at her own reflection. At forty-three, her mom didn't look a day over thirty. And in her own present state, Lily was sure *she* looked like the older one.

"You're gorgeous as always," her mom said. "But something's wrong. Tell me everything."

Lily forced a laugh, then crossed her arms so she wouldn't fidget. "Everything's *fine*. I've just been driving for eight hours. That'll put a damper on anyone's mood." *Or* give a girl enough time with her thoughts that she second-guesses all of her life choices at least six times an hour. "How about *you* tell me about this house?" She raised a brow even as her stomach sank. She and her mom used to know everything about each other. Now here she was at a house she didn't know existed with three years and as many weeks' worth of baggage to unload.

Her mom grabbed her hand. "Come on. We'll order pizza, have some wine, and we'll start with you telling me why you called at six in the morning to ask if you could come home for a bit. You know my answer will always be yes, by the way, right?"

Lily nodded. Ava had picked her up from Luke's without batting an eyelash. Then she'd spent the morning packing—mostly cooking and food storage gear—compiling a list of items and ingredients she'd need to purchase once she got to Phoenix, and composing a text to Luke—one she was sure would make him angrier than any of the arguments they'd had in three long years.

"Pizza and wine sound pretty perfect," she said.

Her mom narrowed her gaze. "You're not even going to fight me on the pizza—tell me anything other than homemade tastes like shit?"

Lily blew out a breath. "I just want one night off," she told the other woman. "Because I sort of need to cook for a small wedding while I'm here." She forced a smile that came out more like a wince.

"Do I even want to know what's in that trunk of yours?" her mom asked.

She let out a nervous laugh. "Just tell me you have room in your fridge and freezer and we'll be all set."

And without another word, the two women unloaded everything from a KitchenAid mixer to a box of various spices to multisize glass storage containers. Basically, Lily had moved her kitchen from Oak Bluff to Phoenix. It was almost as if she had no intention of moving it back.

But she had to go back—for the wedding at the very least. After that?

It took forty-five minutes of rearranging the fridge and freezer, two—okay *three*—glasses of merlot, and one piece of pizza with every topping imaginable before Lily finally broke the silence—her mom having waited patiently for her to make the first move.

She sat cross-legged on the floor in front of the wooden coffee table and finished the last drop of wine in her glass and met her mom's gaze.

She sucked in a breath, hoping it was enough to get

everything out and in the open. "So…Tucker and I got divorced. He's getting remarried in less than a week to this gorgeous, famous, *pregnant* Food Network star who I almost killed with raspberries because I'm catering their wedding. Not that I *knew* it was Tucker's wedding I was catering when I agreed to do it, but you know me—not really good at saying no once I've already said yes. And also it's not like I have a job or anything, since I let him buy me out of BBQ on the Bluff, so my whole new career is sort of riding on this wedding. Then there's the small issue of falling for Tucker's best friend, who was this unbelievable jerk but then somehow turned out not to be until I found out that if he gets one more concussion—which he probably will when he rides this stupid bull—he could suffer permanent brain damage. Or worse. I googled what happens to people who get multiple concussions. He could—I mean, he's risking his *life*, and I'm terrified of losing him. So rather than support him taking a risk he claims he's totally capable of handling, I bailed."

She loved him, and she bailed. Oh God. That was what fear did to her. It turned her into her father.

Her chest heaved as she gasped for more oxygen, her verbal vomit more taxing than she'd anticipated.

"I've been so scared of loving someone and being left that *I* became the leaver. I thought Tucker and I would be safe from that. I fell in love with the picture he painted of what our life would be like, and I still messed up."

Her mom's gaze remained fixed on Lily as she sipped slowly from her own wineglass. Her eyes were neither wide nor narrowed. In fact, her expression hadn't changed at all, which was more frightening than all the scenarios Lily had imagined, because in this one, she had *zero* clue what her mom was thinking.

Finally, her mom set her glass down and rested her hands on the coffee table in front of her. "But you didn't love *him.* And he fell for someone else and cheated on you."

Lily's mouth fell open.

"You didn't answer your phone on your birthday," she said matter-of-factly. "So I called Tucker. Figured I'd catch you two out celebrating or something."

Lily's eyes burned. "You—you knew?" she asked, voice shaking. "You've known for almost three weeks?"

Her mom cleared her throat, and Lily swore the woman's green eyes darkened. "He moved out six months ago." A tear slipped down Lily's cheek, and she swiped it away with the back of her hand. "What in the world made you think you couldn't *tell* me?"

And that was all it took for the floodgates to open. She'd worked so hard to hold it together—not just when her marriage fell apart. But she guessed she'd been holding it together for fifteen long years.

"Because," she said, her word a hiccupping sob. "I feel like I let you down—and facing that felt harder than facing the end of my marriage. You wanted more for me than—"

"Than *I* got. Oh, sweetie. I don't believe you could ever let me or anyone else down."

She'd let Luke down, though, hadn't she? Running like she had? Turned out she didn't know how to stay, not when things got this hard.

"I'm just like him," she said. "Aren't I? Instead of sticking things out, even when they get rough as hell, I bolt."

And there it was—a lifetime of plotting and planning, ensuring she would do better than the man who hadn't loved her enough to even stay in touch—and she'd gone and turned right into him.

Her mom pulled her close, cradling her head against

her chest as she smoothed Lily's hair off her tear-soaked cheeks.

"You're *you*, baby girl," her mom said in that voice that always soothed her as a child, that made her believe everything would be okay as long as they were together. "The only person you ever need to be is *you*. And it's your choice who that is—whether you're the one who stays..." Her chest heaved, and Lily's head rose and fell. "Or goes," she added. "But you can't leave *me*," she said. "I don't care if you're in California or in a different hemisphere. Don't you cut me off because you think I'll be disappointed in you. I've got your back. *Always*. No matter how much you think you've screwed up. I shouldn't have let you think that my baggage had to be yours."

Lily let out something between a laugh and a sob. Then she straightened and met her mom's gaze.

"It's okay to mess up," her mom added. "Learn from it. Get over it. And then let yourself off the hook. Or you might miss the best parts of life." She winked. "It's how I got *you*."

"I missed you," Lily admitted. Because God she had. "And I'm sorry I didn't call." She gave her mom a pointed look. "But you didn't tell me about the house, either."

The other woman blew out a breath. "I was waiting for you to come to me, giving you your space. Sometimes I forget that I still need to *mom* you, though." She put air quotes around the word.

Lily laughed.

"So the inn I've been working at the past few years? It got bought out about six months ago." Her brows drew together, and she hesitated before saying more.

This time Lily's expression fell. "You...you lost your job?" She didn't get it. How could her mom afford this place?

Her mom shook her head, and the corners of her mouth turned up. "The new owner—he asked me to apply for a managerial position—front desk manager." Her brows rose. "And I *got* it!"

Lily flung herself at her mother as all her words caught in her throat. She squeezed her into a hug—a hug that tried to convey everything from the past six months and more.

"You know..." her mom began and then paused. "I was still sort of young and naive when you left after college."

Lily could tell more was coming, so she just listened. Not that she knew what to say anyway.

"Hell, I've been pretty clueless throughout this whole parenting gig, and I'm not sure if it's an age thing or if all parents feel like imposters. But the truth is, I was so, so scared of you getting hurt the way I did that I might have overcorrected. You know?"

Lily nodded against her mom's shoulder even though she wasn't quite sure she understood.

"I never, *ever* saw you as a mistake—despite what my family or your dad's family thought about us having you so young. I've messed up a lot at this whole parenting gig. I'm aware of that. But every time I did it was because I loved you." She blew out a long breath. "So we both married the wrong men. It happens. But you have to let go of the guilt of your mistakes—of the fear of repeating them. Or you will miss out on so much of the joy."

Lily sucked in a breath. *Let go*. How many times had Luke tried to make her see that?

She straightened, looking her mom square in the eye.

"But I am so damned scared," she admitted.

Her mom gave her a slow nod. "Of what?"

Lily shrugged. "Everything? If I let go—if I give in to what I can't control, I could still lose."

Her shot at a new career.

Her confidence.

Her heart.

Her mom smiled. “What have you already lost because you couldn’t?” she asked.

Lily forced a smile. “I’m sorry I disappeared.”

Her mom raised her brows. “Make it up to me by telling me about this bull rider?” She leaned back and raised her brows at her daughter.

Lily laughed, even as a tear escaped.

“Luke,” she said. “His name... is Luke.”

Four days later, with after-hours use of the inn kitchen where her mother worked, Lily and her mom had prepared everything from butternut squash ravioli to her can’t-go-wrong, crowd favorite, no-one-is-allergic, lemon curd wedding cake. She’d done it—without a staff or any other funding aside from the initial deposit and what she’d earned from Tucker buying her out of BBQ on the Bluff. Now she’d either pull this off and get her name on the map, or she’d be back at square one.

She closed the trunk, all equipment packed and all prepared food in airtight containers and coolers.

“Are you going to see him before the wedding?” her mom asked.

Lily shrugged. “It’s in two days. I don’t know if there will even be a chance.” She’d gotten his voice mail but hadn’t known how to respond. She didn’t want to say the wrong thing. She needed to plan it out, get it right.

Lily rolled her eyes and shook her head.

“What is it?” her mom asked.

“Old habits,” Lily said. “Letting fear take the wheel and all.”

Her mom smiled wistfully. “Your dad walking out was

rough, but I have no regrets because I know I did the best I could to keep us all happy. I fought for him, and when he still left, I fought for you to have the best life I could give you. It was scary as hell, all of it. But if you let fear get the better of you when things get tough, then all you'll ever learn is how to run farther and farther away."

Lily sucked in a shuddering breath. She had run—straight out of Phoenix as soon as she'd graduated, then from Tucker the second she knew he'd cheated, and now from Luke. But this was different. So very different.

"He could get hurt," she said. "Irreparably."

"Or he could be fine," her mom countered.

Lily nodded. "I might have asked him not to ride, though..."

Her mom laughed softly. "And now you think he's choosing the rodeo over you. Something it seems he's worked toward for quite a long time—and a relationship that's barely gotten off the ground and you've already got one foot out the door?"

She groaned. "I don't want to be a runner. I don't want to be *him*."

Her mother's eyes softened. "Oh, honey. He wasn't a bad guy. He just made a bad decision. Did I hope one day he'd come back and fight for us? Sure. But even if he tried to, I made myself pretty hard to find after everything went down."

"Did you ever look for him?" Lily asked, something she'd always been afraid of knowing. But now seemed like the right time for putting it all out there.

"No," her mom said. "I fought for us until he left. After that, I wanted to be chased. I wanted someone to fight for me. And he didn't. So that was that."

Her mom pulled her into a hug.

"Only you know what you can handle," she said. "And once you figure that out, you'll have some decisions to make."

And she had eight-plus hours to think about those decisions—and still not feel any less terrified when she rolled into her driveway than when she'd hopped on the highway.

She waited until she'd unpacked and stored all the food, until she knew he'd be done with whatever his day's work entailed, before starting to compose a text.

Hey. Can we talk? I could call you. Or you could call me. Or whatever. We could just text. I just...

"Sound like an idiot?" she said aloud. "Don't know what the hell I want but am hoping you can help me figure it out and then maybe still not get on that bull and put your life in the hands—or I guess *horns*—of some wild beast?"

Screw it.

She closed out of the text and went for the only thing she couldn't chicken out of once it started—a phone call.

It rang once. Twice. So she knew if it went to voice mail before the fourth ring it would be him deciding to send her there. And she wouldn't blame him if he did.

But he picked up before the third, and she felt like she'd just tipped over the top of a roller coaster.

"Lily," he said, his voice low and controlled, only the slightest hint of surprise at hearing from her. But she caught it, and that along with him picking up the phone jolted her confidence enough *not* to hang up and throw her cell across the room.

"Hi," she said, then worried her bottom lip between her teeth. "It's—good to hear your voice."

"Jesus," he said quietly, but he'd meant for her to hear.

"You blow my cover with my family, disappear for five days without calling me back, and now you want to say *hi.*"

It wasn't a question, just a cold realization. Because that's exactly what she'd done.

"Look," she said. "I know you won't believe me, but I told Jack so that someone would have your back when I was too afraid to. I know I didn't handle things well, but I'm back now, and I was hoping we could talk. *Really* talk."

She heard something that sounded like a man yelling through a loudspeaker, and Luke swore under his breath. "I'm at the arena in Anaheim. Something got messed up with my medical release being sent over, so I drove down to deliver it myself and get the lay of the land."

There was a long pause, and because Lily couldn't stand uncomfortable silences, she had to fill them.

"So you're still doing it?" she asked. "You're going to ride that stupid bull?"

She covered her mouth as soon as she said it, but it was too late. The words—and her fear—were out there, and she couldn't take any of it back.

"Dammit, Lily. Yes. I'm still riding the *stupid* bull. If that's the discussion you're looking to have, it's over. Nothing to discuss. Doctor signed off, saying my ribs are healed enough and that I know the other risks. So that's it. End of conversation."

His voice was tight. She'd pushed him too far.

"Luke, I didn't mean—that's not why I called." This was why, at the very least, she should have planned out what she was going to say. When it came to Luke, the words always came first and the thinking second. So far that hadn't boded well for her.

"Then why did you?" he asked.

And because it was either honesty or silence, she told him the truth.

"I don't know."

Because I'm in love with you? Because even though I already lost you, I'm scared of losing you in a whole other way?

He blew out a breath. "I'll see you at the wedding," he said finally.

Shit. This was a mistake. She'd messed up even more. Maybe when they saw each other…

She swallowed hard. "Yeah. Of course. I'm sorry for—I'm just sorry."

"Bye, Lily."

She ended the call.

CHAPTER TWENTY-TWO

The ranch had become wedding central. The small bridal party took over the living room, the bride's two sisters shielding her from Tucker every time he'd walk through the kitchen.

"She's pregnant," he called over his shoulder as he and Luke strode through the back door to meet Jack and Walker on the deck. "I think that whole tradition thing is out the window."

"Then give me this *one* little thing, Tucker Green!" Sara called back, and both men chuckled as they stepped out into the crisp November afternoon.

Tucker handed each of them a longneck before even saying hello, but Luke shook his head.

"Competing tomorrow," he said. "Need to stay clean so I can head back to Anaheim after the ceremony."

"How was two weeks of yoga and being unplugged?" Jack asked Tucker, brows raised.

Tucker pulled his phone from his pocket and opened his e-mail app, then held it out for all to see. "Three hundred and forty-two unread messages. I figure I'll just delete and start over again. And the voice mails—I haven't even started with those yet."

"About our call that got dropped—" Luke began, but Tucker shook his head.

"Hold on. I need to get a look at this," he said. He gave him the once-over, and Luke straightened his tie and brushed nonexistent dust from his tuxedo jacket.

"I'm impressed, Everett," he said. "Haven't seen you in almost a month, and there's not a scratch on you. I half expected to see those damned boots peeking out from the bottom of your pants."

Luke rolled his eyes. "Thanks, asshole. And don't worry. The boots are in the truck ready for the drive to Anaheim in a couple hours."

Jack laughed and clapped his younger brother on the shoulder. "Good to know you use the same term of endearment for those outside the family."

Luke cleared his throat. "Just Tucker," he said. "Brother from another mother."

No one said anything after that, so Luke went back on his promise to himself and grabbed a beer—just one—so he could toast his friend.

"Shit," Walker said. "Someone's about to get sentimental."

Luke shook his head. "I'm not good with sentimental, so I'll make this simple. To the future—and all the best for you and Sara."

Tucker raised his brows. "I'll drink to that."

And they all did, just as Tucker's parents, brother, two nephews, and sister burst through the door and out onto the deck.

"Look at my gorgeous son!" his mother called before grabbing his cheeks in her palms and kissing him square on the forehead. "Don't mess this one up, okay? Especially with my next grandchild on the way!"

Walker's brows rose at the sight, but for once he kept his opinion to himself.

And then it was just a mass of hugging, congratulations, and yelps from inside whenever someone thought Sara got too close to a window.

"Another round before we head to the winery!" Tucker's father exclaimed, and bottles were being handed in what seemed like every direction.

Jack put his arm around his younger brother and pulled him to the side.

"He has *no* fucking clue. Does he?"

Luke's jaw tightened. "No clue about what?"

He was just being a dick. Of course Luke knew what his brother was referring to, and Jack knew he knew, so he said nothing, waiting him out with the quiet patience that sometimes drove Luke up the goddamn wall.

"Look. I tried. I caught him right when he and Sara got to the retreat, and the call dropped before I could tell him. This is the first chance I've had since he's been back." He scrubbed a hand over his face. "And what the hell am I supposed to tell him now? That I'm in love with his ex-wife even though she wants nothing to do with me if I hop on the bull tomorrow?"

Jack blew out a breath, but Luke cut him off.

"You're not going there. Are you? Because I seem to remember you offering your begrudging support. Also I'm not above hitting you at a wedding, since technically the wedding hasn't happened yet."

Jack laughed. As bad as things ever got, he knew as well as his brother did that it wouldn't really come to fists. A standoff was one thing, but the Everett brothers didn't grow up the way they did to then raise a hand to one another.

Sure, Walker raised a drunken fist to plenty of strangers, but never to Jack or Luke.

"I'm not going there," Jack assured him. "You have my begrudging support. But if you get injured—"

"I won't," Luke interrupted. "Not if I can help it."

"What I was going to say"—Jack took a long swig of his beer—"was that *if* you get injured, I'm here for you. All right?"

Luke pressed his lips together and nodded. "Thanks."

They clinked glasses and both drank.

"I was trained and ready," Luke said. "For the last ride. But I got—distracted. That day—"

"Was the day Lily came to finalize her divorce and unwittingly signed up to cater her ex-husband's wedding."

"Jesus," Luke hissed under his breath. "You knew."

His brother grinned. "I know I missed a lot the ten years I was gone," Jack said. "But it doesn't mean I forgot how to read you. Plus you have the easiest damn tell."

Luke crossed his arms. "And what the hell is that?"

Jack raised his bottle. "You're only ever a prick when there's a girl involved." He drained the rest of the beer.

"I have not been…" He groaned. "Fine I've been a fucking prick." For too long. He squinted into the soon-to-be-setting sun. "She's there? At the winery?"

Jack nodded. "She's got most of the staff from BBQ on the Bluff working for her on Tucker's dime. Ava took Owen to her parents and then was going to set up shop with Lily and make sure everything was going according to plan. I haven't heard anything about hot plates catching on fire or ice sculptures melting, so I'm going with no news being good news."

Luke's brows rose. "You're kidding about the ice sculpture, right?"

Jack shrugged, and the corner of his mouth quirked up.

"I made a huge mess of things. Didn't I?" Luke asked. Yes, Lily had run. But Luke hadn't chased her. After she'd betrayed his trust to Jack, he'd let his pride get in the way instead of doing what he should have the night he met her—telling her the truth. The whole truth.

He loved her—had loved her for three damn years but had grown so used to burying the truth that when it finally rose to the surface, he hadn't the slightest clue how to make heads or tails of it.

Walker sauntered over just as those words left his mouth, and the shit-eating grin on his face told Luke he had heard every one of them.

"Made a mess doing what?" Walker asked but didn't wait for Luke to answer. "Falling for your buddy's girl? Or sleeping with her before telling him?"

Luke looked over his shoulder to the Green family, who thankfully weren't paying attention to the three brothers holding private court over his mess of a love life.

"What time is it?" Luke asked, not engaging his younger brother with a response. He knew Lily was working, but maybe there was time to find her and figure this all out before the ceremony got under way.

"Hey!" a voice called from the back door, and everyone's attention moved in that direction to find Sara's sister, Erica, pointing at a nonexistent watch on her wrist. "Ceremony in thirty minutes. You all need to head over first so the bride can make her entrance. Go! Go!"

Luke shrugged. That answered his question.

"Hey, Tuck," he called over to his friend. "Need a ride?"

Tucker's father slapped his son on the back. "Thanks, but no thanks," he said to Luke. "I'd like to have a little prewedding chat with my son before he says *I do*. Again."

Tucker winced, and that one small expression brought Luke back to that morning in Lily's kitchen after the farmers market—to the way it was clear his friend still cared about her.

And he still would now. The question was whether or not he would care enough to want her to be happy no matter who the other guy was—and if there was still a chance *he* could be the one to make her happy. Because that ship might have already sailed.

"All right," Luke said. "I'll see you over there. Do me a favor and meet me in the back office. I need to talk to you before the ceremony."

"Sure thing," Tucker said absently. Since Erica stood like a bouncer in the doorway, making sure the groom did not catch an accidental glimpse of the bride, his family ushered him down the steps of the deck and around to the front yard.

"Well, boys?" Luke said, his heart starting to beat a little faster than normal. "Let's see if I survive this wedding and make it to that damned rodeo tomorrow."

Walker drained the rest of his bottle and shook his head. "You're toast, brother."

"Thanks for the vote of confidence," Luke said, his throat tight. Because his brother was probably right.

Luke didn't even recognize the winery when he walked in. The drop cloths were gone, revealing the travertine tiled floor. While the wood wasn't yet up on the walls, they'd all been painted. There were tables with chairs covered in white cloth and a petal-strewn aisle for the ceremony. And a string quartet played something Luke didn't recognize, but it was beautiful just the same. The place looked fit for a wedding. Good thing that was why they were there.

He saw Ava behind the bar, which looked to be the food service area and was already set with cold appetizers for immediately following the ceremony.

He cleared his throat as he approached. "Where is she?" he asked.

Ava—her auburn waves resting on the thin straps of her blue dress—crossed her arms and blinked, feigning innocence.

"Who?" she asked.

"Come on, Ava. I don't have time for—"

Her gaze softened, and she blew out a breath. "How are you two going to fix this?" she asked, her tone less than encouraging.

"I—I don't know," he admitted, using those same words Lily had when she called last night—when he'd bitten his tongue hoping she'd say something to fix it all when he knew she hadn't messed things up on her own.

"Jack said you're still riding tomorrow." He didn't miss the hint of disappointment in her voice.

His jaw tightened. "Would you have asked Jack to give up his future for you?"

She narrowed her eyes. "You know the answer to that, Lucas Everett. You *know* that everything I did—mistakes or no—was so he could *have* the future he wanted. The future he *needed.* But you get how this isn't the same, right? You get that you might not have the future you think you will after this?"

He shook his head, for the first time with certainty. "I'm not going to fuck up tomorrow," he insisted. "Not if I make everything right today."

Ava sighed. "I hope you're right, Luke. I really do. We'll be there, you know. Jack, Owen, me, and Walker."

"But not Lily."

Ava shook her head.

He opened his mouth to say something else but then looked over her shoulder to where Tucker was just walking into the office.

"Shit," he said. "I'll be right back."

He pulled at the collar of his shirt—at the tie around his

neck—and strode toward either certain death or—no, it was most likely certain death. He'd have preferred the bull. That had to be safer than the fallout of what he was about to tell his friend.

When he got to the office, Tucker was leaning against the desk—arms crossed, his legs out in front of him, one ankle hooked over the other.

"So," he said as Luke stopped just inside the room, the door not even shut before he leveled Luke with his knowing gaze. "Is this where you tell me you're in love with my ex-wife?"

CHAPTER TWENTY-THREE

Lily stood up from where she was squatting behind the bar and dusted off her white chef's coat.

"Do you think he saw me?" she asked.

Ava gave her a pointed stare. "You two are ridiculous," she said. "Seriously. Just go talk to him."

Lily shook her head. "I have to make sure everything is ready before—"

"Enough," Ava said, cutting her off. "Look around you, Lil. Everything is all set. Vegetables are chopped. Food is cooked."

She pointed to the three-tiered lemon curd wedding cake that was simply yet elegantly decorated with white fondant and yellow rose petals, all of which had taken Lily's entire day to prepare yesterday—the one item she couldn't finish in Phoenix.

"The cake is *gorgeous*," Ava continued. "And you've got the whole restaurant staff here taking care of everything else. You did it. You pulled this off. Now it's time to go and fix things with you two already. Because trust me when I tell you that when you fall for one of the Everetts, you never truly right yourself."

Lily's brows rose. "I don't know how to be in love like that," she said.

Ava laughed. “How do you know you’re not already?”

Lily’s stomach flipped back and forth, and she thought she might be ill.

“Where did he go?” she asked.

Ava pointed toward the back of the winery and beamed. “The office. I think he’s with Tucker.”

She blew out a breath. *Perfect*. She could tell Luke how she felt about him with her ex-husband there as witness—right before he married his pregnant bride. This kind of thing happened every day, right?

So she stepped out from behind the circular bar and strode toward the door, hoping that her future lay behind it. Her knees wobbled, but with every step they grew stronger, as did her resolve.

She loved Luke Everett. She loved him. And there was no getting around it. He’d just have to deal with it, and *she’d* have to find a way to deal with the fact that tomorrow he might get injured, worse than he ever had before.

But he also might not.

He was good at what he did. *So* damn talented. And sexy. And she was ready to burst through the door when she realized it wasn’t closed all the way, and she could hear voices rising inside. Even though she knew she shouldn’t, she leaned against the doorframe and listened, unable to see anything other than the shaft of waning sunlight filtering through the small open crack.

“Three years?” she heard Tucker say, incredulity and something unrecognizable in his tone. “What the hell am I supposed to do knowing you’ve been in love with my wife since the day you fucking met her?”

Lily sucked in a breath, then threw her hand over her mouth.

Tucker wasn’t talking to Luke. He couldn’t have been.

Because for three years—up until that night after the ER—he hadn't been able to stand her. They—they didn't like each other. The feeling was mutual. It wasn't—

"*Ex*-wife, Tucker." His voice held a quiet control she hadn't heard before, but it was unmistakably Luke. "The second you left the bar with her that first night, I buried whatever I thought I felt. It was just—I don't know—physical attraction. At least that's what I thought. I didn't realize you were gonna marry her. And I didn't—I didn't *know* I was fucking falling in love with her."

Footsteps sounded on the tile within. Someone was pacing, and she guessed it was Tucker. But considering that she couldn't exactly breathe at the moment, she wasn't entirely sure. A lack of oxygen to the brain could be messing with her perception.

"She told you about the cheating, didn't she? After she promised she wouldn't. This is some sort of retribution? You sleeping with her and then spouting some bullshit about being in love—the guy who doesn't do love?" Tucker asked, and Lily's cheeks burned.

How dare he accuse her? What the hell did he think—

"You…what?" Luke's voice held a measured calm that did nothing to mask the fury underneath. "You cheated on her, and she kept your pathetic secret? You told me you met Sara on that trip to Santa Barbara that was supposed to *clear your head* after Lily walked out. Tell me she's not out there preparing food for the woman you slept with behind her back. Tell me I haven't been piling on the guilt for weeks when you've been lying for months."

Luke's calm was burning away.

Tucker cleared his throat. "So you didn't know," he said softly.

A throat cleared.

"I was shit to her for three years because I loved her. Her plans and her lists and grabbing life by the balls? She is the strongest person I know, and I made her think otherwise because I thought I was protecting our friendship."

"She didn't love me, Everett."

"That didn't give you the right to hurt her. Jesus." He paused. "I beat myself up for three years telling myself I didn't deserve what you had, and you pissed it away."

"I know," Tucker said.

"Then you lied to me, convinced her to lie for you. For what? So you could uphold some goddamn image?"

Lily guessed Luke was pacing. She could picture it, the action so like him.

"Yes!" Tucker admitted. "So you wouldn't look at me like I look at myself in the damned mirror. You saw me as better, and I almost believed it. Well? Now you know I'm not."

"I'm not gonna ruin your wedding," Luke said. "But we're not okay."

There was a beat of silence, then Luke again. "I still love her. I came here to ask you for your blessing, but she was right. You have *no* claim on her, Tuck. No one does. You don't deserve her friendship, but she's still here for you."

"I know."

Still. Luke loved her *still.* That word hung in the silence between the two men—hung now like a weight around Lily's neck.

All these years that he'd been so horrible to her...that she'd wondered what she'd done or why. He'd loved her.

He *still* loved her.

"You wanna hit me or something?" Tucker asked, resigned. "I sure as hell deserve it."

Luke huffed out a breath. "I came here expecting you'd want to hit me. Look how the tables have turned."

Tucker let out a nervous laugh. "If I hit that pretty face of yours and ruin pictures, Everett? Sara will have my goddamn balls."

"You gonna get it right with her?" Luke asked.

"God I hope so," Tucker said. "I'm gonna be a father. I think it's finally time to grow up." He paused for a beat. "Does Lily know how you feel? Does she know how long—?"

"No," Luke said plainly.

"Then I guess you've got some owning up of your own to do." Tucker sighed. "Maybe this is your chance to get it right, too."

There were more words after that, and Lily thought she heard the warning of footsteps, but she was stuck. Frozen where she stood. Only when the door flew open, both men's eyes widening when they saw her there, did she stumble back from the impact of it all.

"Lily. Jesus," Tucker said, then grabbed her hand and squeezed. "I'm sorry. For everything." Then he kissed her on the cheek and headed to his place in the back of the aisle where his parents were waiting.

"Hey," Luke said, his voice tentative. But he made no move to step closer to her. A *smart* move. Because Lily had no idea what she would do if he did.

"I..." Her voice shook on that one word. "I thought you hated me."

"Lily..." He did step forward this time, and she flinched.

A muscle ticked in Luke's jaw, but he halted where he stood. "*Lily...*" he said again, her name a plea, but she shook her head.

"You took my roommate home with you that night. You slept with her."

"And you went home with Tucker. We messed up," he said. "*I* messed up, but I'm trying to make it right."

"Three years, though?" she asked. "Even after my marriage fell apart—did your brothers know?"

He dropped her gaze for just a second, eyes shifting to the floor before finding hers again.

"Oh my God. They *knew*. All this time I was the punch line to some twisted joke."

He reached for her, then thought better of it, hand dropping to his side. "Only Walker knew for sure. Jack suspected, but I didn't know that until tonight."

Her eyes widened. "And Ava?" she asked, voice shaking.

Luke shook his head. "Not if Jack only just figured it out. No."

Lily blew out a breath, wrapping her arms around her torso. "At least the friendship was real," she mumbled.

"So were *we*," he insisted. "So *are* we."

"It wasn't the truth," she told him. "It was enough that you were keeping the seriousness of your injuries from me. But this is *us*, Luke. The truth about us. How am I supposed to reconcile the way we treated each other for *three* years with this?"

His hands fisted at his side. She wanted to take in the vision before her—Luke out of his jeans and boots and gorgeous in his tux—but all she could feel was her throat tightening, her blood pounding in her ears.

"I had to keep the truth from myself, too," he said through gritted teeth. "And from Tucker. I had no choice. And it wasn't like you felt differently about *me*. You were so happy to blame Tucker's behavior on my influence—the guy who doesn't do serious."

She sucked in a breath. "*You* were the one who told me that."

"And you were all too quick to believe it."

He ran a hand through the beautiful blond hair she'd

imagined touching just minutes ago before she made it to this door. But everything was different now.

"I should have told you," he said. "After that first damned kiss, I should have. But I never thought you saw me like you saw him. Tuck messed up, yes. But he's the kind of guy you put on a pedestal. And I know you had him up there. I'm the kind of guy you run to when that pedestal gets knocked down."

"That's not fair," she said. But that wasn't entirely true.

Luke spent so much of his life not feeling worthy. What part had she unwittingly played in reinforcing that belief?

"I did this all wrong," he said. "I got spooked in the beginning, because in my eyes, you were still Tucker's. It doesn't change the fact that I love you."

She inhaled a trembling breath, and he let out a nervous laugh. "I've been so goddamn terrified of saying that, and this wasn't how I planned to do it..."

Butterflies danced in her belly, but at the same time her heart sank. The truth was that nothing was what she'd thought it had been.

"I thought we were falling in love," she said. "Together."

"We were," he insisted. "We *did*."

She shook her head, hands crossed over her chest. "I feel like we lost three years. I feel like I lost something I never had. And now tomorrow?" She couldn't bring herself to say it—to think it. "How do I know you won't leave that arena tomorrow on a stretcher?"

He shrugged. "You let go and have faith that I won't."

The quartet's music changed to the "Wedding March," and both of their heads jerked toward the aisle to see Tucker and his parents as they started to walk.

"Shit," he hissed. "*Shit.* I have to go. I need to head back down to Anaheim tonight, but, Lily...we need to finish this."

She nodded slowly and then let out a shaky breath as she watched him walk away—and then down the small aisle where he stood next to the groom. Who was once *her* groom. And it was all just too surreal. She held his gaze for as long as she could, until it was Sara's time to make her entrance. Even Luke couldn't ignore the beautiful bride, and as she strode toward her husband to be, Luke finally looked away.

Lily made it through the vows. She watched her ex-husband marry the woman he truly loved, and even though there was still a part of her yet unhealed, she was okay.

"I just watched my husband marry another woman, and I'm still standing," she said softly to herself. "I freaking did it."

She pumped her fist in the air ever so slightly, even if she was the only one who saw. Then, half laughing and half sobbing, she sneaked into the office to collect herself—and make sure the guests didn't see the caterer crying. That might not be the best way to sell the menu.

She stepped inside the small bathroom within, pulling the door shut behind her.

Ava was right. Everything turned out perfectly as far as the food was concerned. She'd get herself together and get back out there and figure out how to reconcile the past three years now that she was in love with Luke Everett.

Lily braced her hands on the porcelain of the sink and tilted her head toward the mirror.

"He *loves* you, you idiot. The only thing that's changed is that he's loved you for longer than you've loved him. And you're still scared."

She splashed some water on her face and laughed.

"Okay," she said aloud to her reflection. "Be scared. But be scared with the man you're in love with."

She grabbed the doorknob and yanked hard, then gasped as she stumbled backward into the small bathroom's wall—doorknob in her hand. *Not* attached to the door.

"Noooo," she groaned, remembering Jack's warning that first day she was here to sign her final divorce papers. She'd been in such a mental fog she'd even done something as stupid as hiring herself out to cater her ex-husband's wedding. The muffled music continued to play beyond the walls of her confined space. Of course everything was going to come full circle like this. It was too fitting not to.

"Help?" she said, her voice barely a squeak. She was not about to be the ex-wife caterer who ruined her former husband's wedding.

So she waited. Someone would find her. Someone would notice her phone and purse on the shelf behind the bar.

For now she plopped down onto the toilet seat, shoulders slumping. And the "Wedding March" played on.

"Lily? Honey, are you in here?"

Lily wasn't sure what time it was when she heard Ava call her name, only that she'd never been so happy to hear it in all of her twenty-seven years.

"Yes!" she cried. "Oh my God, I thought I was going to change my address to this tiny little room. I guess the bright side is running water, right? I could probably take a nice shower in the sink."

"Wait…what are you doing in there?"

Lily let out a hysterical laugh. "I'm stuck!" she cried. "The damned doorknob came off in my hand. Is the crew handling hors d'oeuvres okay?"

Ava swore under her breath. "Didn't one of the guys tell you about the door?"

Lily rolled her eyes. "Yes. But I wasn't exactly thinking straight. I'd just found out that Luke—wait, are you going to let me out, or do I have to tell you the whole story from here?"

She heard the unmistakable click of the handle on the other side turning, and then the door flew open.

Lily hopped up from her perch on the toilet seat, her knees stiff and back in major need of a stretch.

"Seriously. How long was I in there?" She chuckled, but Ava didn't even smile.

"Lily," she started, "you've been in there for sixty minutes. You missed the cocktails and the best man and maid of honor speeches."

Okay, so that was kind of a lot to miss when she was sort of in charge of the cocktail hour.

"Why do you sound like I forgot your birthday?" Lily asked. "Is everything okay with the food? I didn't…poison anyone. Did I?"

Ava shook her head. "He thought you left," she said. "We all thought you left until your phone rang and I found your purse behind the bar. Jack looked for your car. Then we remembered you took the BBQ on the Bluff van with the crew."

Lily's eyes narrowed. "What are you *not* telling me?" she asked.

Ava's teeth skimmed her bottom lip. "When you didn't turn up after Luke's speech, he figured that was your answer." She swallowed. "He's gone, Lil."

Lily pushed past her friend and out into the winery, where the reception was in full swing, the small ceremony area now a dance floor.

She scanned the crowd, searching for someone she knew wouldn't be there. He couldn't just be *gone*.

"He went home to pack?" she asked.

Ava shook her head. "Anaheim," was all she said, and that one word made Lily's stomach roil.

Luke was already *gone*?

"Answer?" she asked as she began to pace. "What answer? What was the question?"

Ava held up her own phone. "I recorded it," she said. "He is almost my brother-in-law after all." She pressed her lips into a smile. "You have a big decision to make, Lil. Do you want to watch this video before you decide?"

She took in the room. Food service was well under way. The cake was still standing, and the wine—courtesy of Ava's family vineyard—was flowing.

"I have to go," Lily said absently.

"You're still here!"

Lily spun at the sound of Tucker's voice to find him standing with his beautiful bride, both their eyes wide and blinking.

"Of course I'm still here!" she said, the adrenaline building. "I can't believe everyone thought I just took off."

Jack and Walker approached as the damning words left her mouth, and everyone gave her a glance that said exactly what she knew they were thinking.

You already ran off once.

She groaned. "Fine, okay. I freaked out last week, but I came *back*."

"Where the hell were you?" Jack asked.

"Locked in the bathroom," Ava told him.

He chuckled. "I thought I told you about that door."

Lily threw her hands in the air. "Yeah, well, *you* try learning that the guy you've just fallen for—who's going to risk his life and ride a goddamn bull tomorrow—has been—"

"In love with you for three years?"

Ava, Jack, Walker, *and* Tucker all spoke at once like a Greek chorus.

She threw a hand over her mouth, holding back what felt like a rising sob, and nodded. "I need to go," she said again.

Everyone around her nodded.

Tears sprang from both eyes, and for the first time since she could remember, she didn't care that anyone saw her lose control.

"It's not too weird?" she asked, eyes turned toward Tucker.

He laughed. "Of course it's weird," he said. "But it also seems sorta right. There's no two people I want to see happy more than the two of you, so I guess it's fitting it should happen together." Sara kissed her new husband on the cheek, and Lily realized how happy she was for Tucker, too. Things didn't end well between them or in the right way, but they ended because *they* weren't right.

She and Luke were.

"The food…" she started to say, and Sara nodded.

"The food is delicious. Perfect. I'm going to recommend you to everyone I know. Maybe you'd even like to do a guest spot on my show sometime. We do wedding specials at least once a year."

Lily's heart felt like it would burst right through her rib cage. "Thank you."

"Go get him, Lil," Jack said.

Walker gave her a pointed stare as he loosened his tie and unbuttoned the top of his shirt.

"All this"—he waved his hand in the air—"happiness shit must be getting to me, so I'm only going to say this once. Luke is one of the good ones, and if you give him the chance he deserves, he *will* do right by you. And if you tell him I said that, I will deny it until my last breath."

Lily wrapped her arms around Walker's neck and squeezed him tight.

"I have a feeling you're one of the good ones, too," she whispered.

And just like that she was scrambling to find her purse, phone, and keys.

"My car's at the restaurant!" she gasped.

"I'll give you a ride," Jack said. "You ready?"

She nodded, hugged Ava once, and then followed Jack toward the door.

"Ayres Hotel!" Ava called after her. "And you didn't watch the video!" she added.

"Text it to me!" Lily said over her shoulder, and then she and Jack were out the door.

Whatever Luke said in that speech wasn't important right now. What mattered was getting to Anaheim.

Because she loved him, too.

CHAPTER TWENTY-FOUR

Luke stood with his hand braced against the tile as the hot water tried to ease the ache in his muscles—and failed miserably.

What was he thinking pulling a stunt like that after he'd already freaked her the hell out? He'd *thought* it was what she wanted. But maybe it was too much to put on her shoulders, in front of everyone.

He groaned.

Of course she ran and never looked back. It wasn't enough that she had to find everything out by overhearing him tell Tucker. Then he had to go and hijack the best man speech for his own selfish gain. *Not* that Tucker and Sara hadn't given him permission to do so. The results, however, were not at all what he'd hoped for, so here he was. Alone. Every muscle screaming with tension he knew had nothing to do with the three-hour drive or the final training he'd put himself through this week.

He slammed the water off and wrapped a towel around his waist. That's when he heard the frantic pounding on an adjacent wall.

Great. It was probably a room full of buckle bunnies partying it up the night before the competition.

He opened the bathroom door, ready to be *that* guy—the one who called the front desk to complain—and realized that the sound came from his door and not a rowdy neighbor's room.

He didn't bother to look through the peephole, didn't care who it was. He just wanted the damned pounding to stop.

"*What*?" he snapped, throwing the door open.

Then all his words, along with all of the oxygen, left him. Because there stood Lily, still in her chef's coat, black pants—and the cowboy hat he'd given her the day they rode Ace.

The whites of her eyes were pink, and he couldn't tell if it was from exhaustion or because she'd been crying. Despite everything, though, she was *smiling*, and the beating of his heart went into overdrive.

"Ava told me what hotel," she said hesitantly. "And Jack gave me your room number. Not that it's up to him, but Tucker gives us his blessing, and even Walker said some nice things about you that I'm not supposed to repeat because he'll deny them anyway."

She crossed and uncrossed her arms.

"You know, this is hard enough as it is," she went on. "But having to do it with you standing there all wet and in a towel is not helping me keep my focus."

He felt the corner of his mouth tug upward, but he was too terrified to let himself smile.

"You—*left*," he said, and like it had just happened, that virtual sock in the gut hit him harder than any fall off the back of a horse or bull.

She shook her head. "I was locked in the office bathroom." Then she rolled her eyes. "It's ridiculous. I know. And you Everetts better get that fixed before you start using that place on a regular basis. I didn't leave, Luke. I swear. Not until Ava found me and told me you were already gone." She looked down at what she was wearing, then back up at him. "It wasn't even in my planner to come here tonight."

She laughed. As she did, a tear escaped down her cheek, and he had to fight not to reach for her and brush it away.

"Then why, Lily?" he asked, scrubbing a hand over his jaw. "Why'd you come?"

"Why didn't you come for *me*?" she countered. "To Phoenix?"

He groaned. "You ran away—and made it damned clear you wanted space. I'm not running," he reminded her. "I told you that night, and I'm telling you now. I'm not walking away from this. From *us*."

She shrugged. "Then I guess you should know I came here tonight because I'm in love with you and didn't want you getting on that stupid bull tomorrow without knowing that."

Luke braced a hand against the doorframe to keep himself steady. He dropped his head, letting out a long, shaky breath. When he met her gaze again, it was like his whole world had shifted.

"I thought I had everything figured out. I saw what loving someone could do to a person—how it broke my father beyond repair, how it almost did the same to Jack. And I was so determined to save myself from that." He shook his head. "Then I meet you, and all my careful planning goes right out the fucking window."

A tentative smile spread across her face. "And here I thought I was the careful planner."

He laughed. "Not sure it worked out the way either of us wanted."

She swiped her fingers under one eye and then the other, clearing away the tears even as more fell.

"I'm starting to think the best parts of my life have come out of those unplanned moments. *Not* that some of those moments weren't the hardest parts of my life, but they led me down paths I would have been too scared to take otherwise." She took a steadying breath. "I didn't kiss you that day after your accident because I was looking for a rebound. I did it because despite how I *thought* you felt about me for three years, I felt something when I saw you like that."

His jaw tightened. "Every guy loves a pity kiss."

She groaned. "It wasn't pity, you...you impossible, gorgeous man. It was something I didn't fully understand then. But it had hurt to see you hurting." Her throat bobbed as she swallowed. "Just like it does now."

His chest ached. Because she saw right through him, no matter what mask he tried to wear.

"I should have told you," he said. "I didn't know the right way to do it."

She nodded. "I know. Sometimes there is no right way. There's just the truth."

And there it was. Maybe they'd had a messy beginning. And they were still in it. That was the beauty of it all. Wasn't it? They were just getting started. And they could fix what was broken—clean up that mess as they went.

He took a chance and stepped toward her. She didn't flinch this time. God how it had killed him when she did. Instead she leaned into his touch when he cupped her cheek in his palm.

"Then the truth is simple. I love you—have loved you for three goddamn years when I had no right to do so. And maybe I still haven't earned that right—"

She launched herself at him, her hat toppling to the ground as her arms wrapped around his neck and she pressed her lips to his.

"Didn't you hear me say I love you?" she asked, her mouth against his. "You've earned *every* right, as long as I've earned it from you."

He chuckled. "You don't need to earn anything from me, sweetheart. But I do think maybe I need to hear those three little words one more time to be sure."

She kissed him softly, and finally—*finally*—the tension melted from his shoulders, and the weight on his chest lifted.

"I love you, Luke Everett." She kissed him again. "I love you. *You.* Okay? It's why I ran back to Phoenix when I found out what could happen tomorrow, which was stupid and selfish and... That's not the person I want to be. Someone who runs." She was on her tiptoes, holding steady, with her hands gripping his shoulders as her green eyes stayed locked on his. "But it's also why I ran *here* tonight."

He kissed one tear-soaked eye, then the other, savoring the taste of salt on his lips, the trust he knew it took for her to let him see every part of her.

"Wait," he said, her earlier words registering. "You wanted to tell me all this before I got on the bull. You're... okay with me riding?"

She lowered herself to her regular height, hands splayed on his chest, and shook her head. "No," she said with measured resolve. "I will be there for you anyway. For your last ride. I know how hard it will be walking in there tomorrow knowing that. So I will be there—terrified—but cheering you on."

He held out a hand for her, and she took it and squeezed it tight.

"Stay with me tonight," he said.

She nodded, stepping over the threshold and into his room, closing the door behind her.

"I'm not going anywhere," she told him. "I promise."

She tugged his arm, leading him toward the bed.

"You didn't hear my proposal, then?"

She sucked in a breath, eyes going wide.

"Okay, bad choice of word." He laughed as she backed up against the mattress. "Look, sweetheart," he said with a wry grin. "I love you, but I'm not insane. I know we need time to figure this all out. I did ask you a question I thought you'd answered by bailing from the wedding—which I now know you did not do."

She pulled her phone out of her pocket. "I forgot about the video," she said. "Ava said she'd send it."

He waited as she opened the message and hit play to find it wasn't the whole speech. Just a clip—the part that was meant for her. He watched her watch him. And waited.

He stood at a microphone in front of the room, a flute of champagne in his hand.

"We're all here to celebrate Tucker and Sara, but we're also celebrating this rare thing they were able to find in each other." He paused and shook his head, letting out a nervous laugh. "For anyone who knows me," he continued, "I'm sure as hell not one to shy away from the spotlight, but this is a little different. So I'll just thank Tucker and Sara for letting me steal a bit of their thunder and say Lily, never have I ever loved anyone like I love you. Riding tomorrow means the world to me, but you mean more. I was so stubborn in making sure you understood me that I didn't take the time to understand you and how scared you were. I'll withdraw if that's what it takes to show you I'm all in, that I will fight for us like I should have three years ago. But if you believe in me like I believe in you, come with me tonight. Fight right alongside me, and after I own that bull, let's take our second chance at something *permanent*. All you have to do is come up here and say yes."

The tremble in his words was evident, and he remembered his earnest uncertainty as he looked past the sea of tables, searching for someone he soon realized wasn't there. Everyone else in the room looked for her, too.

"Come on, Lil," Ava mumbled into the phone. "Where are you?"

Then there were the indistinguishable murmurs among the guests.

And after an excruciating pause, Luke finally cleared his throat. "It was a long shot," he said matter-of-factly, but there was devastation behind that smile he wore as a mask. He hoped she couldn't hear it. "To Tucker and Sara," he said, then drained the entire flute. A few guests began to clap and, mercifully, the rest joined in.

Then the screen went black.

She looked up at him, and he held his breath as his heart hammered in his chest.

"I can't believe you did that," she said softly. "In front of everyone. And that you spent the whole drive down here thinking I walked out on you."

He just nodded slowly because what else could he do? She was right. He knew this woman would ruin him, and she had—obliterated him wholly and completely.

She laid the phone on the night table and grabbed his hand.

"You said something that night when I asked you not to ride. You said you'd never ask me to give up on my dream."

"I did."

"Then I accept your proposal, Luke Everett," she said.

His brows rose.

"I will be there tomorrow to watch you get your eight

seconds. And then, when you walk out of that arena injury free, we both get our second chance." She tugged him closer. "If you'll still give me one after what I put you through."

He threaded his fingers into her hair, palms cradling the back of her neck as he rested his forehead against hers.

"You really would have pulled out of the competition for me?" she asked.

"I was banking on you seeing things from my perspective—realizing that with you in my corner there's no way I'm getting knocked down again."

She backhanded him on the shoulder. "Stop being so charming."

He laughed. "I think Lucy was right for once," he said.

Her brows furrowed. "Lucy?"

"Jenna's psychic chicken. I think you two met at the farmers market."

She smiled, and damn if she didn't light up the whole room.

"Thank you," he said, his voice hoarse.

"No," she said. "Thank *you*."

"For what?" he asked.

She tilted her head up and winked, something he'd so often done to her. "For taking that damned towel off already."

He barked out a laugh. "As you wish, sweetheart."

And then he did.

CHAPTER TWENTY-FIVE

First he'd bared his soul to her, and now here he was, bare in the most literal sense of the term, and she was speechless.

"I think this is the part where you lose that extremely sexy chef jacket and let me see what's underneath."

Lily looked down at her attire then back at the beautiful naked man standing in front of her. She imagined the mess her hair must be, the makeup most likely smudged around her eyes and possibly streaked down her cheeks.

"I'm a disaster," she said. "And you're..." She looked him up and down, then threw her hands in the air. "You're *this.*"

He raised his brows, then unbuttoned her jacket, sliding it gently off her shoulders. Then came the tank top she wore underneath and seconds later, her bra. She stepped out of her clogs—because of course she was wearing sensible shoes being on her feet all night—and Luke slid her pants and underwear off in one fluid movement.

He rested his hands on her hips, then spun her to face the mirror on the wall behind him.

There they were, no masks or walls between them.

"And you're *this*," he said from behind her, trailing his hand down her torso, then over her center as he slowly sank one finger, then two, inside her.

She cried out, her head falling back onto his shoulder.

"And what's that?" she asked, barely able to form the words.

"The beautiful, brilliant, sometimes maddening woman I would have given up everything for."

He slid his finger out so achingly slow she thought she might lose it right there. Then he backed her toward the bed, turning to face her before he lowered her onto her back, then climbed over her.

"Maddening, huh?" she asked, her eyes narrowing.

He nodded. "That oil-and-water stuff was no act, sweetheart. We're going to drive each other crazy."

She grinned, hooking her arms around his neck. "Then why don't you take the wheel, cowboy," she said, her knees falling open.

His hard, thick length slid between her legs, and her back bowed. He dipped his head, brushing a kiss over a pebbled nipple, then took her into his mouth as she whimpered and writhed.

He nudged her opening, his tip sinking in with ease, then back out again to swirl around her swollen center. Her fingernails dug into his back.

"Stop teasing," she pleaded, but he only responded with a wicked grin.

"Now where's the fun in that?" he asked.

She pursed her lips and narrowed her gaze at him. "I may be in love with you, Luke Everett, but that doesn't mean you can just—"

He nipped at one of her nipples, and she gasped, back arching.

"Just *what*?" he asked, feigned innocence in his tone.

She hooked her legs around his hips and then, only because she caught him off guard, flipped him onto his back so that she now straddled him.

He laughed, and damn if that grin of his didn't melt her completely.

"I don't think I've ever seen you smile like that," she said, realization in her tone.

"I guess that's what happens when the woman I'm crazy about tells me she loves me. It's an involuntary response. You're just going to have to get used to it."

She kissed him, and his tongue parted her lips so that she tasted nothing but Luke—this man who would challenge her, who would sometimes drive her mad just as she would him, and who would love her through it all.

"I love you," she said again, testing his theory, and those blue eyes crinkled at the corners. Then she sank over him, slowly letting him stretch her, filling her so completely she knew that when this night was over she would come completely undone.

He growled, fisting his hands in her hair.

"I love you, too," he whispered against her mouth.

She nipped at his bottom lip and felt him smile against her.

"Good," she said. "Because it's my turn to drive."

She didn't wake to an empty space beside her the next morning but instead to Luke's alarm clock on his phone. From there everything moved too quickly, and she was kissing him good-bye at the door before she'd even had a chance to have a cup of coffee.

"You need to eat something," she said, playfully tapping the brim of his cowboy hat. She'd seen him on a horse and working at the ranch, but today was different. Clean, polished boots sat below the cuffs of his well-worn, well-fitting jeans. And his red-and-blue-plaid shirt was tucked in. She'd memorized every dip and curve of muscle that lay beneath the trappings of her soon-to-be bull rider. All she wanted was to see it all again that night—to know he was coming back to her in one piece.

"There's a coffee shop on the walk over. I'll grab something on the way. I just need to get there, check in, and sort of be in the space." He kissed the top of her head. "It's okay if you think it sounds crazy."

She shook her head. "I get it," she said. "That's why I liked spending time at the winery in the weeks before the wedding. Getting used to a venue makes it a bit less scary on the big day."

He grinned. "Did it work?"

She laughed. "I think it's safe to say that nothing other than the food went according to plan last night."

"You did an amazing job," he said. "I don't think I told you that."

She held his cheeks in her hands, his stubble scratching her palms. "Thank you," she said. "But I'm glad it ended with me here. With you." She pressed her lips to his, and he hummed a soft sigh against her. "Does it work for you?" she added.

He nodded. "Except once."

Her throat tightened. "What do you mean?"

Luke blew out a breath. "When I got thrown off four weeks ago, it wasn't for lack of training or being reckless or whatever anyone else thinks. It was because I saw you that morning—when you signed the papers and then the whole thing with Sara and the wedding and you not knowing who she was until it was too late. I watched that all unfold and tried to fucking stop it but couldn't."

She shook her head. "None of that was your fault, Luke."

He clenched and unclenched his teeth.

"It was your birthday, and I said nothing. And all I

could think—even when they opened the gate and let the bull out with me sitting up top—was that you'd just had one of your shittiest days, and I couldn't do a goddamn thing about it."

Her hands slid down so they splayed against his chest.

"What are you saying?" she asked.

His chest slowly rose and fell with his next breath.

"That my head wasn't in it," he said simply. "And that's no one's fault but mine. But today is different," he assured her. "Today you're *here*, and everything is different." He kissed her, long and slow and sweet.

"Me being there won't distract you?" she asked hesitantly.

He shook his head, then pressed a kiss to her temple. "I'm not going to fall," he said.

She nodded.

"I believe you," she said.

"Because from here on out, it's like you said—only the truth between us, sweetheart. And I'll be *walking* out of that arena. Not carried on some damned stretcher."

His lips claimed hers once more before he finally said, "I gotta go."

Her throat tightened. "I love you, Luke Everett."

"I love you, Lily Green." Then he grinned.

"What?" she asked as he opened the door and started backing through it.

"I was just thinking about how someday, maybe—should you so choose—that might not be your name anymore."

Her mouth fell open as he winked and then pulled the door shut behind him.

For several long seconds she stayed there, rooted in place, as she let the entirety of the past four weeks sink in. Then she laughed at her reaction to his use of the word *proposal* last night. In the early morning light, it didn't seem so crazy anymore.

"Are you sure you don't want something, Lil? Even a bottle of water?"

The concern was evident in Ava's voice, but Lily just fisted her hands in her lap, her knuckles white against the black pants she'd worn last night. She'd traded her chef's coat for a plain white T-shirt Luke had in his duffel bag. Even though it was clean, she could still smell the memory of him on the fabric. But even that did little to comfort her, especially now that she'd watched three other riders get thrown from the bull's back.

She shook her head. "I'm too nervous."

Walker and Owen sat at the end of the aisle, sharing a box of popcorn. Jack sipped his soda. And Ava—well, she kept trying to be the comforting friend, and Lily kept brushing her off.

She groaned. "I'm sorry."

"For what?" Ava asked.

Lily turned to face her friend, and although Jack kept his gaze straight ahead on the arena, she knew he was listening, too.

"I should have taken him up on his offer not to ride. Then none of us would be sitting through this. And I wouldn't feel so...And Jack wouldn't have to...And Luke would be—"

"Resentful. Regretful. Downright ornery. And we already have Walker to fill that role," Jack said, leaning forward, resting his elbows on his knees. He was joining in the conversation, but he still kept a trained eye on those metal gates, behind which was the bull Luke would be climbing onto any minute. "I'm not happy he's going out there," he admitted. "But I have to believe that he's not being reckless, that he truly does know what he's doing." He turned to Lily now, his blue eyes full of crystal-clear resolve. "I'd trust him with my own life. What kind of brother would I be if I didn't trust him with his own?"

Ava grabbed Jack's hand and gave him what Lily could tell was a reassuring squeeze.

Lily wasn't the only one letting go of control today. Jack was finally stepping back and letting his brother be who he needed to be.

"It's just eight seconds, right?" Lily asked. "Eight seconds and this is all over."

Jack chuckled. "Or longer," he said. "Eight seconds to qualify, but if he stays on longer…"

Lily bit down hard on her lip, and Ava's hand closed over one of her white-knuckled fists. She looked from Lily to Jack and then back to Lily again.

"Just think about how Luke's gonna feel when he sees the two of you out here."

Lily forced a smile. They *were* sitting right up front. If he was looking, Luke could find them.

"Up next is Luke Everett. After getting brutally thrown just four weeks ago, Luke is back in the chute ready to show us what he intended to do on his last ride. For those who don't know, Everett has been an integral competitor in the rodeo circuit for years now, and while today's event will allow riders to qualify for the finals, today will be his last ride before he retires."

Lily swallowed hard at those words, imagining Luke was doing the same. She tilted her head to try and see him behind the gate of the chute, and as she did, he reseated his hat on his head and then looked right at her, like he knew she was there waiting for him.

He smiled and nodded once. And just like that, the gate flew open, and the bull bucked out into the arena, Luke Everett on his back.

Lily stood up against the metal bars separating her and the rest of the audience from the arena floor. She watched in awe of what he was doing—and then in horror as the bull kicked up its back legs and she saw him wince as his shoulder jerked.

"Oh my God," she said, realizing Ava was standing next to her, and then Jack, Owen, and Walker. All of them were on their feet.

"Goddammit," Jack said. "It's dislocated again."

"Three...four...five..." the spectators chanted.

She didn't look away. The worst could still happen, but she didn't look away. Because despite everything, his hand still gripped that rope.

"I'm not running," she whispered, pretending he could hear. "No matter what. So don't. Let. Go."

The crowd continued.

Six.

Seven.

Eight.

EPILOGUE

Close your eyes."

Lily groaned. "Why does it even matter? Your hand is covering half my face. I couldn't peek even if I tried!"

He grinned at the annoyance in her tone, loving that he could still push her buttons.

"*Are* you trying?" he accused.

Another groan. Another button pushed. Another smile from him she couldn't yet see.

"I am *not*."

He laughed quietly, imagining her rolling those emerald eyes, whether they were open or not.

She tripped over her own feet as she made her way around the side of the house—evidence of her innocence.

"Careful, sweetheart," he teased. "We don't want any accidents before the big reveal."

She steadied herself, her shoulders against his chest. But he didn't mistake her hesitation.

"It's okay," he said, his voice softening. "You can lean on me, Lily."

She let out a nervous laugh. "I have seen your backyard before, you know," she said. "How much has it changed since the last time I was here?"

The night she'd walked out—and then run across the state line.

That had already been two weeks ago, but the memory of it still stung. He had to remind himself that she stayed not just after his ride in Anaheim but also while he remained in town to see a specialist about his injury. That she was here now, and that's what mattered.

She stumbled again over a divot in the grass, and the hand over her eyes quickly slid to her torso, catching her before she fell.

"Thank you," she said, and they both paused for several seconds. "And *yes*, my eyes are still closed."

He chuckled softly in her ear. "Maybe I didn't think this through one hundred percent," he admitted. "Probably would have been easier to just walk through the house." He pressed his lips to her neck, and he felt her shiver against his touch.

He urged her to move again, and after only ten more steps he stopped, as did she.

"Okay," he said, letting go of her completely. "Open."

He moved to her side so he could watch her reaction.

She blinked a few times, her eyes adjusting to the sunlight, and then gasped when she saw what he'd kept secret all this time.

The open piece of earth that was his extensive backyard was now fenced on all sides, and out ahead, chomping on a mouthful of grass, was Crossroad Ranch's newest calf.

Lucky.

She turned to him, her jaw hanging open, and he gave her his best cocky, assured grin, one that he hoped said something along the lines of, *I win.*

"It's my cow," she said softly. "You had this all set up while we were away?"

He shook his head. "*Our* cow. And I did the fence while you were in Phoenix. I needed something to keep my mind off—well—you." He shrugged. "But she's just the start. I figure I could build a small arena right there." He pointed toward the right of the field. "And plans for the barn are already drawn up. Contractors are coming over tomorrow."

She narrowed her eyes at him. "And what are you doing with this arena, Mr. Everett?" She took a step closer, ran her fingers along the sling that held his shoulder in place while it healed.

He raised a brow. "I meant what I said about retiring." He kissed that crinkle of worry between her brows. "But it doesn't mean I have to give it up completely. I can teach kids how to trick ride, or I could help the Callahans board horses. I just—I did what I set out to do. On my terms. But I need something else that's just for me. Something beyond the ranch and vineyard."

She nodded. "I'm here," she said. "Whatever you decide, I'm here. In your corner. No more running." She leaned up to press a kiss against his lips.

He'd never get tired of that feeling when the kiss deepened, and her body relaxed, melting into his. He still had a hard time believing any of this was real. But here they were.

He brushed her hair behind her ear as she wrapped both arms around his waist and peered up at him.

"And what about you?" he asked. "After the flawless job you did for Tucker and Sara—other than your minor stint in a bathroom prison—is catering the way of the future for you? Because I know of a few brothers building a winery who *might* want to add some light food service to their patrons. We just need to get the permit, but there's room to add on a small kitchen. You could choose the menu, and we'd even call it Lily's Corner. *If* you wanted."

Her eyes widened and then filled with tears.

"No pressure," he blurted.

She kissed him, then pulled away. "No."

He smiled broadly. Then his expression fell. "Wait... No? I thought—"

She shook her head. "It's an amazing gesture, and I love you for it, but I don't need you to give me a restaurant. I once thought someone could hand me my dream, but I have to make it come true all on my own."

"I wanted to give you what I couldn't before," he said.

She pulled him close again. "All you need to give me is you...and maybe some stories about cows and horses."

His chest tightened at the memory of that first night, of all the mistakes they'd made since then, and of how lucky they were for this second chance to get it right.

"Sounds like it's my lucky day," he said against her. "Because I got stories about cows, horses, bulls, even a psychic chicken for days and days." He kissed her again, each brush of his lips over hers reminding him what he almost lost...and everything he'd found. He may not have walked out of that arena unscathed, but he *walked* out. On his own two feet after dismounting at eleven point two seconds...with Lily at his side. It was more than just that day. Or today. Every day that she believed in him was the luckiest day of his goddamn life.

She pulled away and gave him a mischievous look.

"What?" he asked, his eyes fixing on hers.

"I was just thinking about what you said, that even with the ranch and the vineyard you still want something that's just for you."

"Mmm-hmmm," he said with amusement.

She hooked her finger into one of the belt loops of his jeans. "I might have something to offer. *Just* for you."

The corners of his mouth curled up. "Did you bring me some more white chocolate mousse? Another batch of cookies? Ooh, wait. No. Leftover wedding cake! Or do the bride and groom get to keep that?"

She backhanded him on the chest, then threw her hand over her mouth.

"Sorry! But..." She groaned through gritted teeth. "You are *still* impossible," she said.

He laughed and grabbed her hand, pulling her toward the back door and then inside the house.

"Oil and water," he teased as he led her past the kitchen and straight to the bedroom. "But I'm not exactly hungry for *food*."

He lay down on the bed, crossing one booted foot over the other, and smiled up at the woman he loved.

"Be gentle. I'm an injured man, after all."

She narrowed her eyes, then climbed over him, lowering herself slowly until her lips were just a breath away from his.

"Impossible," she repeated.

"Maddening," he countered. "Good thing I'm crazy in love with you."

"Good thing," she said, then claimed his mouth with her own.

He slid his hand up her thigh and gave her ass a pinch.

She yelped.

He raised his brows. "A little reciprocation?"

She rolled her eyes. "I love you, too—*sweetheart*. But gentle just flew right out the window."

He laughed.

"Like I said. It's my lucky day."

Walker Everett can wrangle cattle, repair a broken roof, and bring in a grape harvest—all before sundown. The only thing he can't handle? Violet Chastain, Crossroads Ranch and Winery's new sommelier—and the most infuriating woman he's ever met.

See the next page for a preview of

HARD LOVING COWBOY.

It was high noon, the heat topping out at an unseasonably high eighty-eight degrees for early March. Walker had been at the circular saw outside the winery's back entrance for the better part of two hours. His T-shirt was soaked through with sweat, his jeans full of sawdust, and his beard was itching his neck something fierce. But when he looked at the perfectly cut pieces of crown molding ready to be stained, he considered it all worth it.

Okay, he was hotter than Satan's pitchfork in a furnace and was sure he'd sweated out fifteen years' worth of alcohol, even if he hadn't had a drink in two months. Nothing was worth this kind of torture, but now that the floors were done and the whole inside of the winery painted, Jack and Luke wouldn't let the sawhorse inside even if Walker used a drop cloth.

"There's air-conditioning inside," he'd argued.

"Fresh air will do you good," Luke had countered.

"Plus Ava and Lily will have our asses if you mess up their space," Jack had added.

Leave it to his brothers to throw their respective partners under the bus when they weren't around to defend themselves *or* hear Walker's side of the argument.

"Do you know how much fresh air I had while I was gone? I've been on hikes, bikes, and—" He'd leaned close to whisper this one to Luke. "And there was outdoor yoga, man. You don't know the fucking horrors."

You'd think a guy would get some sort of recognition for two months of sobriety, yet here he was, tossed outside like his nephew Owen's Lab, Scully.

Who was he kidding? "That spoiled pooch is probably in the ranch, lying belly up next to a vent, getting a belly rub." Damn that sounded nice.

He pulled his shirt over his head, found the one dry spot left, and gave his torso a good once-over. That was when he heard the crackle of tires in the gravel out front and the distinct sound of a car door slamming not once but twice.

Excellent, he thought. *Visitors.*

As he made his way to the front of the soon-to-be Everett Winery, the sound of a heated argument filled the air. At least, he thought it was an argument, based on the rapidly increasing volume, but the words that floated his direction were anything but English.

"*Reviens,* Violet! *Tu sais que tu m'aimes!*"

The male, who Walker could now see was a tall, lanky guy with curly dark hair, was waving his hands in the air as he followed the woman—a curvy brunette with soft waves tumbling over her shoulders, tawny skin, and legs for days that started somewhere under her pencil skirt and ended in the sexiest damn stilettos he'd ever seen—toward the winery's front door.

"*Va te faire foutre*, Ramon! *J'arrête!*" She added a one-fingered gesture, and even though Walker didn't speak what he guessed was French, he did understand the universal language of *Fuck you.*

"We're closed, gorgeous," he said, and without a second glance, she changed her trajectory from the building's entrance to where Walker stood a couple yards to the right.

"*Est-ce que tu vois*?" she called over her shoulder to the other man as she approached. "*Il est là*!" She was close enough to touch him now—and she did, wrapping her arms around Walker's waist.

"Are you married?" she whispered. "Engaged or attached in any way?"

He shook his head slowly. "So you do speak English, huh?"

"Please," she said under her breath. "Just go with this, and I promise to make it up to you."

"Mmm-hmm," he answered without thinking.

She slid her palms up his bare torso and linked her fingers behind his neck. Walker didn't think, just acted. He dropped his balled up T-shirt to the ground, pressed his hands firmly against her hips, and dipped his head so she could brush her soft lips over his. If he thought he was parched from baking in the morning sun, it was nothing compared to the insatiable thirst he felt when her tongue slipped into his mouth. He growled as she let out a soft moan. And then he took all that she gave, and damn this stranger was a giver.

His hands traveled south, and he waited for her to object, but she only kissed him harder. So he squeezed her round, firm ass as their tongues and mouths and lips spoke a language they both understood.

Need.

Sure, the tenets of his therapy strongly recommended no dating within the first six months of his sobriety, but this could hardly be interpreted as dating. He didn't even know this woman's name, only that he'd been in the desert for two months, and she was either an oasis or the best damned mirage he'd ever seen.

"Fine!" Walker heard the other man call, but he wasn't about to cut short whatever was happening to acknowledge him. "*Vous gagnez*. You win. You want me out of your life? *Au revoir*. Perhaps your new man would like to take you home."

His words were heavily accented and dripping with disdain.

She didn't respond, just kept up with the charade as Walker heard the car door slam, the engine rev to life, and then finally, the frantic sound of car wheels spinning too fast to gain purchase before finally squealing onto the main road and eventually, out of earshot.

"You gonna tell me what the hell that was all about?" he said against her lips. "Wouldn't mind your name, either."

She lowered herself onto the spikes of her heels, the shoes apparently not enough to reach Walker's six-foot-four-inch frame. Her pink lips were swollen and the copper skin of her chin rubbed pink from his beard. She absently brushed her fingers over it as her eyes searched far down the now empty road.

"How about I start?" he said when she made no move to answer him. "Walker Everett. You seem to be stranded at my ranch."

She cleared her throat, her eyes—brown with flecks of gold—finally focusing on his.

"I thought this was a vineyard."

Walker grunted. "Depends on if those grapes out there make anything worth drinking, but I'll let my brother and his fiancée worry about that. I'm more interested in that mighty friendly greeting of yours. Not that I'm complaining."

She smoothed her fitted black skirt and refastened the button of her crisp, white shirt that had undoubtedly popped open when she was making his acquaintance. Not before he snuck a glance at the lavender lace that peeked out from beneath.

"I'm here for the interview," she finally said. "Though I realize now I've most likely already lost the job. Dammit, Ramon."

"He your boyfriend?" Walker asked.

The woman crossed and uncrossed her arms, then started looking around frantically.

"My bag!" she yelled. "He left me without my bag!"

Walker squinted, then strode past her to the empty parking area where he retrieved a tan leather tote. Her expression brightened when she saw it, but when she reached for the bag, he retreated.

"First your name," he said.

She blew out a breath. "Violet. Violet Chastain. I have an interview with Jack Everett, and that *was* my boyfriend until a picture of him with his wife and daughter fell out of the passenger side visor and right into my freaking lap. That kiss—I mean, what I did when I got out of the car? I told Ramon I was seeing someone else, too, and you happened to be standing there right when I needed you. Guess that was my pride going into fight or flight, though I'm not sure which category my behavior falls under other than entirely unprofessional." She reached again for her bag, and this time Walker gave it to her. She pulled out her phone. "I'm just going to call an Uber, and you can forget I was ever here."

As she strode to where the parking area met the road, Walker's own phone vibrated in his pocket. He pulled it out to find a text from Jack.

Running late. Supposed to interview sommelier. Wine expert. Fill in for me? Just make sure she knows how to talk about and sell wine. Shouldn't be too difficult.

Walker laughed. Of all three Everett brothers, he was sure he knew the least about wine-making. She could say whatever she wanted, and he'd have no choice but to believe her.

He dropped the phone back into his pocket, then retrieved his shirt from the ground. He beat as much dust off of it as he could before pulling it back over his head. Then he made his way to where Violet stood on the side of an empty road, furiously tapping the screen of her phone.

"How's that Uber going?" he asked.

She groaned. "It's *not*. The closest driver is thirty miles away."

He chuckled. "Not sure where you're from, gorgeous, but you're in Small Town, USA now. Closest you'll get to an Uber is an Everett pickup truck or a horse. Can I interest you in either of those? Also been instructed to fill in for my brother Jack, so if you still want that interview..."

Her head shot up, and she stared at him with wide eyes. "You're kidding, right? After what I just pulled?"

He raised a brow. "Do you hear me complaining?"

"No, but... I mean, you're not... Wait, now that I think of it, you did kiss me back, didn't you?"

The corner of his mouth quirked up. "I sure did."

"Thank you, by the way, for putting your shirt back on. Not that I didn't like what I saw—or felt—but it's making it slightly easier to look you in the eye."

He looked down at his attire, then let his gaze travel up from her strappy three-inch heels all the way to her starched collar.

"I'm not exactly dressed for an interview," he said. "But Jack wants me to fill in. So if you're still looking for a job..."

"I am," she assured him. "I most definitely am."

"Then I guess we'd better head into my office," he said, backing toward the winery's entrance. He held the door open, and she followed him inside. "Why don't you get the lay of the land while I head in back to wash up. Then we can talk about your qualifications as a..." He pulled his phone out of his pocket and opened back up to Jack's text. "Sommelier," he said.

"*Yay*," she said, wincing.

"Glad you're excited."

She shook her head. "You said *suh-mel-yer*. But it's actually suh-mel-*yay*."

He narrowed his eyes. "That French or something?"

She nodded.

"Does it mean someone who knows about serving wine?"

She nodded again.

"Then I'm gonna go wash up. When I get back, we'll talk about your qualifications as a person who knows about serving wine."

He left her standing in the entryway as he headed toward the office on the other side of the building.

"Suh-mel-*yay*," he said under his breath. This woman was in a league all her own. Good thing he was in the penalty box until further notice.

ABOUT THE AUTHOR

A librarian for teens by day and a romance writer by night, A.J. Pine can't seem to escape the world of fiction, and she wouldn't have it any other way. When she finds that twenty-fifth hour in the day, she might indulge in a tiny bit of TV when she nourishes her undying love of vampires, superheroes, and a certain high-functioning sociopath detective. She hails from the far-off galaxy of the Chicago suburbs.

You can learn more at:

AJPine.com

Twitter @AJ_Pine

Facebook.com/AJPineAuthor

Ready for more cowboys?
Don't miss these other great Forever romances.

Second Chance Cowboy
By A. J. Pine

Once a cowboy, always a cowboy! Jack Everett can handle work on the ranch, but turning around the failing vineyard he's also inherited? That requires working with the woman he never expected to see again.

Cowboy Bold
By Carolyn Brown

Down on her luck, Retta Palmer is thrilled to find an opening for a counselor position at Longhorn Canyon Ranch, but she's not as thrilled to meet her new boss. With a couple of lovable kids and two elderly folks playing matchmaker, Retta finds herself falling for this real-life cowboy.

Look for more at: forever-romance.com

Tall, Dark, and Cajun
By Sandra Hill
Welcome to the bayou where the summer is hot, but the men are scorching! Sparks fly when D.C. native Rachel Fortier meets Remy LeDeux, the pilot with smoldering eyes angling for her family's property. He'll need a special kind of voodoo to convince Rachel she was born for the bayou.

Cowboy on My Mind
By R. C. Ryan

Ben Monroe has always been the town bad boy, but when he becomes the new sheriff, Ben proves just how far he will go to protect the woman he loves—and fight for their chance at forever.

Be sure to follow the conversation using #ReadForever and #CowboyoftheMonth!

Valentine, Texas
By Lori Wilde

Can a girl have her cake and her cowboy, too? Rachael Henderson has sworn off men, but when she finds herself hauled up against the taut, rippling body of her first crush, she wonders if taking a chance on love is worth the risk.

True-Blue Cowboy
By Sara Richardson

Everly Brooks wants nothing to do with her sexy new landlord, but, when he comes to her with a deal she can't refuse, staying away from him is not as easy as it seems.

Look for more at: forever-romance.com

Tough Luck Cowboy
By A. J. Pine
Rugged and reckless, Luke Everett has always lived life on the dangerous side until a rodeo accident leaves his career in shambles. But life for Luke isn't as bad as it seems when he gets the chance to spend time with the girl he's always wanted but could never have.

Cowboy Honor
By Carolyn Brown
Levi Jackson has always longed for a family of his own, and, after rescuing Claire Mason and her young niece, Levi sees that dream becoming a reality.

Be sure to follow the conversation using #ReadForever and #CowboyoftheMonth!

9174